Jack didn't say anything, but then he didn't need to.

The look in his eyes, though quickly concealed, was all the proof Lexie Dawson needed. Jack Blade—a man she had slept with and still dreamed about—actually thought her capable of murder.

"Would you be willing to let me test your hands for gunpowder residue?" Jack asked. "I'd like to rule you out as a suspect."

Lexie sat there for several seconds, weighing the request. If her husband had been murdered—no one would believe she was innocent. She had motive, opportunity *and* they would find gunpowder residue on her hands.

"I spent the afternoon at the gun range, trying out a new pistol."

"Any witnesses?"

"Maybe two or three," Lexie said. "And if you're through with me, I'd like to go now."

Jack stopped her with a hand on her arm. "Unfortunately, I'm afraid not," he said. "In fact, I need to read you your rights...."

LORI L. HARRIS

SECRET ALIBI

HARLEQUIN®

TORONTO • NEW YORK • LONDON
AMSTERDAM • PARIS • SYDNEY • HAMBURG
STOCKHOLM • ATHENS • TOKYO • MILAN • MADRID
PRAGUE • WARSAW • BUDAPEST • AUCKLAND

For Mavis Allen, with gratitude.

ISBN 0-373-22907-0

SECRET ALIBI

Copyright © 2006 by Lori L. Harris

ABOUT THE AUTHOR

Lori L. Harris has always enjoyed competition. She grew up in southern Ohio, showing Arabian horses and Great Danes. Later she joined a shooting league where she competed head-to-head with police officers—and would be competing today if she hadn't discovered how much fun and challenging it was to write. Romantic suspense seemed a natural fit. What could be more exciting than writing about life-and-death struggles that include sexy, strong men?

When not in front of a computer, Lori enjoys remodeling her home, gardening and boating. Lori lives in Orlando, Florida, with her very own hero.

Books by Lori L. Harris

HARLEQUIN INTRIGUE
830—SOMEONE SAFE
901—TARGETED*
907—SECRET ALIBI*

*The Blade Brothers of Cougar County

CAST OF CHARACTERS

Jack Blade—He worked undercover on some of the meanest streets in America before taking the job as Deep Water's police chief. But he knows even quiet streets aren't always safe. And justice isn't always so easy to find—even for the innocent.

Lexie Dawson—Without an alibi, this pharmaceutical rep might just find herself on Florida's death row.

Dr. Dan Dawson—A successful obstetrician and Lexie's ex-husband. Who would want him dead?

Dr. Fleming Whittemore—Dan Dawson's partner. Lexie considers him a close friend. But is he? Or does he have his own agenda?

Alec Blade—Jack Blade's older brother. A top FBI profiler, Alec retired from the FBI after his wife's brutal slaying and moved to Deep Water, hoping to rebuild his relationship with his brother. It seems as if Alec has brought Jack only more trouble.

Katie Blade—Less than a year ago, targeted by a brutal killer, she fought back and survived. Now she and Alec Blade are happily married.

Chapter One

10:30 p.m. Deep Water, Florida

What had happened to him?

Unable to move, unable even to lift his head off the desk blotter, Dan Dawson attempted to focus on his surroundings, but couldn't. The room—his home office—seemed to be a mishmash of colors, one bleeding into another.

The objects closest to him were clearer—the paper clip and the gold pen appeared almost jewel-like as they floated against a bloodred background. Those a few inches beyond were blurred and indistinct.

As he was staring at the paper clip, his eyelids slammed shut, cutting off the one sense that seemed to be working, the one thing that kept him feeling connected to his surroundings. Even as the panic ripped through him, he tried to fight it. But it was as if he'd been closed into a box—a coffin.

His eyelids suddenly sprang open, the sharp reentry of light painful but not unbearable.

Don't panic. Panic was...was counterproductive.

Stay calm. Approach it as if it was one of his patients who was in trouble. He needed to...he needed to do...

What? He tried to focus, but it was as if his brain had locked him out.

Vitals. Like a life ring, the word suddenly floated past in the black sea of nothingness, and he grabbed on tight. If he really concentrated, he realized he could feel the air moving in and out of his chest. Respiration slow and shallow, but steady.

A sudden explosion of pain struck at the base of his skull, then ravaged downward through him, sucking the air from his lungs. His throat muscles contracted hard, and he felt his body gasp for oxygen.

What the hell was wrong with him?

His sluggish mind grappled with and discarded possible diagnoses. Stroke? Too young. Cardiomyopathy? Overdose? He hadn't taken any drugs in months…or had he? Had he taken something tonight?

Sweat slid slowly down his back, morphing into a living thing, a parasite that devoured his life force before escaping through his pores and oozing downward toward the floor, toward escape. Like rats from a burning building.

A distorted sound shattered the silence. Not in the room with him, but in the foyer or the kitchen. He felt a warm rush of relief. Rescue. He would be rescued.

Dan again tried to raise his head, but it was like trying to lift a watermelon that dangled from the end of a swizzle stick.

When he attempted to speak, the muscles of his throat refused to cooperate, the sound coming out more a cough than a plea.

More noise drifted from beyond the room. Drawers opening. Closing. Not in a hurry, but slowly, as if someone wanted to go unheard.

A shapeless shadow entered the room. For a moment, he

thought he'd imagined the movement, but then, as the form passed in front of the flickering light from the fireplace, he realized he hadn't.

Dan again tried to speak, but the pitifully weak sound that came from his lips was barely audible. "Help…"

The shadow made no attempt to render aid. Dan's vision partially cleared, and he made out a hand encased in latex. The disembodied hand hovered ghostlike, and then slowly slid open the top right drawer of the desk.

With sudden lucidity, Dan knew what had left him paralyzed. Worse, he knew what was about to happen.

And this time, there was no controlling the panic.

LEXIE DAWSON GLANCED longingly at the exit of Baldacci's.

Even before she had arrived for this business dinner, it had been a long day for her, and the conversation among the three surgeons at the table had drifted into more technical realms. As a pharmaceutical rep of a large drug company, she was well versed in her product, but not this stuff.

Fortunately, none of the three seemed to notice that her attention had shifted.

Dr. Dennis Rafferty, the oldest and least forward-thinking of her three guests, had chosen the upscale, overpriced restaurant, which was located in what eighty years ago had been Deep Water's theater house. Back then, the interior would have been quite ornate, but now, all that remained of the once-gracious building were exposed brick walls and large, unadorned windows, giving it the warmth of an empty operating room.

Small wonder that Rafferty had chosen the place. She didn't even want to think about what this one night was going to do to next month's expense report. But if it paid off, if she sold another doctor on using Talzepam, the meal would be well worth it.

"What's your opinion, Lexie?"

Lexie refocused her attention on the man directly across from her. Ken Lattimer was a thirtysomething orthopedic surgeon with dark hair and liquid brown eyes. Good-looking by most standards, but not by hers. He was reputed to be the Southeast's best hand and wrist surgeon. But his nickname around the hospital—Dr. Hands—had nothing to do with surgical talent.

The third man at the table was Joe Lemon, a slightly overweight, fortysomething pulmonary specialist with a wife, two kids and a booming practice.

Straightening in her seat, she hoped to buy some time by reaching for the glass of water. With any luck, someone would unknowingly clue her in on the direction of the conversation. When she lifted her gaze above the glass rim, though, she realized all three doctors were waiting for her to respond.

It was Ken who rescued her. "I was telling Joe and Rafferty that I've been using Talzepam for about two months now. Or has it been three?"

"Three." Lexie had started repping the drug about six months ago and had found it a difficult sell. Most anesthesiologists and surgeons were slow to make changes. In fact, Ken was one of the few doctors at Cougar County Regional Hospital who embraced Talzepam.

She understood the reluctance the others had. Talzepam's competitors, Valium and flurazepam, had been used in the operating room with good success for years. Why take a chance on a new drug—even if it offered some advantages to the patient?

"Like Ken, most surgeons who have tried Talzepam have found it to be fast-acting and dependable," Lexie continued.

Ken agreed. "And so far I've seen very few post-op side effects. At least with my patients."

She scanned the faces of the other two men—the unconverted—then swung her gaze back to Ken. "Not just your patients. I've been hearing the same from all my accounts. In every trial, Talzepam outperformed its counterparts. There were fewer reports of vision changes post-op, as well as problems with breathing or a slow heartbeat."

Rafferty leaned forward. "Perhaps fewer incidences of respiratory problems, but those that did occur were more severe."

Lexie maintained her relaxed posture. "You're right. Several early studies did suggest that when breathing problems occurred with Talzepam, there was greater difficulty stabilizing the patient's respiration—especially during long procedures. But it was found that, in all but one case, the anesthetist had overcompensated for the patient's body weight. Talzepam is a powerful drug and dosing guidelines have to be strictly adhered to."

His expression thoughtful, Ken nodded. "I've been following Talzepam since the trial stages. I think it has something to offer both the medical community and the patient."

"In what ways?" Joe Lemon asked, and in the next instant, Ken was off and running, discussing his experiences with the drug.

Lexie knew that doctors tended to listen to other doctors more than sales representatives. Which made sense, really. The key was to pick the right doctor—usually the young ones were more open to new drugs. And if you could nab one who was both well-liked and respected by his peers, as Ken Lattimer was, the selling became that much easier.

She still was puzzled, though, by Ken's phone call this morning. He'd asked her if it would be possible for him to join the group. That had never happened to her before, and she couldn't help but wonder what was in it for him. It could hardly be the free meal. Or that he was without other social options for the evening. Reaching for the nearly full glass of red wine, she realized what she was most afraid of was that his interest was not in Talzepam, but her.

The cell phone tucked discreetly beneath her black tweed jacket vibrated. Pretending to smooth the napkin in her lap, she glanced down. Her ex-husband's home phone number appeared on the backlit screen.

Great. She'd been expecting some form of communication from Dan all day. Dreading it, actually.

Lexie straightened her jacket, concealing the phone once more. Even if it had been someone she was interested in talking to, she would have ignored it. She'd already been caught once being less than attentive; she wasn't about to look unprofessional a second time in one evening.

The discussion at the table again drifted away from her product, briefly touching on hospital politics and the current shortage of nurses. When the conversation veered to Tampa Bay's chances in the playoffs, she excused herself from the table and headed for the ladies' room. She'd nearly made it there when her phone began to vibrate again.

Flipping it open, she scanned the text message: have anniversary surprise stop by drink.

What in the hell was wrong with her ex-husband? Didn't he understand that as far as she was concerned the only anniversary worth celebrating was March 15, the day she'd been awarded a divorce from him?

Fed up, she stopped just inside the short hallway where

the restrooms were located and quickly manipulated the phone pad keys.

Don't drink with murderers. Cruel words, but Dan would know exactly what she meant.

Only after hitting Send did she notice her hands were trembling. *Calm down,* she reminded herself. *He's just doing this to get a rise out of you.* Or because he was drunk…. It didn't really matter why he was doing it, though. She was pissed.

She clipped the phone to her waistband again. Right now, she needed to forget about Dan and keep her mind on business.

When she returned to the table a few minutes later, something in her face must have given her away, because Rafferty leaned toward her. "Everything okay?"

She glanced at him. He'd always seemed like such a cold fish, so she was surprised when he picked up on her emotional state. "Everything is fine." She offered a tight smile. "Can I interest anyone in some coffee and dessert?"

Rafferty shook his head. "I have an eight o'clock surgery scheduled." He placed his napkin on the table. "Time to call it a night, gentlemen."

"I'll drop by with samples of Talzepam in the morning," Lexie said as she, too, stood.

"Sounds good. Wait up, Dennis." Joe Lemon shook her hand, then hurried after Dr. Rafferty. Lexie caught the words *prolapsed* and *ICU,* and knew the two men were discussing a mutual patient.

Ken was the last to get to his feet, and he made no move to follow the other two men.

Here it comes, she thought. He's going to suggest a nightcap or something. How was she going to turn him down without damaging the professional relationship?

She bent to retrieve her briefcase. By the time she straightened, Ken had walked around the table.

"Care to come by my place for that dessert?"

He didn't look quite as confident as he usually did. Which surprised her. She tried to formulate some type of reply in her head, but after several seconds realized that the longer she waited to say something, the more awkward it was going to be for both of them. She settled for simple and direct. "No, thanks."

He nodded, his mouth tightening ever so slightly. "I didn't think so, but figured it was worth asking."

He offered his hand, and she took it without hesitation. "Thanks, Ken, for helping tonight."

Again, his mouth tightened briefly. "It's a good product, Lexie. In time, it will outsell its competitors. Can I see you to your car?"

She had barely declined his offer when he tossed his jacket over his shoulder and, with one hand tucked into a pants pocket, strolled toward the front door. Several women a few tables over watched with interest. For a moment, Lexie envied them.

What did they see that she didn't? She was twenty-seven, not ninety-seven. Sex was a healthy part of being an adult— one of the few perks, when you came right down to it. But in the eleven months since she and Dan had gone their separate ways, she'd had sex only one time. With a stranger who hadn't stayed a stranger. Her abdominal muscles tensed at the memory of all the things they'd done that night. But more than the mechanics of sex, she'd been able to do something she hadn't done in months—she had cried. He'd held her while she sobbed, never asking why, seeming to understand that her pain couldn't be mollified with words.

"Excuse me, ma'am."

Lexie realized she had no idea how long the busboy had been standing there looking at her.

"Sorry," she said, embarrassed. Ducking her head, she moved away from the table. She had to stop thinking about that night, glorifying it as something more than it had been. Pity sex. That's all it could have been for him. What was more embarrassing and depressing than that? To know a man had taken you to bed because he felt sorry for you?

After leaving the restaurant, she dropped last month's expense account report into the box in front of the post office, and then took Alligator Creek Road toward home.

Temperatures had taken a hard dive into the high thirties—uncommon for early December in central Florida. A misting rain forced her to turn on the windshield wipers. She was used to the fifteen-minute drive, having moved out to River-house, her grandparents' old weekend retreat on the river, when she and Dan had separated. She'd expected the move to be a temporary one, lasting only until Dan vacated the house in town.

The majority of the land out this way belonged to the state now, so she was unlikely to see another car at this time of night. The dense line of vegetation, mostly palmettos and scrub oaks, with a few slash pines mixed in, formed a wall on either side.

Usually the drive relaxed her, but not tonight. She couldn't seem to quite let go of her irritation over Dan's interruption, or her uncertainty over the dinner meeting's success.

Her headlights skimmed across a small family of arma-dillos that had wandered out of the undergrowth toward the road. Braking, she hit the horn and watched them scatter back into the brush.

She had just stopped in front of the house when her cell phone went off again. She checked the message screen.

paprs signd last dink

"Do you really think I'm that stupid, Dan?"

That was a fatal drawback to text messaging—you couldn't really tell with any certainty the condition of the person on the other end. But the dropped letters in his message suggested that Dan was at least on his way to being drunk.

She should never have answered the first text message, she realized. As soon as she had, she'd given him what he really wanted from her. Not to be ignored.

Which was exactly what she needed to do. She reached for her briefcase and then paused, staring down at the phone she still held in her left hand.

But what if he wasn't screwing with her? What if this time was different? What if he had signed the amended property settlement? She'd heard talk about his seeing a woman. Maybe he had finally started to move on.

She glanced through the rain-pocked window toward the front door of Riverhouse, wanting a hot shower and a soft bed. Wanting to forget about her ex-husband and legal documents. She wanted the mindless oblivion of sleep.

Lexie rubbed her forehead. No. As much as she would like to believe this time might be different, it would be like all the others. She'd lost count of the times he'd agreed to sign the papers, only to refuse when they were face-to-face.

She flipped the phone back open and, after briefly debating what her response should be, settled for being brutally frank. F off

She'd wanted to say that for months now, but hadn't. Partially because she wanted to keep things as civilized as possible between them, figuring as long as she played nice, Dan would also. Boy had she been wrong.

She was reaching for her briefcase again when the phone vibrated in her hand. Startled, she dropped it on the floorboard. As she picked it up and straightened, she read the screen.

Pick up tnight Or brn them n house.

"You wouldn't dare!" Lexie took a deep breath and let it out slowly. Calm down. Just a head game. That's all the threat was. He might burn the papers, but he wouldn't burn the house. He wasn't quite that crazy.

As she sat there in the dark, though, she realized that she was wrong. Drunk and mad, Dan might be capable of almost anything.

"Okay, Dan. We'll play it your way one last time."

She tossed the phone on the seat and turned the key in the ignition. If the papers weren't signed, that was it. She'd kept her mouth shut for way too long. But no more.

Ten minutes later, Lexie paused at the end of the driveway leading down to the Victorian that she'd once shared with Dan. This house and Riverhouse had passed into her hands nearly four years ago with the death of her grandparents. Just the thought of losing it frightened her. As Dan had known it would.

Unlike most in the neighborhood, the large home with its deep, wraparound porch sat well off the boulevard. Several ancient live oaks blocked the view of the house from the road, their dark limbs so low-slung they appeared to rest on the lawn before rising skyward. As a child, she had spent summers crawling on those sturdy branches, climbing upward to where a thick bounty of leaves had made her invisible. At least once, when her mother had come to collect Lexie at summer's end, she'd sought refuge there.

And there had been unpleasant consequences for that action.

Lexie took her foot off the brake and let the car creep down the brick drive. Some lessons stayed with you for a lifetime. Avoidance was an option, but it was rarely a solution.

The front light wasn't on, and large, dense hedges blocked any light from neighboring homes, making the yard extremely dark. A lamp in the foyer and the one in Dan's office were on, though.

With the rain having increased to a steady drum on the car roof, Lexie removed her coat before getting out. She held it over her head as she made a run for the door. Her eyes darted toward the wide set of stairs that climbed from the brick walkway to the porch, but just as quickly she looked away. She couldn't go up them. She would never use those stairs again.

As she started for the back of the house, she saw movement, a shadow, just inside the front door. He must have seen her headlights. He'd know to meet her at the back door.

Lexie sprinted across the thick St. Augustine grass, now slick with rain, and ducked under the back porch covering. She shook the dampness off her jacket. Shoving her arms back into the sleeves, she peered through the glass, waiting for Dan to come into view.

They'd remodeled the kitchen two years ago, replacing the ceramic tile countertops of the 1920s with granite and the original cabinets with new ones that had been made to look old. The under-cabinet lighting they'd added gave the room a peaceful glow.

As she stood there, though, the knot in her stomach tightened. The last time he'd gotten her over here with a promise of signed papers, there had been candles, wine and a diamond bracelet waiting instead of the papers.

One look and she'd been out of there.

When she didn't see Dan after half a minute, she knocked. Pulling her damp suit jacket closed, she crossed her arms to hold it that way. "Come on. It's too damn cold for this."

Several seconds later, when there was still no Dan, she tried the door and, finding it unlocked, debated going on in. Was that what he wanted? For her to come in? Was he waiting for her naked on the couch again?

She stood there weighing her options. She didn't relish the idea of dealing with a drunk, naked man, but it wouldn't be the first time. There was also the possibility that he had simply passed out. If he had, and if by some miracle the papers were signed, she could just grab them and leave. No confrontations.

Lexie pushed the door open. The first thing that struck her when she stepped inside was the silence.

Dan liked noise. He always had the television going, or left a CD on. He couldn't handle being alone. It was the same reason he drank. The same reason he occasionally abused Valium.

"Dan?"

When he didn't respond, the knot in her chest tightened. Something didn't feel quite right....

"Dan? Where are you?"

As she crossed the kitchen, heading for the door leading into the dining room, she opened her jacket. The house was unusually warm, which wasn't like him, either. He always kept the place cold enough for a polar bear.

She shoved open the swinging door. When she let it go, it closed behind her, the only light now coming from the lamp on the old English chest in the foyer.

"Dan?"

Her footsteps echoed on the oak flooring, and then were

muffled by the foyer's Persian carpet. A thin swath of light spilled out from where the door to his office stood ajar. She called out one last time when she was still several feet away.

Two scents registered simultaneously. Blood. Fresh blood. She remembered it from the few times she'd entered an operating room. And the underlying scent, the much more subtle one—cordite.

"No!" Her heart crashed inside her rib cage as her gut twisted in fear. Her palms slammed into the door, her forward momentum carrying her halfway across the room before the scene registered: Dan slumped at his desk, his head resting in a large pool of blood. Lexie kept going, something inside her refusing to believe—until she touched his hand.

Releasing cold fingers, she jerked backward, almost as if something had struck her a physical blow. Her hand came up to cover her mouth. Too late, she realized there was blood on it.

She stared at it, then at Dan. She tried to take a deep breath, but couldn't. It was as if her brain, her body, had forgotten how, had been short-circuited by what was in front of her.

The first wave of nausea hit her, forcing her to stumble backward, toward the door. She clamped a hand over her mouth as if that could stop the vomit. She made it as far as the small bathroom beneath the stairs.

When the retching passed, she leaned against the sink, afraid her legs would give out. Dear God, this couldn't be happening! Not to Dan. What would make him commit—?

When she lifted her gaze to the mirror, her thoughts suddenly derailed.

She hadn't closed the door behind her. She was sure of it. But it was shut tight. And everything inside her told her there was someone on the other side.

Waiting for her.

Chapter Two

Rain came down hard and steady as Deep Water's chief of police, Jack Blade, was waved through the barricade by a slicker-clad patrolman.

Wadding up the wrapper from a greasy cheeseburger, Jack tossed it back in the sack, then rolled down the window to speak with the officer.

"Who's all here, Hank?"

"Ellis, Martinez, Shepherd, Fitz. The D.A. did a quick walk-through about forty-five minutes ago."

"What about our illustrious medical examiner? He make it by yet?"

"Been called." Hank nodded toward the food bag. "Thought you were swearing off fast food, Chief."

"Yeah." Hitting the gas, Jack nosed the car forward before casting a jaundiced glare down at the bag.

Hank was right. He really had to start eating better. He also needed to begin carving out some kind of life for himself. He'd thought making the move to Deep Water would be enough, that with the change of scenery, he would also change. But he hadn't. It was pretty much business as usual, his life revolving around police work, and not much else.

Except, of course, for that one night nearly two months ago when he'd met a woman. A very intelligent and beautiful woman.

He'd thought they'd made a real connection. He'd called several times after that, hoping to pursue something with her, but she had been pretty blunt the last time he'd contacted her.

Just his luck, the only woman he'd met who interested him wasn't interested in return. And to make matters worse, he couldn't seem to get her out of his head.

Reaching down, he switched on the defroster to clear the windshield. Though he'd relocated from Atlanta nearly two years ago, he still couldn't get used to the damp cold of a Florida winter, where thirty-nine degrees cut through you like thirteen. And where three days of gray skies felt like an eternity.

There was no sign of any media yet, but he suspected it would be only a matter of time before they made an appearance. Reporters and bluebottle flies. Both fed on the dead, but it was the reporters who usually showed up first.

Like any midsize, modern city, Deep Water had its share of murders, but up until tonight, none of them had taken place in Thornton Park, an affluent area of large, historic homes with sweeping, deep-green lawns and brick streets.

Jack looked up as the house came into view. Most of the homes in the area were dark now, but light flooded from this one, and vehicles crowded the driveway as if some swank gala was under way. And in some ways, it was a party—a morbid one—attended by crime scene techs and police officers, and with the host already dead.

Jack swung in behind the department's white crime-scene van—a recently purchased, fully equipped vehicle. It had taken him nearly a year to convince the city council that the vehicle wasn't a luxury, but a necessity.

Jack grabbed gloves and shoe covers, dug a roll of mints out of the center console and flicked off two. He could still taste the cheeseburger. In another hour or so the sour taste in his mouth would be even worse.

A patrol officer, Billy Ellis, stood just outside the front door, hunched in a jacket that was too lightweight for the weather, stamping his feet against the cold. As Jack approached, Ellis scribbled down his name in the security log.

"You first officer on the scene?" Jack asked.

"Yes, sir."

Still outside, Jack slipped on vinyl gloves—he was allergic to the more common latex variety. Glancing up as he was tugging on the second shoe cover, he noticed the kid's lack of color and shell-shocked expression. "First homicide?"

Ellis nodded nervously. "Yes, sir."

Jack suspected that no matter how many other homicides Billy Ellis worked in his career, tonight's would always be the most vivid. At some point during the next week or so, the kid would probably tell himself that the next one would be easier. It wouldn't be. In Jack's experience, they never got easier—a man just got better at coping.

Another new recruit looked up as Jack stepped into the foyer. The officer, who stood in front of the chest against the opposite wall, was sifting through what appeared to be mail, and used his head to motion toward a set of double doors. "Body's in there."

"Who called it in?"

"The ex-wife. Fitz is in the kitchen with her now."

After the week he'd had, Jack would have liked to bypass the room with the body—to spend time with the living instead of the dead. But no matter how much he wanted to, he wouldn't. Because when it came right down to it, homicide investigations weren't about the living. They were about the dead—about attaining justice for those who were beyond needing it.

Jack stepped inside what appeared to be a home office. Every lamp had been turned on and additional lights had been brought in to flood the space.

It wasn't the type of room you expected to see in one of these older homes. The wood floor had been left bare and the walls were a stark white, as was just about everything else in the room. Even the large brushed-metal-and-glass desk seemed too cold and sterile for the space.

The body was slumped over the slick surface and belonged to a white male with his head—at least what was left of it— resting on the desktop.

It was always the odor that hit Jack the hardest. With a new body, there was the raw, metallic scent of fresh blood, sometimes so strong that when you opened your mouth to speak, it seemed to collect on your tongue. If the victim had gone undiscovered for a longer period of time, the odors were even stronger, but no more unpleasant. Death was simply death.

Two men worked the room. Detective Frank Shepherd was a 30-year veteran of Deep Water PD. A tall, rail-thin man with sharp features. Even though the department had relaxed its dress code for detectives, Shepherd continued to wear starched shirts and neckties. And freshly polished shoes. Jack liked him for his intellect and his thoroughness—both important qualities in a detective. At the moment, Shepherd was shining a flashlight at an oblique angle, looking for prints around the front window.

"Window's unlocked. And I have what appears to be a decent thumbprint," Shepherd called over his shoulder. Neither man had yet seen Jack.

The other man was 26-year-old Andy Martinez, the only crime scene tech currently employed by Deep Water PD. Where Frank wore a starched shirt and a necktie, Andy wore a white T-shirt, with CRIME SCENE printed on front and back, and jeans. A black ball cap turned backward and athletic shoes encased in paper covers completed his uniform. At the moment, Andy was digging through the large, black case that he liked to call his toy chest. The box contained everything he needed, from pencils and pliers to dusting powder and a strong flashlight.

"Been expecting you, Chief," Andy commented without looking up.

Everyone in the department knew that Jack showed up at every homicide. Mostly to make sure his detectives were getting what they needed to do their jobs. Sometimes, especially if there was DNA evidence involved, that meant contacting the Florida Department of Law Enforcement lab in Daytona Beach, and other times it just meant handling the media and running interference with several town councillors.

"I didn't get the call until the plane hit the ground," Jack said.

Shepherd had turned as soon as Andy had spoken, and nodded a greeting in Jack's direction before going back to studying the area near the window.

"That explains the suit," Andy said as he walked across the room to hand Shepherd dusting powder and lift tape.

"How'd it go in Philly?" Andy asked as he passed Jack the second time.

Jack had flown up to Philadelphia to be at his brother's side. Not because Alec wanted company, but because Alec's eight-months-pregnant wife, Katie, had wanted Jack there.

"Jury deliberated for six hours before coming back with a guilty verdict," Jack said. "Penalty phase starts next week."

"Let's hope the bastard gets what he deserves," Andy said.

The man on trial was responsible for the brutal slaying of Alec's first wife nearly two years ago. At the time of her murder, Alec had been a criminal profiler with the FBI. He'd retired only months after his wife's death so that he could, with his usual tenacity, devote every moment of his time to bringing down her killer.

Alec didn't know how to fail at anything. It was one of the things Jack admired about his brother. It was also one of the characteristics that at times could get under Jack's skin.

He moved farther into the room, careful to stick with a straight path that he could later backtrack. "What do you have so far?"

Andy had closed in on the body's right side and seemed to be examining its position. "The victim is a 36-year-old male. Cause of death appears to be gunshot to the head at very close range. By the look of it, he didn't go right away. Too much blood."

"I assume we have a name?"

"Dan Dawson. Local doc."

At the name, Jack looked up from the body, everything inside him tightening. If this was Dr. Daniel Dawson, then that made the woman in the other room… Not a stranger.

Andy, who had been examining the floor beneath the victim, stuck his head above the desk edge, but didn't seem to record Jack's reaction to the name.

"I completed the video and sketches, as well as the preliminary 35 mms and a few digital shots. There was a nickel-plated .357 revolver on the floor on the victim's right, and I found powder residue on the victim's right hand, right cheek and shirt collar."

"So you think it was self-inflicted?" Jack asked, and waited tense seconds for Andy's answer.

"You'll have to ask the medical examiner that one."

"I'm asking for your opinion, Andy."

The crime scene tech looked up from what he was doing. Jack wasn't surprised to encounter speculation in his eyes. Andy was probably wondering what was different about this murder, why his boss had just asked him to comment on an aspect of the scene that was clearly the M.E.'s territory.

After nearly a half minute, Andy looked down at the corpse. "I obviously haven't moved the body, so the most I can tell you is that the bullet appears to have entered just behind the right condyle and then exited low on the left side of the skull."

"Not the usual positioning of the weapon for a suicide," Jack said.

Shrugging, Andy started to collect items from the desktop. "The bullet trajectory pretty much did away with any chance of survival. Which is usually the goal."

"Damn," Jack whispered. "What drives a man, a seemingly successful one, to just give away his life?"

Andy picked up a photo that had been facedown on the desk. Blood dripped from the frame edge as he held it for Jack to see. "Maybe losing something like that."

Both men knew who she was. Andy because he would have seen her when he arrived, and Jack because they'd met once before—under very different circumstances.

The photograph was a close-up and had been cropped so

there was no background—just hair and face. An interesting face with a strong chin and steel-gray eyes so direct that some would find them intimidating. Then there was all that dark gold hair, not smooth and neat, but full and, from the looks of it, hard to restrain. What the picture didn't show was the supple, well-muscled body. Jack's fingers curled into a loose fist as he tried to forget the warm, satiny skin.

Andy placed the frame in the box with other items that would be transported to the lab for evaluation.

Jack scanned the room again. With the exception of the evidence markers scattered about like a toddler's toys, the space looked tidy. Definitely no signs of a struggle.

"Were there any indications of forced entry?"

It was Shepherd who responded this time. "No. At least not on the first floor. When I finish up in here, I'll check upstairs."

Andy had collected a pile of manila files from one corner of the desk and was placing them in another cardboard box.

"What are those?" Jack asked.

"They look to be patient charts."

As Jack moved closer to the victim, he was still very aware of where he placed his feet. "It appears as if he may have been sitting here reviewing them."

On the surface, the pieces seemed to fit, but…

Jack lifted his hand, intending to massage the stiffness in his neck, then realized he was still gloved, and allowed it to drop again. "He brings work home with him, and then stops in the middle to put a gun to his head? Why look over charts if you have no intention of seeing or treating the patients?" Jack paused. "Unless you were being sued?"

"And the charts belong to women who might be called as witnesses at a trial?" Andy had keyed in on the direction Jack was going. "He realizes he's screwed and reaches into the drawer…. Bam. No suit. No trial."

"Just happy trails," Shepherd chimed in.

Jack took a deep breath and let it out slowly. "Or he brought the charts home because he hadn't had time to take care of them at the office. Someone comes in here and puts a gun to his head." He looked over at Andy. "The powder residue on his hand—any possibility that it got on him when he was trying to grab the gun from someone else at the time it went off?"

"Sure."

Shepherd moved in closer to the body. "The only entrance is in front of the desk. If he didn't do this to himself, then whoever did knew him well enough to get in close and personal."

Jack scanned the room again. Shepherd was right. There was no way anyone could've snuck up on him.

Shepherd handed the dusting powder back to Martinez. "My money is on the ex-wife."

Jack's mouth tightened. The possibility that the woman in the other room—the same woman who had too briefly shared his bed two months ago and who had haunted his mind ever since—had put a gun to a man's head and pulled the trigger left him feeling exposed.

LEXIE HAD BEEN SITTING in the kitchen's breakfast nook for nearly two hours now. For the last hour, she'd been answering questions asked by Detective Joe Fitz. He was somewhere deep into middle age and had one of those Moon Pie faces that would go unnoticed in a group photo.

"So you arrived around eleven-fifteen?" Fitz asked.

"No. I arrived at eleven-thirty." How many different

ways were there to ask the same question? She leaned back, pressing her spine against the hard surface of the bench. She was so tired. Not just physically exhausted, but she was weary of answering the unending questions from the police.

"I know you're just trying to establish when it happened, but I guess I don't see why it really matters when Dan…when it happened."

"It's just routine procedure, ma'am."

She nodded in understanding, and solemnly waited for the next question.

Fitz glanced at his notes. "You came in through the back door?"

"Yes. It was open."

"Was it unlocked, or was it open?"

"Unlocked." Lifting her chin, she massaged the back of her neck slowly. Even without the black tweed jacket that was folded on the banquette next to her, the room was suffocatingly warm. There was blood on the coat, just as there was on one sleeve of her blouse. Unable to face the sight of it, she'd concealed both—that on the jacket by removing the garment and carefully folding it in half, and that on the blouse by turning back the cuffs. But it was still there. Just as the bloody images of Dan were there when she closed her eyes. Just as the smell of blood and death seemed to cling inside her nostrils.

"Was it normal for the door to be left unlocked?"

Shaking her head, she hunched forward, her fingers tightening around the mug on the table in front of her. She didn't want the coffee, but couldn't seem to let go of it, either—just as she couldn't seem to let go of what was happening inside her head.

If she had arrived earlier, would Dan still be alive? Could she have talked him out of it? Or would he only have killed her, too? Was that his intention when he'd called? Had the anniversary gift been a bullet and not signed legal papers?

The thought that Dan had hated her enough to want her dead left her fighting to breathe. How could two people who had once loved each other end up as they had? How did that happen?

"Mrs. Dawson?"

She looked up, realizing Fitz must have asked her another question. "I'm sorry. What did you say?"

"Did you see anyone when you arrived?"

"No." She pushed the coffee to one side. Obviously, she'd imagined the shadow inside the front door, just as she'd briefly imagined she wasn't alone in the house. Of course, as soon as she opened the bathroom door and there had been no one waiting for her on the other side, she'd realized her mistake.

Just then the door into the dining room swung open. Her chest instantly tight with renewed apprehension, Lexie looked up, praying that it wouldn't be Jack Blade.

She relaxed as soon as she realized that it was one of the officers who had been in and out of the kitchen several times in the past few hours.

"Medical examiner's here for the body," the officer announced.

Detective Fitz flipped his notebook shut and stood.

She looked up at him. "Can I go now?"

"You're free to go at any time, though it would be helpful if you could stick around a bit longer." The detective shrugged. "At least until we finish processing the crime scene."

Lexie nodded with resignation. It wasn't as if she'd be able to sleep even if she did go home. Better to stay here. To help as much as she could.

As soon as the detective left the room, she closed her eyes and leaned back, resting her head against the wall behind her. Her backside ached from the hard seating and her head hurt. There would be aspirin in the cabinet next to the sink, but she didn't seem to have the energy to get them.

She still couldn't get her mind around it. Dan was dead. He'd put a gun to his head. It just didn't mesh. He was a doctor. If he'd wanted to take his own life, why not end it with pills?

Lexie let go of that line of thought because it wasn't helping anyone. Certainly not Dan, who was beyond help, or herself.

For a period of time, in a numb trance, she listened to the clomp of feet just beyond the door and those overhead on the second floor. The not-so-quiet opening of doors and drawers as not only Dan's death was probed, but his life, as well.

She recalled how when they were first married, she'd awaken early on Sunday mornings sometimes. She'd be sitting in the very place she was now, sipping coffee and reading the paper, when Dan, having slept in after a late night at the hospital, would come stumbling downstairs. They'd talk about the baby he'd delivered and about the three or four they wanted. He'd reach across the table, his fingers capturing hers, and he'd tell her that he wanted to make a baby with her, not sometime in the future, but right then. Had that all been an act?

What she wouldn't give to go back to one of those uncomplicated mornings right now. To feel about Dan the way she had before everything went so wrong between them.

Reaching for her phone, needing to hear a familiar voice, she tried Fleming's number again. Dan and Fleming were—

had been—partners. As it had the last time she'd called, which had been just after she'd dialed 9-1-1, Fleming's voice mail picked up. She hadn't left a message before, but did this time. "Fleming, I really need to talk to you. I'm at Dan's. Something awful has hap—" Voice mail cut off the rest.

And when it did, she realized just how alone she felt sitting there in the kitchen. The house was full of people, but she felt isolated, as if she'd been shut out, shut away.

Lexie scooted to the end of the bench and climbed to her feet. How pathetic was that—feeling sorry for herself? She had a dozen friends she could call. Who would do whatever she asked of them. But she was stronger than that.

She located the aspirin and poured water into a glass. As she took the pills, she thought about what morning would bring. Funeral arrangements needed to be made. And someone should call Dan's parents. It would be easier on them if the news came from someone they knew and not from the police. Not from her, though.

Up until she filed for divorce, she'd always gotten along well with her in-laws. Better than she had with her mother and stepfather. And because she had, she felt the loss of them in her life more than she did the loss of her own parents, who, when the divorce was announced, had cut off all contact with her, but not with Dan.

Something banged in Dan's office, a loud sound followed by tense voices. What was going on in there now? Had Dan's body been carried out? In her mind, she envisioned him being placed in a body bag. She could almost hear the hiss of the zipper closing over his face.

Lexie turned around and stared at the door leading into the dining room. A sense of claustrophobia closed in on her. She couldn't stay any longer. She had to get out of here. Go anywhere. She crossed to the bench where she'd left her purse and jacket.

Straightening, she came face-to-face with Jack Blade.

A solid jolt of panic shot through her. The last time they'd been this close he'd been smiling down at her, the look in his pale blue eyes… She derailed all thoughts about what she'd seen in his eyes that night.

She had been praying he wouldn't show up. It was hard enough keeping herself together in the presence of strangers, of people who didn't know her, who hadn't seen her without the protective armor of clothing. Hadn't held her during the most vulnerable moments experienced by a woman.

The warm rush of heat hit her cheeks at the same time that cold dread settled at her core.

"Hello, Lexie." There was an edge to his voice that had also been absent during their last conversation.

She offered a tight smile and a brief nod, but decided to wait before saying anything. At least he wasn't pretending they were strangers. It would have been even more awkward if he had.

He motioned for her to sit. "I know you've already answered a lot of questions for Detective Fitz, but I need to ask you a few more."

She slowly sank onto the bench. Instead of also sitting, as she'd expected, Jack crossed to where the coffeepot remained nearly full. He was dressed in a suit. Had he been out on a date? Had he sat across from a beautiful woman tonight in an expensive restaurant?

Lexie retrieved her cold cup of coffee. Where Jack Blade went or what he did when he got there was none of her business. In every way that was meaningful, they were strangers.

So why couldn't she just forget about that night two months ago? They'd met in a restaurant bar. He'd been wearing faded jeans and an equally faded T-shirt stretched tight across his shoulders. He'd looked very male, not as civilized as he did now. And by the end of the evening, the T-shirt had been smeared with her tears and makeup.

It had gotten only worse from there. He'd driven her home to her place and taken her to bed. She became uncomfortable at the memory of the gloriously hot sex they'd shared.

He'd phoned several times after that night. Finally, she'd lied, telling him that she wasn't interested. The pathetic and cowardly truth, though, was that it was easier to pretend she was okay when there was no one there to see her fall apart.

As she watched, Jack poured two cups. Putting both on the table, he slid in across from her, facing her as Fitz had, but because he was taller than the other man, his knee brushed hers. Both of them ignored the contact.

He looked better than she remembered. Blond hair, longer on top and with some darker streaks running through it. Penetrating, deep-blue eyes; a strong jawline. But it was his mouth that was the real attention grabber. No woman would be able to resist imagining how it would feel. And not just on her lips.

Lexie pushed the old cup of coffee to the side and pulled the fresh one toward her, then waited in silence.

"Was your ex-husband right- or left-handed?"

It wasn't a question that she'd been expecting, so it took her a second to answer it. "Actually, Dan was ambidextrous. He did some things with his right hand and others with his left." She leaned back. "He was born a lefty and still played most sports that way, but during medical school he trained himself to use his right hand for just about everything else.

Said it made things easier for everyone. That nurses didn't have to spend a lot of time changing setups and rearranging the equipment in operating rooms."

"How about with a gun? Would he have used his right or his left hand?"

She fiddled with the cup handle. "I don't know. I never saw him pick one up."

He seemed surprised by the answer. "There was a .357 found next to the…next to your ex-husband. Nickel-plated, which means it was sort of a silvery color."

"I'm familiar with the term." The words came out sharper than she intended, but Lexie wasn't in the mood to apologize. She took a hurried sip of the cooling coffee. That she hadn't seen the gun or given any thought to the weapon that had been used bothered her. She should have, she realized. Was the revolver hers? She hadn't been worried when she'd moved out and left it secured in the gun safe. Dan had never shown any interest in her grandfather's collection of weapons.

Jack seemed to study her for several seconds. "So, as far as you knew, Dr. Dawson didn't own a .357?"

"No. But when I moved out I left one locked in the gun safe upstairs."

"So the weapon may be yours?"

"If it's the one from the safe, it would be registered to my grandfather."

"But you had possession of it?" Jack said.

Lexie frowned. "Yes. I suppose you could say the gun was mine."

"When was the last time you shot it?"

"Never."

"Why keep it then?"

"Sentimental reasons." She drew air deep into her lungs,

let it back out. The questions were really starting to get to her. She was beginning to wish that she'd left when Fitz had said she could.

"Most people don't consider guns to be very sentimental."

"I kept it because my grandfather enjoyed taking it to the range and shooting with his buddies. When I visited as a little girl, he'd take me with him. When I got older, he taught me how to handle a gun. After that, it became something we shared. The gun meant something to him, so it means something to me."

"When's the last time you saw your grandfather's gun?"

"Eleven months ago."

"But not tonight? When you found the body?"

She shook her head. "As soon as I saw Dan, I called 9-1-1."

"The call came in around eleven-forty," Jack said. "What were you doing here at that time of night?" Unlike Detective Fitz, he wasn't making notes, so his gaze never left her face. It had been the same the night they'd met. But it hadn't been just his eyes that had seemed completely focused on her; it had been everything else, too. Every movement, every touch had seemed meant for her. Had seemed meant to heal her deep down inside. It was no wonder she couldn't get him out of her head, and yet at the same time couldn't allow him anywhere near her.

She realized that he was waiting for her to answer, but it took her a moment to recall his question. "I had come by to collect some documents."

"What type of documents?"

"Property settlement papers," she said. "Dan called me earlier. He'd signed them and wanted me to pick them up."

"At eleven-thirty at night?"

Lexie felt her pulse pick up, but tried to ignore it. She had nothing to worry about. She hadn't done anything wrong. Everyone became a little nervous when a cop asked questions.

"Dan was a night owl," she said after a several-second hesitation.

"How did he seem when he contacted you tonight?"

"Fine."

"Who wanted the divorce?"

"This is a no-fault state." As soon as she said it, she realized that, though she didn't like the direction the question had taken, it was still a police investigation and personal feelings shouldn't play into it. "I was the one who wanted out."

"May I ask why?"

"Irreconcilable differences," she offered. It was nothing more than a twentieth-century sound bite that explained very little, but then, she'd learned that pigeonholing the reason a relationship failed was nearly impossible.

His mouth tightened. Jack had yet to take a sip of coffee, and she suspected that he'd poured it only to give the illusion that they were two people having a conversation. But that's where the illusion started and stopped, she realized, wondering why she hadn't sensed it earlier with Detective Fitz.

What Fitz had labeled an informal, fact-gathering interview had deteriorated into something more intense. More uncomfortable for her. Had the police found something that led them to believe Dan's death wasn't suicide? Did they think she was somehow involved? She almost wanted to laugh at the idea. Great. She'd gone from terrorized to paranoid in a matter of seconds.

"Was he alone when you spoke to him?"

Leaning back, Lexie folded her arms. "I don't know. He was text messaging me."

"Did you erase his messages?"

"No." She dug the phone out of her purse and placed it on the table in front of her. "I usually make notes of important calls when I get home at night."

"May I look?"

She slid the phone across to him, and then watched as he manipulated the buttons. After several moments, he turned the screen and held it up for her to see.

Anniversary surprise stop by drink.

"That was the first one," she said.

"Wedding anniversary, I assume?"

She nodded solemnly.

He looked at the phone again, though she suspected he really didn't need to.

"The call came in at ten-fifteen. Where were you when you received it?"

"Dinner."

"Kinda late for dinner. Were you alone?"

"It was a business dinner. At Baldacci's. My guests were Drs. Rafferty, Lemon and Lattimer. We were discussing a new drug, one that I rep. The reservation was for eight o'clock. We finished up a little before eleven."

"Eleven," he repeated. He hit a few more keys and again turned the screen so she could see it.

paprs signd last dink

"This one came in at 11:05. Were you still at the restaurant?"

She shook her head. "I had just arrived home."

"Alone?"

The question bothered her. Perhaps because of what had happened between them two months ago, and what she sensed to be the underlying suggestion that she often spent the night with near-strangers.

"Very alone."

If she hadn't been watching his face closely, she wouldn't have seen the barely perceptible tightening of his mouth and the infinitesimal narrowing of his eyes.

He nodded. "So why don't you tell me more about these property settlement papers? Was your divorce not final?"

Again, she sensed a hidden question—had Lexie been married when they'd slept together?

"The divorce was final six months ago. However, there was a problem with the paperwork, something fairly minor that only recently came to light. Dan took advantage of it, though, and filed an appeal of the original settlement, claiming that the division of property hadn't been equitable, and that he should retain possession of this house."

"And you didn't agree?"

"No. The house belonged to my grandparents and had been willed to me nearly a year before Dan and I married. Besides, he didn't really want the house. He hated it. He just wanted to drag things out."

"What makes you say that?"

"This wasn't the first time he claimed to have signed the documents," she said.

Instead of commenting, Jack punched more keys. He held up the phone.

Pick up tnight or brn them n house

"Where were you when this came in?"

"At home. I was still sitting in my car, debating what I should do."

"Did you believe that he might actually burn the papers and the house?"

"Dan never threatened. He warned of consequences."

"So you thought him capable?"

"Of burning the papers?" She glanced away. "Yes. I thought him capable."

"And the house?"

She rubbed her forehead. The headache really pounded now, making it difficult to think.

"Lexie, did you think he might burn the house?"

She shoved the hair that had fallen forward off her face as she looked up, meeting his gaze. "Intentionally? No. Accidentally? Maybe. If he'd been drinking," she admitted.

"Did he have a drinking problem?"

She fiddled with the charm bracelet again, her fingers automatically searching out and finding the smooth, heart-shaped locket. "Not as far as he was concerned."

Once again, Jack's eyes narrowed, but this time that wasn't the only change. It was like watching an approaching tornado, the clear skies of a summer afternoon suddenly turning dark and lethal. Treacherous and unpredictable.

And in that moment, it hit Lexie that she wasn't being paranoid earlier. Jack did think she might somehow be involved. Probably Detective Fitz did, too. How had she not picked up on it sooner?

Without saying a word, Jack got up and left the room briefly. When he came back, he had a cell phone encased in a plastic bag, the inside of which was smeared with blood. He wasn't alone this time, either. A Hispanic man followed him in, dressed in jeans and a T-shirt printed with CRIME SCENE, but stopped just inside the door.

This time Jack didn't sit down. Deep Water's police chief held up the phone, as he had the last one.

Silently, she read the screen: Don't drink with murderers

"Care to explain that?"

She realized that if they'd been looking for motive, she'd given them several in a matter of minutes. Her ex-husband was bullying her on a property settlement. He'd threatened to burn a house that she obviously wanted enough to fight him for. And then there was the most damning reason—the one they didn't even know about yet.

"Lexie?" There was menace in Jack's tone.

She lifted her eyes to his but remained mute. Should she ask to see an attorney? No one had read her her rights yet. Didn't they have to do that? Wasn't anything she said up until now inadmissible in court?

Jack punched more buttons, held the phone up yet again.
F off

"Were you angry?"

"Irritated. And…" Lexie closed her mouth, worried that her response would be misinterpreted.

Jack placed the phone on the table in front of her, the screen still lit and the words still there. The smeared blood on the inside of the bag blurred the screen. She looked away, her gaze stumbling onto Jack's as he watched her.

"You don't believe Dan's death to be a suicide?" Her voice was pitched lower than usual. This couldn't be happening. Not to her. Lexie looked toward the Hispanic man, who hadn't moved. "Do you?"

Jack's voice came as if from a distance. "It's up to the medical examiner to make that determination. Our job is to do a thorough investigation in the meantime. Anytime there is a questionable death, we have to approach it as if it's a homicide."

She didn't believe him. Maybe they had to wait on the official word, but her gut told her they were already building a case. Against her.

"Would you be willing to submit to a gunpowder residue test? Just to help rule yourself out?"

Lexie sat there for several seconds, weighing the request. She was really and truly screwed, wasn't she? If Dan hadn't killed himself—if he had instead been murdered—no one would buy her innocence, would they? She had opportunity and more than enough motive. And now they would have a residual test?

She stood slowly, her gaze moving from the man who waited near the door—the reason for his presence now obvious—to the man in front of her, who stood between her and the back door.

"It would be a waste of time," she said.

"Why's that?"

She lifted her chin and squared her shoulders. "I spent part of my afternoon at the gun range, trying out a new pistol."

Chapter Three

Jack didn't say anything for several moments, but then he didn't need to. The look in his eyes, though quickly concealed, was all the proof she needed. Jack Blade—a man she had slept with and still dreamed about some nights—actually thought her capable of murder.

"Any witnesses to that?"

"Two or three." She cast a quick glance in the direction of the crime scene officer. Fitz had returned and now stood next to him. Great. Just what she needed, a bigger audience.

"What gun range?" Jack asked, and she returned her attention to him.

"Frankie's on Sabal Run." She gathered up her purse and her jacket. "Now, if you're through with me…" She adjusted the purse on her shoulder.

"Unfortunately, I'm not." He looked over at Fitz. "Please inform Ms. Dawson of her noncustodial rights."

She couldn't breathe. "Am I under arrest?"

Fitz shook his head. "No. You have the right to leave at any time. And you have the right to hire an attorney and have him present before this interview continues."

"It's the middle of the night." She glanced from Fitz to

Jack. Asking for an attorney would only serve to make her look guilty. And while she may have entertained the thought of killing Dan once in sheer frustration, she hadn't ever done anything to harm him.

"What is it that you want?" she asked.

"For starters? For you to submit to gunpowder residue testing," Jack said.

Lexie put her jacket back on the table, as well as her purse. The procedure, nothing more than a swab of both hands, took a matter of minutes.

"Anything else?"

"Your shirt. There's blood on the right cuff."

Involuntarily, Lexie's hand flexed. The vision of Dan's bleeding, shattered skull swam before her eyes. Nothing would have saved him. "I tried to help…."

"Help how?" Fitz asked politely. Too politely.

Lexie glanced up, taking in the three identical expressions of professional skepticism. Ignoring Fitz's question, she met Jack's stare. "You want my shirt? What would you like me to wear home?"

As she continued to meet his gaze, another vivid memory of the night two months ago surfaced. Jack unbuttoning her blouse, his warm hands pushing it off her shoulders and down her arms. She wanted to glance away but didn't.

Jack nodded to the heavyset detective. "Fitz, get something for Ms. Dawson to put on."

Fitz brought her one of Dan's shirts. She opened the kitchen door into the dining room, heading for the small bath beneath the stairs, but when she reached the foyer, a sharp breeze whipped in through the open front door. In the next instant, she realized why it stood open.

Everything went cold inside her as she watched two men

maneuver Dan's body out of the den. Dan hadn't been a big man, just shy of two hundred pounds, but they still struggled, their feet shuffling noisily against the wood floor as they made a wide turn to avoid the entrance table and a small side chair. Only when the load was aligned with the front entrance did they carry their burden out into the frigid December night.

Dan was dead. Was inside that heavy bag. Tonight was the last time she would see him. She wouldn't attend the funeral. Not because she didn't want to, but because her presence there would upset Dan's parents. And she understood just how difficult it was to lose a child.

The body bag was loaded into a waiting vehicle. She should feel something. Grief. Sorrow. Maybe even outrage. But she felt none of those things. She simply felt empty and scared.

The men moving the body hadn't noticed, but a detective who she'd been introduced to earlier but hadn't seen since—and whose name she couldn't remember—walked out of Dan's office at that moment and stood staring at her, his gaze direct and condemning.

Immediately bowing her head, she ducked into the bathroom, closing the door behind her. She'd been in such a hurry that she hadn't turned on the light, so now was forced to fumble for the switch. The few seconds that she was trapped there in the dark pushed her to the edge of her already tenuous hold on her control.

Had the timing been on purpose? Had they hoped seeing Dan's body would force her to confess?

Turning, she caught her reflection in the mirror. Her eyes appeared dazed and slightly red. Some of it was the late hour, the fact that her contacts were beginning to feel scratchy, but mostly it was the shock. Not just Dan's death, either. She'd gone through her whole life trying to do the right thing. Believing that as long as she did, everything would be okay. Tonight showed her just how stupidly naive she'd been.

After removing the blouse, Lexie shoved an arm into one of the long sleeves. She could smell Dan's cologne on the shirt. Not strongly, but it was still there. Her fingers felt stiff, unresponsive, so buttoning the shirt took some effort. As she lifted her hands to do the topmost button, the material brushed across her rib cage. The sensation of cloth across skin tightened her apprehension. Dan's fingers. That's what the contact felt like. As if it was Dan touching her.

When she lifted her gaze to the mirror this second time, she saw a familiar stranger. Someone terrified and lost. She recognized that face, but the last time she'd seen it, she'd been twelve years old.

Maybe she'd had it all wrong earlier. Perhaps Dan hadn't brought her here tonight to kill her, but to frame her.

Was it possible to make a suicide look like murder? Could Dan have hated her enough to do that?

Lexie turned her back on the mirror. She had to pull herself together. She couldn't go out there looking the way she did now. Beaten. Frightened.

Someone knocked on the door. "You okay, ma'am?" Fitz asked. Was he waiting for her to come out? To confess?

"I'm fine," she said, but realized she didn't sound that way, her voice pitched higher than normal. She slumped against the wall and waited until she heard Fitz move away.

But he was waiting for her when she opened the door, and took the blouse and jacket from her.

He placed them in separate evidence bags. "We need to inspect the contents of the gun safe."

With a sharp nod, she immediately headed for the stairs.

It was easier to give them what they wanted. Besides, if the gun was her grandfather's, they'd find that out soon enough.

She led the way upstairs, Fitz and the tall, rangy detective whose name she didn't remember trailing behind her. The master bedroom had been redone since she moved out, the antiques replaced by contemporary pieces. The bed was neatly made, but there were signs that the room had been searched—drawers not quite closed and the closet door left open.

Taking that first step into the master bedroom closet, suddenly surrounded by Dan's personal things, it seemed as if he was there in that small space with her.

She remained unmoving after that initial step, her eyes focused on the door to the gray safe. One of the two men behind her cleared his throat, reminding her that she was not alone. They probably thought her hesitation was motivated by fear over what they would find inside. Maybe she should be.

She took the final steps. As she lifted her fingers to the dial, she realized they trembled. Her companions would no doubt have already noticed. Lexie manipulated the combination lock, then reached for the lever handle. With the scent of gun oil suddenly overriding that of Dan's cologne, she thought of another man—of her grandfather. It was his presence that she felt as she scanned the lineup of shotguns and rifles, the shelves where automatics and revolvers were arranged neatly.

Out of habit, she started to reach for the Colt 1861 Navy revolver, but Fitz stopped her. "We can take it from here, ma'am."

After Fitz escorted her to where Jack was waiting for her in the kitchen, he left, presumably retracing his steps.

She wrapped her arms in front of her. "If we're done here, I really would like to go now."

Even though she was standing right in front of him, her gaze meeting his, she didn't see the man who had made love to her two months ago. At that moment, he was just a stern-faced professional doing his job. She knew it was too much to expect one night together to make any kind of real difference, but still found herself oddly angry with him.

"We're done for tonight," he said.

Instead of maneuvering around him as most people eager to escape would have, she remained where she was, her body only inches from his, and waited, eyes reflecting what she hoped appeared to be confidence and not the fear she actually felt.

Jack didn't step aside, but did turn enough to let her past. At the last moment, he wrapped his fingers loosely around her upper arm, forcing her to turn back, to lift her gaze to his again. She felt a sharp stab of awareness run through her, accompanied by the memory of his hand closing around her upper arm, his mouth coming down hard on hers. But not this time. This time his mouth only flattened with… Disgust? Distrust? It didn't really matter, she realized.

Jack's fingers flexed. "Where will you be staying?"

"Detective Fitz has the address, but then you already know the way, don't you?"

The pressure of his fingers increased and his eyes briefly lost some of their remoteness. "Hire a lawyer."

She frowned. "I didn't kill my ex-husband, Jack."

He looked as if he planned to say something more, but didn't. Releasing her, he stepped back.

Once outside the back door, Lexie fought the urge to run. The rain had stopped, the night clearing so that stars hung overhead now. Without the protective blanket of clouds, the temperature had continued to drop toward the low thirties, and without a jacket, she was shivering before she'd made it halfway around the side of the house.

Had she made a mistake in answering questions, in submitting to the residue test? In opening the safe?

It was too late to worry about it now. What was done was done. But she'd do as Jack suggested; she'd contact an attorney first thing in the morning. If Jack or his men had more questions they wanted answered, she'd only do it if her attorney was present.

A wind gust went through the material of the shirt as if it wasn't there. Wrapping her arms around herself, she kept walking, faster now, with her shoulders hunched and her head bowed. She was suddenly eager to reach her car, not just for the warmth it offered, but also for the privacy.

As she turned the corner of the house, though, she realized that getting in her car and leaving wasn't going to be so simple. When she'd arrived earlier, the drive had been empty, but now a dozen or so police vehicles packed the area in neat order, one beside the other. At least two of them blocked her company sedan.

She took a few more steps forward, wondering how long it would take to get them moved. It was two-thirty in the morning. Even if she called a cab, it would take at least a half hour for one to show up. All she wanted was to go home. Maybe with a lot of luck, she could get a few hours of sleep. Maybe even for a span of hours forget about the nightmare that had suddenly become her life.

Hearing the front door open, she turned. Jack stepped out onto the porch. Maybe he'd been watching from the window and, recognizing the parking problem, was coming to rectify it.

He walked down the steps and headed across the damp grass toward her. Tightening her arms across herself again and locking her knees, she bounced in place on the balls of her feet as she waited on him. He moved easily, his stride loose. She'd noticed that about him even before they'd actually met. Her awareness of him had gone beyond that, though. But then, if you asked any woman in Deep Water to describe the chief of police, the word *hunk* was bound to come up.

Hearing rushing footsteps behind her, she glanced over her shoulder, catching only the glimpse of a woman's white face and dark hair before she felt the blow to her left cheek that landed openhanded and with stinging force.

"Evil bitch!"

As spittle splattered Lexie's face, she fell back a step, confused. She wiped the spit off. "What do you…who the hell are you…?"

Instead of answering, the woman picked up a fist-size rock from the ground and rushed Lexie, who was still backing away. "You're going to pay!"

At the last moment, seeing the rock driving downward toward her head, Lexie ducked and immediately lashed out with a fist. Pain exploded in her hand as it connected with the woman's shoulder. What seemed like a thousand kilowatts of electricity shot upward into her elbow.

Jack grabbed the woman and dragged her backward. Lexie doubled over her injured hand and turned her back as several other officers arrived.

"Don't you understand? That bitch killed him!"

She heard Jack handing off the woman, who continued to rail as she was led away.

Then he approached Lexie. "You okay?"

She tried to form words, but couldn't seem to push them past her lips. Where she'd been freezing seconds earlier, now sweat clung to her, and her chest felt painfully tight. But it wasn't until her vision tunneled toward black and her knees started to buckle that she realized what was happening to her.

"Lexie? Are you all right?"

What the heck was wrong with the man? She was anything but okay. Still cradling the hand close to her body, she sank to her knees.

Jack squatted down in front of her. "Do you think it's broken?"

"Yes." She took a deep breath and tried to let it out slowly. Another knifelike pain climbed her arm. "That's the problem with being a girl," she managed to mutter between gritted teeth. "No one teaches you how to throw a punch. How to protect yourself. Because they figure there's going to be a man around to do it. Well, I got news for them—"

"Come on, Sugar Ray. You're going to the hospital." Jack helped her to her feet. She wobbled slightly and he steadied her. When she looked up into his face this time, she thought she saw concern. In the next instant, though, it was gone. Or perhaps it had never existed.

"Did you want to press charges?" Jack asked.

"No. I think I have enough problems, don't you?"

She took a deep breath. With even the least bit of jarring, it felt as if someone was stabbing her wrist with a very dull knife. All she wanted was enough medication to deaden the pain. Since hands and wrists were his specialty, she thought about calling Ken Lattimer. If only she'd accepted his invitation—if she'd said yes instead of no to dessert—tonight would have turned out so differently. For her, at least.

She was so intent on keeping the hand and wrist steady, she didn't see the newcomer.

"Lexie?"

At the sound of Fleming Whittemore's voice, she turned. He stood five feet away, dressed more casually than she was used to seeing him, his expression grim. He wasn't alone. One of the officers, the kid who'd been guarding the front door, was with him.

When Fleming tried to approach, the officer stopped him. "What's going on, Lexie?"

"Dan's dead."

"Dead?" Fleming shook free of the officer's restraint but didn't make any move to reach her. "What happened?"

"Suicide, they think." She shook her head. "Maybe murder."

"Are you okay?" Fleming asked, his glance traveling from her face to the face of the man beside her.

She nodded as Jack's fingers closed around her upper arm. Lexie glanced up at the man who held her. Why was he suddenly holding her? To keep her from Fleming? "This is Fleming Whittemore, Dan's partner. I called him earlier. He…he should be the one to phone Dan's parents." She looked at Fleming again. "I need to go to the hospital. Do you think you could drive me?"

Jack's fingers tightened their hold. "One of my men will take you."

"But I'd rather—"

"Andy," Jack interrupted. He motioned to the woman who had assaulted Lexie. "Put her in the back of a car for now. I'm sure Fitz and Shepherd will want to talk to her and to Mr. Whittemore." He looked at Fleming. "I assume you have no objections to answering a few questions?"

Fleming shook his head.

It was only as her attacker was being led away that Lexie recognized the woman as one of Dan's nurses. What was she doing here at this time of night?

Taking off his coat, Jack draped it around Lexie's shoulders. "Come on."

The gesture surprised her. But as the weight of the coat settled around her, she realized it shouldn't have. Wasn't that one of the first things she'd noticed about Jack the night they'd met—his ability to make a woman feel very alive, but also safe?

IT WAS NOW NEARLY 4:00 a.m. Jack had stepped outside, hoping the cold air would stave off the exhaustion that seemed to be gaining on him. He'd already been up for more than twenty-three hours and figured he had another couple to go before he could catch a few hours of sleep.

News crews were setting up out on the street. The dispatcher at the police station had relayed the message that calls were coming in requesting interviews with Jack. Word had gotten out about the prominent doctor's death. One persistent reporter had already called the mayor at home, waking him from sleep with the news and asking for a reaction. Luckily, or perhaps more accurately, unluckily, the mayor had refused to comment until morning. At which time he promised to hold a joint press conference with Jack.

That was just what Jack wanted to do first thing in the morning. Share a microphone with a man who had publicly criticized him on more than one occasion. The friction between Jack and the mayor, and even with several members of the city council, was no secret, and the press was likely to play on that angle if they got the chance.

Jack's cell phone rang. It was Fitz. "I've invited Whittemore into the kitchen for questioning. I thought you might want to join us."

"I'll be right there."

The doctor was already sitting in the breakfast nook, Fitz's bulk squeezed in on the opposite side of the table.

Jack grabbed a cup of coffee and took a seat at the island counter where Fitz had been earlier, content to just watch and listen. If it had been anyone but Lexie, he would have done the same earlier, been a spectator during her questioning.

Dr. Fleming Whittemore, one of the city's preeminent obstetricians, looked as tired as the rest of them. He'd shed the heavy leather jacket and was now dressed in jeans, a brown flannel shirt and work boots. Both the boots and jeans had mud on them. But not the hands, Jack realized as Whittemore reached for the foam cup of coffee. Skin pink, nails clean, as if they'd been scrubbed aggressively.

"Looks as if you're a bit of an outdoorsman?" Fitz commented. Building rapport by establishing common ground with the interviewee always came first.

Jack had intentionally skipped that step with Lexie. They'd previously established common ground—one he hadn't been anxious to have revealed to his men. Though Jack wouldn't be surprised if their previous relationship came out at some point.

Fleming looked down at the chunks of mud he'd left on the floor. "I have a cabin in the Ocala Forest. I was out there checking on it earlier."

"Do you hunt, then?"

Whittemore slumped. "No. I just keep it as a retreat."

"Does your wife go with you?"

"I'm not married." Whittemore glanced over at Jack.

Jack sensed that instead of relaxing, the casual questions that were unrelated to what had taken place here tonight put the doctor on edge. Jack wondered why, and suspected Fitz did, as well.

"How long had you and Dr. Dawson been partners?" Fitz asked.

"Just over three years."

"How did the two of you meet?"

"My practice had grown to a point where I couldn't handle it any longer alone. I took out an ad in a medical journal. Dan had finished up his residency in obstetrics down in Miami and, because of his relationship with Lexie, wanted to relocate to Deep Water."

Jack wasn't surprised when Fitz avoided showing too much interest in Lexie. The detective had obviously sensed that it was still too early. That if Fleming guessed they were focusing on Lexie as a suspect, his responses might become more guarded.

After all, the fact that she'd called Whittemore suggested that the relationship between them was a strong one. Just friends? Or something more? Jack didn't try to deny that his interest in the answer to that question wasn't strictly professional.

"Would you say he was a good doctor?" Fitz asked.

"Yes. A very good one. He tended to take plenty of time with his patients, and most of them seemed to like him. Of course, there's always one or two who don't."

"No impending lawsuits?"

Whittemore shook his head. "No."

"How was he around the office and with the staff? Was he easygoing or uptight?"

"You could tell when things weren't going well."

"So he had a bit of a temper?"

Whittemore glanced away briefly. "I never saw him really lose control in the office," he said when he looked back.

"What about outside the office?"

Again, Whittemore looked away.

Fitz changed tack with the next question. "What about his divorce? Did he ever discuss it?"

"No. But then I would be the last person he would talk to about it."

Jack could think of several reasons why a man might not discuss a divorce with a business partner, the most obvious being a love triangle. Was it possible that that was what was going on here?

"Why would you be the last person?" Fitz asked.

"Because I was the one Lexie came to the night she lost the baby."

Lost a baby? Fitz glanced over at Jack, speculation evident in the detective's face.

Had they finally hit on something? Whittemore hadn't said "miscarried." He'd said "lost." How many ways were there to lose a baby? Problems in the delivery room? No. There was more to it than that. Whatever had happened had created tension between the two doctors.

Fitz straightened. "Okay. Maybe you should tell me about that night."

Whittemore didn't answer right away, the pause once again suggesting he was choosing his words carefully. Why? Who was he protecting? Himself? Dan Dawson? Or Lexie?

"It was about eleven months ago," he said. "A Sunday night. Late. I'd just returned from vacation and was at the office catching up on some files."

Whittemore took another sip of coffee, the last. Normally Fitz would probably have refilled it, but didn't this time.

Possibly because he was afraid that given too much time to think, Whittemore might stop talking altogether.

"You were at the office?"

He nodded again. "If it hadn't been the private line, I wouldn't have even answered the phone." He looked as if he wished he hadn't. "It was Lexie. She was hysterical. Dan had pushed her down some steps." He glanced over at Jack. "It wasn't the first time."

Jack felt his gut tighten. Domestic violence, crimes against women and children, topped every cop's list of most hated call-outs. But the anger he felt now was more personal than that, he realized. Lexie wasn't a stranger.

Up until that moment, Jack had been telling himself that, despite the fact that he knew her, he'd be able to maintain a professional distance. He now realized just how difficult it was going to be—almost as difficult as it would have been to keep his hands off Dan Dawson if he was still alive.

"How far along in the pregnancy was she?" Fitz asked.

"Over eight months."

"Nearly full-term then. Any problems with the pregnancy before that night?"

"No."

"So you met Lexie at the hospital and—"

"I tried to get her to go to the hospital, but she insisted that the office was closer. I figured I'd stabilize her there and then get her transferred. Of course, I didn't know how bad it was."

"How bad was it?"

"When she arrived, she was already in hard labor. I don't know how she even managed to drive, but I knew immediately that stabilizing and transferring wasn't an option."

"So you attempted to deliver the baby in the office?"

"Yeah. Things seemed to be going fine until halfway

through the birth. The baby's heartbeat suddenly bottomed out completely. I did everything I could, but it wasn't enough."

"Did you dial 9-1-1?"

Whittemore rubbed his face, his color having gone from washed-out to a shade resembling that of a dead man's. "No. There was no reason to."

"Was an autopsy done on the fetus?" Fitz asked.

"Yeah. Dan insisted. I think he desperately wanted the baby's death to be caused by something other than the fall."

"What were the medical examiner's findings?"

"That if Lexie hadn't fallen, the baby would have been born in perfect health."

Jack stood. It wasn't looking good for Lexie. Whittemore's statement had given them an even stronger motive for her to have killed her ex-husband.

"Did Lexie make a report?"

"No. She's a strong woman. So I could never understand why she put up with Dan's treatment of her." The doctor frowned. "That night wasn't the first time I suggested she do something about the situation, but I think she felt that she shared in the blame."

"Why?"

"I don't know." He lowered his head again as if in exhaustion. "All I know is that she didn't deserve the way Dan treated her. She's a good lady. Caring. Maybe too much so for her own good."

"Why do you say that?"

"Because as crazy as it sounds, I think she was worried about what would happen to the medical practice if it came out that Dan had some personal problems."

"Did Dan ever indicate that he was afraid of his ex-wife?"

"Yeah. He called me the night before the memorial service for the baby and told me he wasn't going to be able to attend. That Lexie had told him if he did, she'd kill him."

"Is that something you would have expected her to do?"

"No. And I'm not even certain it's true. I think he may have been trying to cast her as being on the edge of a mental breakdown. I think he was worried what she might say, and that if she talked, he'd have to leave Deep Water in order to continue practicing medicine."

"So why would he give her a hard time on the property settlement? I would think that he'd be willing to hand over just about anything she wanted."

"He did the first go-round. But when he got the opportunity to take her back to court… I think he felt a little braver by then. Probably figured if she talked at that point, everyone would believe that it was just the typical mudslinging of a vindictive ex-wife. Especially in light of his new relationship."

"Any chance that Lexie Dawson was jealous?"

He frowned. "I suppose it's possible."

Jack stood. Whittemore had just handed them possible motive number three.

THE CAB SHE'D TAKEN from the hospital let her off in front of Riverhouse. She'd opted not to collect her car from the house in town, partially because she'd been afraid the police would still be there.

A slow drizzle had started again. With one arm in a cast, her briefcase and house keys in the other, handling an umbrella was out of the question.

The rain started to come down a bit harder as Lexie propped the briefcase against the door.

"Of all the times for the front light to burn out, it had to be tonight." Lexie tried to stab the key into the lock, but using her left hand made it extremely awkward.

As she lost her hold on the key ring for the third time and heard it hit the deck, Lexie prayed the set of keys wouldn't slip between the boards.

Locating them, she straightened and tried the lock again. This time she managed not only to get the key in, but to open the front door. Bumping it closed with a hip, she turned on the foyer light with her left hand and was greeted with… Sameness?

It wasn't as if she'd expected the house to look any different. Maybe, as crazy as it sounded, she'd expected to see it through different eyes.

She sagged against the door. What was she going to do? Beyond calling an attorney in the morning? Just wait to see what happened next?

Was she supposed to just get up in the morning, run her Saturday errands, pick up groceries for the week, clean the house, do laundry? Pretend that nothing had happened?

Lexie slowly slid down the door until she sat on the floor. But something had happened. Dan was dead. Why hadn't she cried yet? Was there something wrong with her? Was she some kind of monster who couldn't forgive even in death? Dead. The man she'd married. The father of her baby was dead.

And she felt nothing. Not grief. Not even a tiny bit of sorrow. She just felt numb. As if someone had reached inside her and unplugged her emotions.

After several long moments, Lexie climbed to her feet and doggedly walked into the kitchen. She grabbed a water glass from the cabinet and took one of the pain pills Ken Lattimer had prescribed.

She was innocent. In time, the police would realize as much. She just needed to sit tight on this scary roller-coaster ride until it pulled into the station. And it would be easier to do if she had some clue to the ride's duration. Would it be days, weeks or would it be hours?

She glanced at the clock. Though it was already past four o'clock in the morning, it was still too early to call Fleming. What kind of questions had they asked him? And what kind of answers had he given?

Lexie left the glass in the sink and headed for bed. As it always was, the door to the second bedroom was closed. She opened it and looked in, and it, too, was the same. Nearly eighteen months ago she'd redone the room into a nursery, fully expecting that once the baby came she and Dan would spend more time out here. She knew she needed to dismantle the room, pack away or donate the contents of the drawers, but so far she hadn't been able to do it.

Lexie changed into plaid boxer shorts and a white T-shirt in the dark, then crawled into bed, too weary even to wash her face. She rolled onto her side awkwardly, attempting to find a comfortable position for her injured hand.

Closing her eyes, she waited for the drug to dull not only the pain, but also the overriding sense of doom that seemed to have taken hold of her. It felt as if her feet had been laced inside lead boots and that she was standing on the edge of the dock, waiting for that final push into the dark waters below her.

She was beginning to wonder why she just didn't let it happen.

THE BABY. It was screaming.

Fighting her way up from sleep, Lexie shoved the sheets off her and staggered out of bed. Disoriented, she felt her way to the bedroom door and opened it.

As soon as she did, everything went silent. Motherly concern escalated to fear. Something was wrong. Very wrong. A baby didn't just suddenly stop crying.

A hallway linked the two small bedrooms on this side of the house. The night-light in the small bath between the rooms was bright enough that she could see the closed door of the second bedroom. Dread tightened her chest, as she opened the door. The drapes hadn't been drawn, and the last of the night's starlight slipped in through the large, multi-paned window and onto the pastel-colored carpet.

As she leaned over the crib, her lungs suddenly locked tight and her world—the one she sometimes managed to escape into while she slept—came crashing down around her.

Not just the night eleven months ago, when she'd briefly held her baby daughter in her arms, but the nights and days since that had been filled with emptiness and remorse.

Crossing her arms on her chest as if she could protect her heart, Lexie stumbled through the living room and out onto the back deck.

She stood at the railing dragging in the cold air. It had been months since the last nightmare. She'd convinced herself that she was doing better, that she'd finally come to terms with losing the baby. With her own culpable negligence.

She should never have gone anywhere near Dan the night he'd pushed her down the stairs. She knew what he was capable of. It wasn't the first time he'd shoved her when she tried to stop him from leaving the house after he'd had too much to drink.

She hadn't been thinking about the baby, though. And a good mother always thought of her baby first. Always protected her offspring. Even at the cost of her own life.

In reality, Lindy's death was as much Lexie's fault as it

had been Dan's. And she was beginning to believe that she would never be able to put it behind her.

She looked down at her fractured right hand. The anesthetic was wearing off and she was beginning to feel the sharp aching brought on by movement. Ken had assured her that in a matter of weeks it would heal. And if she lost any range of motion, rehab would restore it. She'd had no trouble believing him.

So why didn't she believe the psychologist she'd seen right after she'd lost Lindy? The speech both doctors had given was eerily similar. Take it easy. Don't overdo. Don't push. She'd done all those things.

And look at her now. She was still just as screwed up.

Tonight's awful events and the surreal accusation that she was somehow involved didn't help. Part of her didn't believe Dan was dead. The same part that didn't believe her baby was dead.

Lexie looked out at the river, allowed her gaze to climb the low bank that gave way to a grassy expanse. The open space had been left by the harvesting of logs for the house. Several of the pines that hadn't been harvested—perhaps because they'd been too small at the time—appeared to have broken away from the forest behind them. If she stared at them long enough, they seemed to be moving closer and closer.

As a child she'd pretended the trees were actually coming for their downed brothers and sisters, and that in time, they would reach the house and reclaim their family.

But even then, she'd known it was nothing more than childish imagination and a trick of the eye. Trees couldn't walk. Just as she knew that her daughter couldn't be alive.

So why did everything inside her tell her otherwise?

Chapter Four

Lexie glanced around the hospital's meeting room at the other members of the Saturday morning Sisters-in-Loss, a support group for women who had lost an infant. Since the last time she'd attended was nearly six months ago, most of the faces were new to her. She'd been hoping that would be the case.

Before she'd left home this morning, three friends who had heard about Dan had phoned to ask if she was okay and to suggest that if she didn't want to be alone she could come stay with them. Lexie had declined the invitations. Partially because she didn't want her problems overflowing into their lives and partially because she believed it would be easier to be among strangers.

Several women came up behind her.

"It happened sometime last night," one of them said. "It was all over the news this morning. Dr. Dawson was found dead in his home."

"Was it a burglary?" another woman asked. Lexie wasn't about to turn around to see who was speaking.

"No comment. At least that's all Chief Blade was willing to say when they interviewed him this morning."

Lexie pushed past another small group of women talking at the door. Maybe coming here had been a mistake. Maybe she should just leave. Maybe, given the situation, anonymity was impossible. Even among strangers.

But go where? Her appointment with the attorney wasn't until one o'clock.

Taking a seat, Lexie focused her attention on the serenity garden just outside. Instead of appearing serene, the space looked sad and empty. With the cold temperatures of two nights ago, the usual profusion of impatiens had melted into decaying masses, and because of poor drainage and the recent heavy rains, the pine nugget mulch that had once tidied the planting beds now resembled brown flotsam scattered across the lawn.

"Ladies," the leader announced several minutes later, clapping her hands. She was somewhere in her early sixties, wore a denim jumper with a black turtleneck, sneakers and an energetic smile. "Please come find seats. We need to get started."

A latecomer took the vacant seat on Lexie's right. She'd seen the attractive Eurasian woman enter the room. At first, she'd thought that the woman had mistakenly wandered into the wrong meeting. Mostly because of her age, which had to be somewhere in her late forties, or even early fifties.

The woman hung her red leather jacket on the seat back and placed her clutch across her lap before glancing at Lexie. "You weren't saving this chair for anyone, were you?"

"No. I wasn't holding it." Lexie said. "My name—"

The woman turned to the young mother on the other side of her. For several seconds, Lexie found herself staring at the back of the woman's head. Had she just been snubbed? By someone she didn't even know?

With a mental shrug, Lexie shifted her attention to the other women in the circle. Most of them were in their mid-twenties to late thirties. Only the Eurasian woman and a young girl of perhaps eighteen or nineteen, who sat opposite Lexie, fell outside that range.

"Okay." The leader remained seated. Her job was to keep everyone on track, but not intrude. "I suppose I should ask who would like to open the session. And please remember, ladies, that we use only first names here."

For several seconds no one said anything, everyone looking around to see who was going to be the first.

The young girl across from Lexie climbed to her feet.

In spite of her untrimmed and slightly messy dark hair and her wrinkled cargo pants and sweatshirt, she was pretty.

"My name's Amanda." Her eyes were large and brown and filled with uncertainty. "Most of you…" She fiddled with the zipper on her red sweatshirt. "You lost your babies." She lifted her gaze. "I gave mine up."

No one in the room said anything. No murmured words of understanding as there had been in the past when someone finally worked up the courage to speak. No gentle touches on the lower arm or shoulder to encourage the speaker to go on.

She must have known what they were all thinking. That she wasn't one of them. That every member of this group would have gladly given their own life for that of their baby.

After another few seconds of strained silence, Lexie uncrossed her legs. Wasn't someone going to say something? Though the leader's job was only to observe, was she going to leave this young girl standing there emotionally naked?

Lexie scooted to the front edge of her seat. "Aren't we all here because we need to talk about a painful time in our lives?"

Most of the women immediately bowed their heads. Only two members continued to stare at the teenager. But under those stares, Amanda appeared to shrink. Her shoulders rolled forward so that they appeared even narrower than they had previously, and her spine seemed to collapse, stealing inches from her frame.

"Ladies," the group leader said at last. "Isn't this group about nurturing and support?" She got to her feet. "We're not here to judge, are we?"

The nods of agreement from those with bowed heads were barely perceptible.

The leader reached out and touched Amanda on the shoulder. "If you don't want to talk just now, you don't have to."

The young woman gave a hesitant nod. "I want…um…I don't have anyone else to talk to about it, ma'am."

"Then you talk."

"Yes, ma'am." She released the zipper. "The doctor let me hold her before he took her away." She looked down. "Until a couple months ago, I was okay with what I'd done. He said it was better for Janie. That she'd go to a good family who could give her things I couldn't. Her father wasn't around and my mom, she was sick, and I didn't have no insurance…." She started to break down, but quickly caught herself.

Her lips pressed together, she swallowed hard two or three times. "I tell…I tell myself she's okay, that she's out there with that other family and that everything is good for her…." She looked down at her hands. "But I can't stop thinking about her. About what I did. About how a baby belongs with its mama." She stood there, tears streaming from her eyes, and yet the other common signs of sorrow—the shaking shoulders and features twisted with emotion—were oddly absent.

Such despair and sorrow in one so young. Where was her mother? Where were her friends? Lexie realized that where most of the women in the room had a spouse, a significant other, a mother of their own to talk to, Amanda didn't. Lexie and the young woman were alike in that way.

Amanda sat suddenly, almost as if someone had placed a hand on her shoulder and shoved her back down. As soon as her buttocks met metal, her hands folded on her lap and became still. In another few seconds, her spine relaxed against the chair back. She had essentially pulled on her armor. Had walled herself off from pain by retreating inwardly.

More than a half-dozen other women stood up after that, talking about the past week and their emotional obstacles. When the meeting broke up, Amanda bolted for the door.

Lexie was intent on catching up to her when the Eurasian woman grabbed Lexie's upper arm.

"I kept thinking your face looked familiar."

Only half listening, Lexie watched Amanda slip out into the hallway. The girl had seemed so alone that she had wanted to suggest they could go somewhere to talk.

"But it wasn't until just a few moments ago," the woman continued, still holding on to Lexie, "that I realized where I had seen you before."

Lexie turned to her. "I don't mean to be rude, but I need—"

"You were married to Dan Dawson, weren't you?"

The room went instantly silent. Conversation ceased. Those still in the room turned and stared at Lexie.

Lexie pulled free of the woman's grasp. "I really do have somewhere I need to be."

So much for anonymity.

JACK WAS SITTING in the back booth of Alligator Café having breakfast with his brother, Alec, on Sunday morning. As usual,

the restaurant was crowded with both locals and tourists
headed out to Deep Water Springs to see the manatees that had
made their way up the river and into the springs after the cold
snap.

Jack and Alec had already done their five-mile run out at
the springs and, as they did nearly every Sunday these days,
had stopped for breakfast at the small restaurant where Alec
had met his wife, Katie.

It was here at the Café that Jack had first seen Lexie, too.
Over a year and a half ago.

She'd been sitting with a group of nurses when he'd
entered. Initially, as he walked past her table, he'd noticed
her attractiveness. Nice features, lots of blond hair, well-
dressed and well-groomed. But it wasn't her appearance that
had held his attention after that, it was the way she'd seemed
so full of energy and life. She talked with more animation
than the other women and laughed more freely. There was
no hesitation when she reached out to touch those closest to
her. *Warm* would have been the word he would have used to
describe her.

He'd been so intrigued by her that when done with his
lunch, he'd lingered with a second glass of sweet tea and a
slice of key lime pie just so he could watch her.

It wasn't until the group rose to leave that she looked in
his direction. Her smile had hit him dead center of his chest
and gone through him like a thirty-eight caliber slug.

Person of Interest. That's how he'd labeled her that day,
using cop jargon.

As chief of police, he hadn't found it difficult to learn her
identity. What had been hard was curbing his disappointment
when he'd discovered she was married.

Jack unwrapped the napkin from around the silverware.

She was still a Person of Interest—and, if the M.E. ruled Dan Dawson's death a homicide, Jack wasn't going to be the only one interested in Lexie Dawson. The state was going to be interested, too.

He'd been trying not to form any opinions about the case, but hadn't been completely successful. Partly because of what had happened between them two months ago and partly because of what he'd seen two nights ago when he'd interviewed Lexie. She'd been shaken. She'd been scared. But she hadn't acted guilty. Even when he'd pushed her. Or maybe, if he was being completely honest with himself, it was that a part of him just couldn't accept the possibility that she'd killed a man.

"What about the autopsy?" Alec poured coffee from the carafe. "Any idea when you'll get the report?" The Sunday paper, minus all the advertising inserts, was piled on the end of the table between the two brothers.

Though they hadn't been discussing Dan Dawson's case, Jack knew which autopsy Alec referred to because it was the department's only open murder investigation.

"The medical examiner's office promised everything but the tox screen by Monday afternoon."

"That's quick." Alec located the sports section, but didn't open it.

"Yeah. Dan Dawson played racquetball with Brian Huffer and Harvey Sanderson." Sanderson was the mayor and Brian sat on Deep Water's city council.

"Even in death, it's not what you know, but who you know," Alec offered.

"Yeah." Jack decided a change of subject was in line. This wasn't a big city where a discussion of an ongoing police investigation would go unheard. Even in a busy restaurant. "How's Katie doing?"

"I think she's ready to get the show on the road. She's not getting much sleep. Baby's been keeping her up at night, doing a lot of kicking."

Jack smiled. "I hear it only gets worse once they're born. At least for the father."

"Katie and I have that all worked out. If the baby wakes up before 3:00 a.m., she gets it. After three, I do. Every third night, one of us gets a night off."

"Well, we know who came up with that plan. It's a damn good thing you married someone who doesn't mind having her life organized for her."

Alec's expression eased. It was obvious that he loved his wife.

Jack took a sip of water. "You intend to cut back on your travel after the baby?"

As soon as he said it, Jack recognized his mistake. He watched his brother's expression stiffen, the comfortable atmosphere of moments earlier evaporating.

Alec jerked open the sports section. "As much as I can."

As hard as it was for Jack to hold on to his anger and his words, he did.

Three years ago he had been visiting with Alec and Alec's first wife, Jill, at Christmas when his brother, who was with the FBI at the time, had been called away on a child abduction case in Arizona. Normally Jack would have cleared out when his brother did, but Jill had been having a hard time of it right then. Alec was gone more than he was home. And even when he was home, he was distracted with his job. She wanted a baby, but couldn't get pregnant. Wanted her husband's attention, but couldn't seem to capture it.

She'd begged Jack to stay. She didn't want to spend the

holidays alone. He'd had nowhere that he had to be, and the request had seemed reasonable. He'd even thought he was doing Alec a favor by sticking around.

The first night they were alone in the house, she'd drunk too much wine and cried on his shoulder, telling him more than he'd wanted to know about his brother's marriage.

Jack had known he should leave the next morning, but he hadn't. Instead, he'd taken his brother's wife hiking through the snow. He'd taken her to dinner. And, because he was a man and she was an attractive woman, he'd wanted to take her to bed. But he hadn't. Because he didn't do that kind of thing.

When Alec returned unexpectedly that night, though, he'd found his wife and his brother sitting on the couch, Jill's head resting on Jack's shoulder—and he'd assumed the worst.

And obviously, he now assumed that if he turned his back for too long, Jack would make a play for Katie. In Jack's book, it couldn't get any rougher than that between brothers.

The waitress arrived at that moment to take their order. As soon as she left, Alec went back to the sports page, and Jack picked up the local section. Like two strangers stuck sitting together because there weren't enough tables, they hid behind their papers.

There had been moments when Jack considered just having it out with Alec. But he wasn't completely sure the relationship would survive. So he allowed things to continue as they had for several years now, with each of them pretending all was okay between them.

After a period of time, Alec lowered the paper. "Any progress with the contract negotiations?" Since there hadn't been an open statement of war, there really couldn't be a peace offering, and yet the simple question clearly was an attempt to pretend that the tense moments had never happened.

"Not really." When Jack had been offered the job as Deep Water's chief of police, he'd agreed to a two-year contract. The two years were up in less than a month, and he had yet to be presented with a new one.

Jack sipped his coffee. "I spent last Tuesday night justifying my job performance to the city council and the mayor." It wasn't an experience he'd particularly enjoyed. "The Dawson case hasn't helped. Half the city council lives in that same neighborhood. Several of them have pointed out that if it was a random act of murder, one of them could have been the victim."

"So they're implying the department should have done more?"

"They're implying that the department should have prevented it."

Alec folded the newspaper in half. "You could always join me in the private sector." After leaving the FBI, Alec had turned the experience and the security clearance he'd achieved while with the Bureau into a career. Today he was a much sought after security consultant, both nationally and internationally, and was occasionally even called on by police departments he'd worked with in the past for a profile.

"Thanks," Jack said. "But I like police work." He did like police work, but that wasn't the reason he turned Alec down each time he asked. Jack wasn't certain how comfortable he'd feel working for his brother. The friction of business might create additional stress in their relationship.

Alec nodded. "If you change your mind, there's always a spot waiting."

Their breakfast arrived at the very same time as the mayor.

Harvey Sanderson was in his late thirties, had a long face and a set of recently planted brown hair plugs that reminded Jack of rows of dried cornstalks.

The mayor dragged a chair to the end of the booth and sat. "I was down at the Crab Shack last night, and the bartender was telling me how you were in there a while back." Harvey leaned closer. "You came in alone, but left with Lexie Dawson." He sat up straight. "Is that true?"

Jack exchanged a look with his brother that said being the chief of police got you noticed, even when you didn't want to be.

"True enough," Jack said simply as he added horseradish to the top of his over-easy eggs.

"You don't see that as a problem? Your having a relationship with the main suspect in a murder investigation? Because I do."

The mayor glanced from Alec to Jack and back. Following his brother's lead, Alec had already added butter and pepper to his grits. "Nothing worse than cold eggs," Alec commented, and dug in.

"First off," Jack said to Harvey, "my personal life is none of your damn business."

"It is if it's the reason an arrest hasn't been made."

Jack laid down his fork. He didn't like having his integrity impugned, and if they hadn't been in a crowded restaurant…

"The reason an arrest hasn't been made is that the detectives assigned to the case haven't completed their investigation, nor have the autopsy report and tox screen come back." Jack's ability to curb his temper was getting a real workout this morning. "In police work you get your facts and substantiating evidence in order first, and then you make an arrest." He pushed his uneaten breakfast away, his appetite suddenly gone. "Unless you want a false-arrest suit. Which can run into millions when you're talking a murder charge." He leaned toward the mayor. "I'm assuming the city doesn't want that kind of trouble."

Irritation creased the mayor's brow. The man never liked to hear no, so it didn't surprise Jack that he wasn't taking it well. Jack would have liked to tell him to get his nose out of police business, but, having tried it more than once in the past, knew it would be a waste of time.

"We need to move on this one." Harvey still pushed his agenda as he stood.

"As soon as the autopsy confirms that it isn't suicide, and Fitz and Shepherd complete their investigation."

"The sooner the better," Harvey pressed.

"Sure," agreed Jack. As Harvey made his way to the front door, he stopped to offer a handshake here, a quick slap on the shoulder there, working the diners as if there was an upcoming election.

When Jack turned back, Alec was watching him. A little too closely. "What is the relationship between you and the ex-wife?"

"There is none."

"That's not how it sounded."

Jack tossed a ten on the table. "How things look and even how they sound isn't always an indication of how they are, Alec."

IT WAS STILL BEFORE NOON when Jack opened the Deep Water Police Department's glass door. Having served on the larger police department in Atlanta, he couldn't quite get used to how quiet the stationhouse could get on a Sunday afternoon. As if even those bent on crime were taking a day off.

Jack hadn't planned to come in today, but Frank Shepherd, the lead detective on the Dawson investigation, had phoned, asking to meet. The request hadn't particularly surprised Jack. During any homicide investigation, he met with the detectives periodically. Sometimes just to keep abreast of progress and sometimes because, having come from a city with one of the highest homicide rates in the nation, he'd just about seen it all and could offer some insights and suggestions to his men. He was always careful to let them run the investigation, though.

The complaints desk was being manned by two officers—Louise Saint and Dean Parker. Both were on the phone as Jack came in, but they made eye contact and nodded a greeting.

Jack grabbed a soft drink out of the vending machine and headed to the interview room.

Frank Shepherd looked up as Jack entered. "Sorry to cut into your Sunday, Chief."

"No problem," Jack said as he set his soda can on the table. As he'd entered, he felt a sudden spike of tension in the room. But it wasn't so much what was in the air as what wasn't on the table that tipped him off. Usually there'd be thick files with interview notes and lists of evidence. Photos taken at the scene would already be spread out for viewing and discussion. Today, there was a single closed folder on the table in front of Frank.

Instead of sitting across from his detective as he normally did, Jack chose a seat at the head of the table. "Fitz running late?"

"He's not part of this meeting."

"Why?"

Frank folded his hands over the file. "You made me the lead detective on this case."

"And I gave you a damn good partner to work it with you. He's not here. I want to know why." As he took a sip of the cola, Jack watched Frank over the edge of the can. "Does he even know we're meeting?"

"Sure."

Jack lowered the drink. What in the hell was going on? Fitz wasn't the type of cop who would drop the ball during an investigation. He understood that the job came before family sometimes, that there were occasions when dinners were missed, when anniversaries or birthdays were celebrated days or weeks after the actual date.

Frank flipped open the file folder, revealing the typed affidavit. "We're burning department time. We have enough to take to the State Attorney."

"Everything you have is circumstantial." Jack leaned toward the other man. "Why the hurry? The medical examiner hasn't even ruled it a homicide yet. You might want to at least get the M.E. to sign off on it first."

"And we both know what he's going to say, don't we, Jack?" Frank climbed to his feet. "And we know damn well who did it."

"Well, if you do, then I'd say you missed one of the most important steps in a murder investigation—keeping an open mind." As the other man paced, Jack settled back in his chair. "I'll grant you that a suicide ruling is a long shot, but have you even considered what will happen if that's how the M.E. calls it and you've already made an arrest? Well, I have. The department either ends up looking incompetent, or even worse, as if we were on some kind of witch hunt. Lexie Dawson gets herself an attorney and files a wrongful-arrest suit. The city loses a huge chunk of change. We all lose our jobs."

"If it's a suicide, where's the suicide note? Why doesn't even one person that I've talked to mention that the man was upset over anything enough to want to end his life? Most people think he was too ego-driven to have killed himself."

"Maybe you just haven't spoken to the right person yet. And that lack of a note isn't unusual."

Shepherd leaned across the table. "The evidence may be circumstantial, but there's a load of it. Even the weapon is hers."

"And as of now," Jack said, "the only prints found on the weapon belong to the victim."

"She's in and out of hospitals every day, has easy access to latex gloves." Frank held up a hand. "Before you say anything about the gunpowder residue test results—"

"You mean the ones that were consistent with her story of having shot a weapon earlier in the day?" Jack said. "And not within hours of when Martinez swabbed?"

Jack had never seen Shepherd so anxious to make an arrest. It almost seemed personal with him. As if he had a beef with Lexie. Or had some kind of run-in with her? Or perhaps it was something more physical than a run-in? There were women who went after cops. Groupies. As soon as the idea ran through Jack's brain, he tossed it. He'd known his share of badge bunnies. Lexie didn't fit the profile.

"Have you ever seen her handle a gun, Jack? It's like second nature to her. At twenty-five yards, she can clean out the center of a target faster than any man on this force." The detective pointed as if he had a gun in his hand. He pulled the invisible trigger. "And I'm not talking just with her right hand, but with her left, too."

Jack looked up. "The shot that killed Dan Dawson wasn't fired from twenty-five yards away." He took a deep breath. "What's your best guess, Frank, on distance for that shot? Somewhere between point-blank and three inches?" He didn't wait for the detective to answer. "An eighty-year-old grandmother with cataracts couldn't have missed at that range. Nor could someone who had never picked up a gun before. So I don't think the fact that Lexie knows weapons means a whole helluva lot here."

Frank jerked back the chair he'd been sitting in earlier and sat. "I've already called the State Attorney's office."

"Damn it, Frank, when's the last time you ever had evidence this neat? This boxed-and-ready-to-go?" Jack leaned across the table. "Let me rephrase that. When's the last time you had this damn much evidence going into an investigation where your main suspect made the 9-1-1 call and was willing to answer questions?"

"It wouldn't be the first time that a perp realizes someone has seen her entering or leaving the crime scene and decides she can throw off the police by making the call. Then she sits there and answers questions, secretly thumbing her nose at all of us."

"I saw no signs during the interview that she was being anything but truthful. Fitz didn't either. But then he probably told you that, didn't he? And that's the reason he's not here now. Because even he thinks you're making a mistake."

Frank glanced down at the open file folder, at the neatly typed forms, his expression grim.

"Did you even look at other suspects?" Jack asked. "Or did you, right from the start, close yourself off from the possibility that Lexie Dawson didn't kill her ex-husband?" Jack got to his feet.

Shepherd remained seated, but threw up his hands. "Are you suggesting I haven't done my job?"

"Well, have you? Did you check for patients who might have a beef with the doctor? The charts on the desk that night? Why were they there? What about the office staff? Did you question them?"

"Yes. Yes. And yes!"

"What about the relationship between the partners? Any problems there? You drove out to the clinic in Pierson and checked to be sure Whittemore was actually there seeing patients on Friday?"

"Damn it, yes!"

"What about when he left the clinic?"

"Everything checked out."

"So you didn't find anyone who had seen him between the time he left the bar and when he showed up at the Dawson house?"

"No. And it's no wonder. His cabin is well hidden in the trees."

"He spoke to his answering service twice during that time, though."

"So?"

"So why didn't he return Lexie Dawson's call? Why did he claim that the reason he didn't was because he was out of cell tower range and didn't get the message until he was on his way back to Deep Water?" Jack straightened. "Maybe you should pull the records for his cell phone, determine where he was when he contacted his answering service that night?"

Shepherd looked down.

"We're talking a man's death here. And a woman's life. Don't you think we can spare both some time and the resources?"

Shepherd shoved the file off the table. "Oh, what the hell! Maybe a one-armed bandit did it."

Jack leaned down so that they were face-to-face. "I'm going to let that last remark go. Pretend I didn't hear it. You're the best detective I have, and you know it. I'm just asking you to do your job! And not be in such a damn big hurry that you make a mistake that the whole department will end up paying for. Or an innocent woman."

Shepherd eyed him for several seconds. "Maybe what I've been hearing is true." The detective lifted his gaze. "That you got something going with Lexie Dawson."

"Watch your step, Frank." Jack headed for the door. "No arrest until after the autopsy tomorrow morning. And I want everything you have, every piece of paperwork you and Fitz have generated on this investigation, on my desk in the next hour."

Chapter Five

Jack figured he had eighteen hours to find a killer.

Otherwise, Lexie was going to be arrested for a murder that he knew in his gut she hadn't committed.

He opened the throttle on the motorcycle. The weather was still cool, hovering just above fifty, but cloudless, which, if you strapped on leather chaps and a leather jacket, made it a good day for a ride. His destination was the Ocala National Forest, a nearly four-hundred-thousand-acre parcel of land, bisected by several state highways and home to everything from black bears and bobcats to wild pigs and possibly, if rumor was to be believed, a few undiscovered, shallow graves.

Jack downshifted and swerved to avoid an alligator that had crawled out onto the road to sun itself, then opened her back up.

If it had been just the mayor pushing for an arrest, Jack wouldn't have been worried, but it appeared that his lead detective may have also developed a case of tunnel vision. And tunnel vision was very dangerous when working with only circumstantial evidence. Focusing in on one suspect too soon left an investigator open to the possibility of error. And such mistakes meant that the true perp walked.

After reading over everything in the case file, Jack had decided that the best place to start was with the partner. Whittemore had been overspending for years and was in the kind of debt that most people would never be able to dig out of. At least not without some substantial help.

Shepherd had been aware of Whittemore's financial situation, but hadn't felt it was relevant, since there had been no recent significant changes in the doctor's debt load. Jack wasn't so inclined to go along with that assessment. At least not until he'd nailed down Whittemore's movements on Friday night, and if he stood to gain financially in any way from his partner's death.

The obstetrician had seen patients at the clinic in Pierson late in the afternoon, the last one sometime around five-thirty. From there he claimed to have stopped for a beer and burger at Clive's Joint, a local hangout on Route 40, and then headed out to his cabin, located near the town of Lynne and close to Halfmoon Lake. When asked, Shepherd had claimed to check out the alibi, but there was nothing in any of the investigation notes to indicate that he had. Perhaps just an oversight when he was typing the report, or perhaps Shepherd wasn't as thorough as Jack had believed him to be.

It was nearly a half hour later when Jack pulled into the parking lot of Clive's Joint. With the painted plywood siding and tar paper roof, Clive's Dive would have been a better name for it. It certainly didn't look like the type of place a successful doctor would frequent. And it didn't look like the kind of place where a professional man would go unnoticed, either.

If Whittemore had been here Friday night, someone would remember.

The inside of the dark restaurant smelled of smoke and

mildew. Just below those scents was the yeasty scent of spilled beer.

The clack of pool balls competed with that of two televisions, one tuned to a football game and the other to a NASCAR race. There were just over a dozen customers—three at the bar, six at a table near the kitchen and four shooting pool. Most of them looked as if they considered Clive's their home away from home.

Jack chose a seat at the bar and in front of the beer taps. Back in college, when he'd had the hots for a good-looking female bartender, he had learned the trick of parking himself in front of the taps. It was easier to strike up a conversation with someone when he or she was forced to be face-to-face with you while drawing beer.

The bartender, a man in his early sixties or late fifties, wore a leather vest over a dingy white T-shirt. He'd pulled his gray hair back into a single braid that hung to a point several inches below his belt. Jack figured that the navy-blue bandanna hid a receding hairline. The forest drew all kinds, the ones who wanted to be surrounded by nature and those who just wanted society to leave them alone. The bartender was the latter.

"What can I get you?" he asked. Several bikers walked in. The bartender nodded at them as they filed past where Jack was sitting, and took seats at the opposite end of the bar. Jack nodded at the new arrivals. It never hurt to be friendly, and the greeting also furthered the illusion that he was just out for a Sunday afternoon ride.

The bartender placed a napkin on the bar top. "What's it going to be?"

"The coldest beer you have."

The bartender plopped a mug down, poured a bottle of

domestic beer into it, and then set it in front of Jack, almost immediately turning away. Sipping the beer, Jack pretended to be interested in the stock car race. The bikers discussed an upcoming charity ride.

The heaviest of the four men looked up and, catching Jack glancing in their direction, motioned toward the front door. "That your vintage bike out there, surfer boy?"

Jack smiled. Because of his blond hair and blue eyes, the easy smile, people occasionally called him by the moniker. And at the same time underestimated him. He normally saw no reason to correct the assumption. The ability to appear laid-back even during the most stressful of times had been one of the reasons he'd managed to last as long as he had undercover. Jack lowered the beer. "Yeah. She's mine."

"You do the restoration?"

"Yeah."

As the bartender returned to draw a couple of beers, Jack drained his. "This is my first time through here. A friend of mine recommended I stop. Said the beer was cold and the food was good."

For a second the bartender studied him, his expression far from friendly, but then he asked, "Beer's sure enough cold and the food won't kill you. Who's your friend?"

"Fleming. Fleming Whittemore."

The bartender nodded. "He comes in once or twice a week during good weather, less often when it's not."

"You probably haven't seen him in a while, then?"

"That's right. Been two or three weeks maybe."

Jack looked around. "You the owner?"

"Yeah, that's me. Owner, bartender, cook."

"Been around these parts long?"

The bartender turned off the tap. "Long enough to know a cop when I see one. And smart enough to keep my mouth shut about other people's business."

MONDAY MORNINGS WERE always the pits, Lexie noted.

Given the way her life was going, why would she expect this one to be any different?

Holding it awkwardly in the hand with the cast, Lexie stared numbly at the plus sign on the home pregnancy test strip. The kit was a leftover from when she'd been trying to get pregnant with Lindy. She scanned the outside of the box, looking for an expiration date. Maybe the thing was past its prime. Maybe the result was just a false positive.

Unable to find any date on the box, she checked the instructions again. As she did so, she pressed a hand over her left breast. The test might be wrong, but her body wasn't. She just hadn't been paying attention to it recently. The nausea that she'd attributed to coffee. The too-tight jeans and her recent mood swings. The fact that she was tired and found concentrating difficult...

And last, but certainly not least, tender breasts.

The fear in her middle expanded upward, taking over her chest, too. A baby? How was she going to handle that along with everything else?

With her eyes filled with tears, Lexie swept the packaging from the kit into the trash, where it landed on top of the shirt of Dan's that she'd worn home Friday night.

It wasn't as if she hadn't thought about the night with Jack often as she'd laid in bed alone, remembering his hard body, his deep thrusts. But because they'd used protection, not even once had she considered the possibility of a child. She knew darn well that he hadn't, either.

What was she going to do? Lexie raised her eyes to the mirror above the sink. Tell Jack? She couldn't tell him she was carrying his child. She couldn't even begin to imagine how he would react to the news. Especially given the current situation.

She rested her bottom against the vanity as she stared down at the strip.

Pregnant.

Her left hand stole lower, running over her abdomen. She looked down at her still-flat stomach. A life was growing inside her. A child. Her child.

To bring into this world.

She unzipped her jeans and pulled them open so that she could place her palm against bare skin, closer to the baby. The realization that she was going to be a mother washed over her. The panic in her middle eased, replaced with the low hum of excitement. What was wrong with her? Wasn't this what she wanted? More than anything else? To be a mother?

Her hesitant smile grew stronger, then wavered. What if something happened again? What if her injuries had left her incapable of carrying a baby to term? Just because Fleming had assured her there wouldn't be a problem...

Closing her eyes, Lexie drew a deep breath. It would be okay. She wouldn't let this one down. She was strong, physically fit. She would bring the baby into this world. She would love it and nurture it. Most of all, she would protect it.

For the first time in days, she was feeling something that was almost like hope. How long had it been since she'd felt it? The day nearly two years ago, when she'd discovered she was pregnant, had been filled with the kind of elation that had made her feel invincible. Then there was that very first introduction to her daughter during the sonogram. Lindy's first kick. There'd been so many firsts after that, and yet there hadn't been quite enough of them. No first smile. No first tooth. No first step.

This time, though, would be different.

Lexie lifted her right hand, intending to rest it over her belly, too. Only when she saw the cast did she think about the pain medication she'd taken that first night, the aspirin she'd consumed once or twice since. What if she'd already done something to hurt the baby? What then? Forcing a deep breath, letting it out slowly, she thought of calling Fleming, but quickly decided against it. They'd spoken only once since Friday night. She'd made the call, catching him as he was picking up Dan's parents at the airport. Out of necessity, the conversation had been stilted and short. He'd promised to call when he was alone, but he hadn't. She suspected it was because he didn't really know what to say to her. And to be honest, she was almost relieved that he hadn't contacted her. Because she didn't know what to say, either.

And given the current situation, calling him about the possible impact of class three narcotics on a fetus would be the same as announcing her pregnancy.

When the knock landed at the front door, Lexie zipped her jeans and smoothed her hair. But didn't make any move to answer it. Two reporters had ambushed her as she came home last night, appearing out of nowhere, cameras flashing, microphones shoved in her face. It had been all she could do just to get in the door.

When they gave up and left, she'd driven to the end of the gravel lane and stretched the chain with the No Trespassing sign across. In the way of deterrents, it wasn't much.

When the knocking came again several minutes later,

she walked out into the hallway, but still made no move to answer the door.

Would whoever was there just go away if she didn't? Even with her car in the drive?

When the pounding became more emphatic, she decided that she was going to have to answer it. The autopsy had taken place this morning. There was a good chance that it was the police. That she was on her way to jail for a crime she hadn't committed.

Yeah. Mondays were the pits. And this Monday most of all.

JACK TRIED TO TELL himself that he didn't have a choice, but he knew better. There was always a choice to be made. Evidently, he'd made his. Didn't mean he was completely comfortable with it yet.

It was nearly ten o'clock on Monday morning when he opened the screen door of Lexie's house and knocked on the front door. Even when she didn't answer after a reasonable length of time, he assumed, since there had been a chain with a No Trespassing sign hanging across the drive and the white Taurus was still in the drive, that she was home. He'd give it a minute and try again.

Shoving his hands into the pockets of his jacket, Jack scanned the front of the house, focusing on details that he hadn't seen the night he'd brought her home.

The structure was low-slung and built mostly of logs, except for one wing that was frame construction with cypress siding. The front door and shutters were red, as were the flowers in the pots next to the door. Not fancy like the Thornton Park house, but homey.

As he turned to check out the surrounding woods, he realized there was a stillness, a peacefulness to the morning, and having just come from the medical examiner's office, Jack welcomed it. But even as he inhaled the cool, fresh air, the scents of death and Vicks VapoRub lingered in his nostrils. Of all the senses, the olfactory carried the longest "memory," and even now, if he closed his eyes, he'd be standing over the body again. Listening to Dr. Silas Ecker as he dictated his findings, as he answered questions. As he described the last minutes of a man's life.

This morning's autopsy was the first Jack had attended since taking the job as police chief. Several times, as the gazes of Fitz and Shepherd had met his over the body, he could see them wondering just how involved he was with Lexie.

He suspected his brother's answer to that question would be "too involved."

Maybe he was. In the past, when he'd been working undercover and dealing mostly with prostitutes and drug dealers, he'd been careful not to let himself get too close or too mixed up with a suspect or an informant. It hadn't always been easy, especially when it was a woman and the situation was a bad one.

Pounding on the door this time, Jack stared inside. Maybe she thought he'd give up and go away. If she did, she obviously didn't know him.

Jack let the screen door swing shut again. He'd give it a few minutes and try yet again.

The house sat on the bank of Deep Water Run, the surrounding deck acting almost like a dock linking house to water. Jack walked to the railing and rested his elbows on it. In spite of the fast moving current, the surface barely rippled. The water was perhaps ten feet deep but looked shallower because of the river's clarity and white sand bottom.

What made a woman choose to live way out here? It

seemed an odd choice. Jack straightened. Perhaps it had been an easy spot for her to run to when she lost the baby and her marriage broke up. He was still having a hard time seeing Lexie as an abused wife. Not because he doubted it was true, but because she seemed too strong to have put up with any type of abuse.

Jack stared down into the water. The night they'd met, she had been very upset about something. He had assumed it was the breakup of the marriage. He now suspected that the loss of the baby was more likely the cause behind her emotional state.

He felt regret for what had happened the night they'd met. He'd been surprised when she sat down next to him at the bar where he'd been nursing a beer. She ordered a martini straight up and had downed it immediately. The next one pretty much went the way of the first. It didn't take keen investigative skills to detect that she was a woman eager to forget something. When she ordered a third, he'd made the decision to drive her home. The decision to take her to bed wasn't so easy to nail down, though. He wasn't even sure it had been his, and yet he'd been the one who was stone-cold sober that night. Looking back, he realized that he should have stopped at her front door.

Hearing the screen door whine open behind him, Jack turned and saw her standing there, wearing jeans, a bulky black sweater and a wary expression.

She didn't say anything, just met his gaze. He realized that she did that a lot. Waited for other people to take the lead in conversation. Which seemed out of character in some way, since she obviously wasn't a follower. She wore her thick hair up, anchored by some type of clip. And because loose strands clung damply to her neck, he decided the reason she hadn't answered the door sooner was because she'd been in the shower.

As he closed the distance between them, she glanced toward the drive, almost as if she expected him not to be alone.

"I'm here just to talk."

"I don't think that's a good idea."

When she started to close the door, Jack's hand shot out and grabbed the wood frame just above hers. "You could use a friend, Lexie. Especially now."

Her fingers tightened on the doorknob. "Why especially now?"

"I just came from the autopsy."

The look on her face said that she'd already guessed the medical examiner's ruling. Though she didn't offer a verbal invitation, Lexie stepped back.

As he slipped past her, Jack checked out the living room. It wasn't all that surprising that he didn't remember the space. It had been dark the last time he'd been inside her home, and his mind had been on other things. His body tightened at the memory of the night, of how it had been between them. He actually dreamed about her some nights, and when he did he'd awaken aroused. He hadn't jerked off since high school, but there had been a time or two recently when he'd wondered if it would come to that.

Was it the same for her? Did she ever think about that night? Did she ever *want* the way he did?

Probably not. If she had, she wouldn't have turned him down when he'd called.

Because it was safer, Jack refocused on his surroundings. A stacked-stone fireplace covered the largest of the interior walls, a fire filling the grate. The furniture appeared comfortable but not stylish, the kind that invited rough use. Several faded rugs covered the stone floors. There was little artwork, but then, even if there had been more, it would have rarely been noticed because of the view outside the French doors. Once again, as he looked out across the river to the opposite bank and beyond that to the thick woods of pines and oaks, he was struck with the remoteness.

When he turned back, he caught her watching him.

"I didn't make any coffee." She locked the door, her movements awkward because of the cast. "But I can offer you a cup of tea or a glass of water. If you haven't already had breakfast, I was just about to make myself some toast."

"Tea sounds good." He couldn't actually remember the last time he'd had hot tea. Perhaps when he'd had the flu as a kid and his mother had forced a doctored version on him.

He followed Lexie toward the kitchen. "How's the hand?"

"Okay," she said over her shoulder. "It's just a fracture."

Like the living room, one wall of the kitchen was all windows. A small television on the counter was tuned to the morning news. The fact that it was worried Jack. Typically, a victim's family tended to isolate themselves from the outside world. They didn't want to see or hear their personal tragedy dissected by strangers. In his experience, the only time that didn't hold true was when a family member needed to keep tabs on the progress being made by law enforcement—because he or she was the one who had committed the crime.

As Lexie poured water from the kettle into two mugs and added tea bags, he checked out the room a bit more. A pot rack loaded with cookware hung over the table in the center. A small wall next to the back door held a dozen or so photographs, some recent, others appearing to be very dated. They were obviously family shots centered on the outdoor activities that would have taken place during stays in the cabin. Fishing and picnics, and even some hunting shots. One of them showed a much younger Lexie with a man that Jack assumed was her grandfather.

"I don't suppose I need to ask how the medical examiner ruled this morning." The slight elevation of her tone revealed just how nervous she was, just how much she wanted the answer, but at the same time dreaded it.

"Homicide," he said as he faced her.

Her pupils constricted, her eyes going from dark gray to nearly silver. She turned away and took a deep breath. Obviously, she hadn't been nearly as prepared as she had thought. Had she held out hope that her ex-husband's death would be ruled a suicide?

"Did you contact an attorney?"

Her back still to him, Lexie nodded. "Garland Ramsey has agreed to represent me." Arms folded in front of her, she faced Jack with a grim expression. "Would it be better if I turned myself in?"

The question surprised him. Even to ask it took courage. "No. Just make yourself available."

"In other words, wait for them to come for me?"

"Yes." Why couldn't he get a real read on her? She seemed so controlled and contained at times. So different from that first day he'd seen her having lunch. She'd been open, reaching out to those around her.

Using the fingers of her injured right hand, she lifted a tea bag and then let it sink into the hot water again, all the while watching it as if it were some kind of scientific experiment. "When?" she asked as the bag went down for the third time.

"Soon. The paperwork is ready to take to the judge, so it won't be long."

Her left hand was unsteady when she passed him one of the mugs. As he took it, the now empty fingers curled into a loose fist and her mouth tightened as if she found her inability to control her body as unsettling as the news.

Jack sat at the table, assuming she'd follow suit. But instead, she crossed the room to turn off the television, and then leaned against the counter. She was waiting for him to speak first—to give some indication of his stance. Obviously, she understood how an interrogation worked. That the power was usually in putting her cards on the table last.

But he wasn't looking for power; he was looking for the truth.

"Do you own a twenty-five automatic?" Jack asked.

"No."

Jack tasted the tea. "It's a woman's gun."

Lexie pushed away from the counter. "Maybe a woman who's afraid of anything bigger. I don't have guns for protection. I have them for competition. A twenty-five is worthless." Looking only slightly less nervous, she crossed to where she'd left her mug. "Why all the questions about a twenty-five?"

"Because on Friday night someone first used a twenty-five and then followed up with the .357. Not right away though. There are indications that there was up to half an hour between the two shots."

Lexie reached for the counter edge with one hand and covered her mouth with the other. For several moments, she just stood there, looking as if her knees would go out from under her. Then, after dragging in a deep breath and letting it out, she turned and stared out the window.

Jack stayed where he was.

"So they think I shot Dan with a peashooter first and then went and got the larger caliber weapon?"

"You have both motive and opportunity. And there was gunpowder residue on your cuff—"

She faced him, the counter now at her back, supporting her. "I'd been to the shooting range."

"The prosecution will argue that the reason you went to the gun range was so you'd be able to explain away the positive result. Premeditation, Lexie. If the prosecuting attorney can convince the jury of it, instead of doing twenty to life, you'll be staring at the death penalty."

She tightened her arms across her. Her color had drained to the point that even her lips looked pale.

"You had blood on your clothing—"

"From when I bent over Dan! To make certain that he was dead!"

Jack stood and walked toward her. "Checking to see if someone is dead, Lexie, is what killers do. Checking to see if someone is alive is what the rest of us do."

He stopped in front of her. "So which was it? When you bent over him were you hoping to find him alive or dead?"

"Alive, damn it." Pulling back, she took a deep breath. "No one could survive what was done to him. No one. Even before I bent over him, I knew it was hopeless." She lifted her chin. "I didn't kill Dan. I wouldn't kill anyone! No matter what they did to me!"

Jack saw the truth in her eyes. Even if no one else did. But her last words rang in his head. *No matter what they did to me!* What had been done to her?

When she tried to push past him, he wrapped his fingers around her upper arm, staying her. "I believe you, Lexie."

She studied his face as if she wasn't certain she'd heard him right. "You believe me?"

He couldn't remember the last time he'd ever seen eyes so filled with both hope and fear. "Yes. I do."

Tears collected in them. Her lips trembled. When she started to turn away, Jack reached out and, hooking a hand around the back of her head, pulled her into his arms. As soon as he did, she broke down completely.

As he tightened his arms around her, Jack realized that for the first time since he'd made his decision, he was comfortable with it. What he'd done, what he was about to do, was the right thing.

After a period of time, when she seemed to be in better control, she backed out of his arms. Using both hands, she scrubbed away the last remnants of tears. "I'm confused. You come in here telling me that I'm about to be arrested, and then you tell me that you believe me?"

"The fact that you will be arrested today hasn't changed."

"But can't you do something?"

"No. As of this morning, I resigned as police chief."

TWENTY MINUTES LATER, hands shoved into his pockets, Jack headed for his car. Halfway down the walk, something—a sensation that he was being watched—made him stop and look toward the woods.

The low cloud cover of earlier had settled to a point where the tops of the trees seemed to pierce the sky's exposed, soft gray underbelly. A breeze kicked by, bringing the first mist of rain.

Atlanta weather, not Florida. He found himself almost wishing he was back there, working undercover, dealing with pushers and druggies, hookers and pimps, instead of the beautiful woman he'd held in his arms this morning. Maybe only because as much as he wanted to help her, he feared he might not be able to. The mountain of circumstantial evidence they had on her was damn impressive. Arguing reasonable doubt wasn't going to be good enough. He was going to have to find the real killer, or watch Lexie go to prison.

Jack was nearly at his car when he saw the blue strobe of rack lights through the trees. Shepherd had made fast work of getting the arrest warrant signed by a judge. There'd be a search warrant, too. Because the main item that they were looking for was a twenty-five automatic, they'd have pretty much free rein to go anywhere inside the house they wanted to—anywhere a small caliber pistol could possibly be concealed.

He glanced back at the front door, where Lexie still stood. He knew the moment she, too, saw the blue lights. He'd heard the term *struck with fear,* but had never seen it so clearly demonstrated.

Jack waited beside his car.

Fitz and Shepherd pulled in behind. They didn't get out immediately, instead conferred for more than a minute. When they emerged, their expressions were grim.

Fitz turned up the collar on his wrinkled sport coat. Though still more a mist than a real drizzle, the precipitation was more enthusiastic now. But it wasn't just rain that Jack saw on Fitz's plump face as he strode past. There was also perspiration there. He knew the detective well enough to recognize that Fitz wasn't comfortable with what was going down, that it was Shepherd who was in control. But unlike Jack, Fitz was letting it happen.

Shepherd didn't say anything, just pulled the arrest warrant from the inside pocket of his black wool coat and held it up as he passed. "Stay out of our way, Jack. This can be as easy or difficult as you want it."

"I wasn't the one who made it difficult. You did when you failed to do your job."

Frank Shepherd stalked back to where Jack stood. "I respected you, even went to bat for you last year when the town council wanted to flush you. But what you're doing now... there's no damn excuse for it." He jabbed a finger in the direction of the house. "Lexie Dawson isn't worth it, Jack! She already ruined one man's life. You going to let her do the same to you? Is a little sack time really worth losing your career over?"

"Better my career than an innocent woman's life." When Frank started to turn away, Jack grabbed him by the upper arm and stopped him. "What is it, Frank? You figure you're going to get offered my job?" Jack allowed his hand to drop.

Shepherd made a show of straightening his coat. "I've already accepted the position of chief of police."

Jack wasn't surprised that Shepherd had been offered the job, but he was somewhat surprised that the detective had accepted. Or was he? Maybe Shepherd was more ambitious than Jack had realized.

Shepherd walked away.

"You're buying a career with that woman's life, Frank," Jack called at the man's retreating back.

"Go to hell, Jack."

Joining Fitz at the front door, Shepherd jerked open the screen and pounded with his fist. "Police. Open up."

As if she had been waiting just inside, Lexie immediately stepped out. She'd pulled on shoes and wore a leather jacket over her jeans and sweater.

Jack started up the walk toward them, but Shepherd lifted his hand. "Come any closer, Jack, and I'll arrest you, too."

Jack found a confident smile. "On what charges?"

"Interfering with a lawful arrest."

The charges wouldn't stick, but they would keep Jack busy for a few hours—time better spent helping Lexie.

As Jack watched, Fitz Mirandized Lexie as Shepherd placed the cuffs. Lexie flinched slightly as the steel closed around her right wrist.

The two of them led her down the stairs, one hand wrapped around an upper arm. She looked at Jack when she was led past, but didn't speak.

Nor did he.

Shepherd placed her in the back seat. As he closed the door, he glanced toward Jack again. "It wasn't a witch hunt, Jack. As much as you don't want to believe it, she did it."

Frank climbed behind the wheel. When the car swept past where he stood, Jack ignored the two men in the front of the car, instead focused on the woman in back. She didn't glance at him even once as the car pulled away, but as it headed down the driveway he saw her turn and look back.

It was only then that he realized just how tightly their fates were now linked.

Chapter Six

Lexie sat on the narrow stainless steel "cot" anchored to the wall, her back pressed against the concrete block, her knees collapsed beneath her. The mattress was hard and, despite the lingering odor of antiseptic in the cell, there was no way she was going to lie down. No reason to, anyway, since she wouldn't be able to sleep.

How many hours had it been now? She tried not to think about the grueling interrogation, the horror of the booking process, of being photographed and fingerprinted. She'd been frightened and then indignant, then frightened again, each emotion rising and falling and escalating as the hours dripped by too slowly.

Incarcerated. Even the word was scary as hell. She shifted, pushing her spine flatter to the painted wall as the muscles of her abdomen clenched with a mixture of fear and dread. How in the hell could this be happening to her?

She was innocent.

She closed her eyes and rested her head back. She no longer believed that she'd been unlucky, that she'd simply been in the wrong place at the wrong time. Someone had intentionally done this to her.

In an effort to sort it out, she had replayed that night in her head over and over again. Had Dan already been dead when she received the first text message? Or had his killer simply taken advantage of the fact that her ex-husband had already contacted her, following up with the other messages?

Someone in a nearby cell let out a sharp cough and a grunt. She could hear the person moving around, the sound of urination.

She glanced around her cell. What time was it? How much longer to dawn, to the possibility of freedom? Lexie climbed to her feet, stretching her cramped muscles as she went.

A door opened somewhere down the corridor. Probably a guard on rounds. Lexie had been here only a matter of hours and already she knew the routine.

She looked at the stainless steel toilet in the corner. She'd been considering using it but, with the possibility of an audience, decided she could wait a bit longer.

When she'd been stripped of her personal possessions yesterday afternoon, she'd thought the loss of freedom was going to be the most difficult thing for her to cope with, but now realized that the loss of dignity was nearly as hard.

Lexie swallowed the saliva that suddenly pooled in her mouth. A warm flush washed over her. Light-headed, she quickly plopped down on the hard mattress. No matter how unappealing, she should have eaten some of the food on her dinner tray. In the next instant, she was diving toward the stainless steel fixture, retching uncontrollably even before she reached it. Not trusting her ability to maintain her balance, Lexie held on to the bowl.

Sweat clung to her skin by the time the dry heaves faded. If she went to prison, what would become of her baby? She couldn't give her child away. Even to the father.

What if he didn't want the baby? Would the child be taken from her, placed in foster care or put up for adoption? Who would want the child of a convicted killer? What if no one did?

Sinking back onto the floor, she realized that she was crying, hard and uncontrollably and silently. Not for herself, but for her baby.

Lexie washed her hands and face, then climbed back onto the cot, resuming the position that she had retained through most of the night. She wouldn't think. She would just exist. She would think about the next five minutes and no further. Placing her left hand over her abdomen, she shut her eyes.

They were closed only momentarily.

"Hey, you, sitting there. What's your name?"

The prisoner in the cell across from hers, a woman somewhere in her late fifties, stood at her cell door, her hands gripping the bars as she stared out.

Her gaze met Lexie's. "What day is it?"

"Tuesday."

Nodding, she turned away and slunk back to her cot, where she collapsed once more.

Was that how it would be inside prison, one day bleeding into another, with no real mile markers to tell you when one week, one month, ended and another began?

Someone was crying now, soft mournful sobs that neither became louder nor faded. Lexie rested her head against the wall and closed her eyes again, praying not only for help but for sleep, too.

The rattling of her cell door as it was being unlocked startled her awake, but she had no sense of how long she'd been asleep.

"Time to head next door, Dawson."

She peered up at the hefty, dark-haired woman with features that looked as if they belonged on someone half her size. "Do I get to change first?"

Lexie wore the orange jumpsuit she'd been given the previous afternoon, but it was now extremely wrinkled.

"Nope. You'll be back here before you know it."

"I'll be brought back here afterward, then? Until bail is posted?"

"If the judge allows bail," the guard said. "Usually doesn't happen when the charge is murder."

"But I thought—" She took a deep breath and let it out slowly. The idea of staying in this cell for even one more day was unbearable. She'd been so numb when she'd talked to her attorney yesterday that she'd asked few questions of him. Garland Ramsey had been a friend of her grandparents, so Lexie had known the well-respected lawyer for years.

She dragged herself to her feet. "I need to wash up at least."

The guard waited while Lexie made a quick attempt at grooming. The only mirror was a polished piece of stainless steel. The closer she leaned into it, the more distorted her already indistinct image became. Her nose and mouth grew in prominence, the distance between her eyes narrowing. But even with all the distortion, there was no disguising that the woman in the mirror was frightened.

Turning her back on her image, Lexie saw the cuffs the guard had in her hand and held out her wrists, one bare, the other encased in plaster. She'd expected to be loaded into some type of vehicle, so was surprised when she was escorted outside and through an alley to the courthouse a block away. The day was overcast and cold. The guard was dressed for the weather; Lexie was not and the breeze seemed to go through the jumpsuit.

While the jail was a new facility, the courthouse had been built in the latter days of the nineteenth century, when Deep Water had been the county seat. Over the years, it had undergone numerous remodelings; none of them had attempted to meld the present with the past, though.

The original floors had long ago disappeared beneath brown linoleum tiles. The guard unlocked and relocked doors as they went. With each turn of the key, Lexie's chest tightened and her respiration quickened.

There were no windows in the short hallway that led from the back entrance to a small vestibule, and because of the lack of air circulation, there was a mustiness to both spaces. The guard's hand remained wrapped around Lexie's arm the whole time, and glancing down at it, Lexie was reminded of the way her stepfather had sometimes grabbed her when she was a child. It wasn't a pleasant memory.

As soon as the guard opened the door into the courtroom, conversations stopped. People turned and stared in her direction as she entered. She saw five or six friends in the crowd, but she didn't see Jack or Fleming. And because she didn't, she felt as if she was about to face the worst situation in her life completely alone.

It was possible that Fleming been called out with an emergency delivery, but what about Jack? Why wasn't he here? Desperate, she scanned the crowd. Had he changed his mind about her? She tried to contain her growing panic by telling herself that it would be Garland Ramsey who got her off, not Jack. That as long as her attorney stuck by her, she'd be okay.

"It's just stage fright, hon," the guard said, urging Lexie forward.

Lexie managed to respond to the guard's tug, but nearly

stumbled over her own feet because she was still madly searching the crowd. She spotted Dan's parents. Jessica Dawson was a rail-thin and unusually tall woman, while Jeffrey Dawson was nearly a foot shorter. Mutt and Jess. That's how Dan had introduced his parents to her the first time. She'd been instantly certain that she was going to love them. And she still did—in spite of the animosity between her and their son.

When Jessica realized that she was looking in her direction, the woman quickly turned away. Though Lexie hadn't expected her ex-mother-in-law to respond any differently, it still hurt.

The guard pulled out a chair for her, but when he would have retreated, Garland stopped her. "Please remove the cuffs."

Lexie lifted her wrists to allow the guard to comply. She realized her hands were both freezing and shaking, as was everything inside her. As she turned in her seat to face forward again, her eyes went to the imposing, mahogany edifice of the judge's bench.

Taking a deep breath, Lexie let it out slowly. Above all else, she needed to stay calm. She didn't want to fall apart in front of Garland or the courtroom full of people.

Garland leaned in closer. He was a man in his upper sixties now, with silver hair and the tanned, lean face of an athlete. He wasn't much over five-seven or -eight, but his restless energy made him seem larger. "Are you okay, Lexie?"

Because she was afraid to speak, she nodded.

"You were treated well?"

"Yes," she managed to answer, and turned to look at him. "Did you reach Fleming?" she asked in a tone just above a whisper.

Garland Ramsey nodded, but then shook his head. "He says he'd like to help, but he doesn't have that kind of cash and doesn't think he can raise it even if we give him a few days."

She fought to stay calm. When her attorney had told her that the bail amount could be upwards of a million dollars, she'd realized that she was going to have difficulty coming up with the ten percent required by a bondsman. She'd been hopeful that Fleming would make her the loan.

But if Fleming wasn't able to, where was she going to come up with that kind of money? On paper, she looked pretty good, especially if you didn't check her current credit card debt. With Dan having cleaned out the bank accounts, she'd been forced to use her salary to pay attorney fees, and her credit cards for the other necessities. It had been the first lesson she'd learned during the process of her divorce. Possession was everything in the eyes of the law, especially when it came to a joint bank account.

Getting a signature loan was unlikely. No bank board would approve one for someone in her current situation. She'd taken out a mortgage on Riverhouse to pay for the kitchen remodel on the house in town earlier that year. Getting a mortgage on it would be impossible, since it was tied up in the property settlement dispute, and would likely remain that way until after the trial.

Garland reached over and covered her hand with his, offering what was undoubtedly intended to be a bolstering smile. "One step at a time. Let's just get through this morning's proceeding, and then we'll regroup and consider our options."

"Did he offer to help with some of it, at least?"

"No." Garland frowned. "To be honest, I don't think it's

so much a matter of not being able to come up with the money as that he's worried about how it would appear to his colleagues and patients."

She turned away. She couldn't cry. Not now. Not in front of all these people. So Fleming probably hadn't been called out on an emergency. Was it actually possible that he believed she'd killed Dan? Was that why he was refusing to help her?

"It'll be fine, Lexie," Garland said. "You have friends. True ones."

She nodded, but felt certain he was wrong about the number of people who would come forward to help.

He had been reviewing his notes when she arrived, and now went back to them.

She didn't turn around again until the courtroom suddenly went quiet. When she did, she realized that Jack had just stepped into the room. The hard knot of apprehension at her center didn't completely disappear, but it eased some. He wore dark slacks and a blue dress shirt. A second man had followed him in, and though she had never met him, she recognized Jack's brother, Alec Blade. What was he doing here?

When Lexie's gaze connected with Jack's, he gave her a small smile and nod as he took a seat in the second row—the closest he could get. His brother didn't sit. Instead, he stood at the back.

"All rise for the honorable Judge Lloyd Meeks."

The judge took his seat behind the bench. He was an older gentleman, and with his black robe and bald head, he looked like a henchman.

Charges were read by the bailiff.

The judge shifted his attention toward where they sat. "How does your client want to plea, Garland?"

"Not guilty."

The judge addressed the court reporter. "Enter a plea of not guilty, order state to provide discovery and set pretrial status." He glanced at what Lexie assumed was a copy of the charging document. "That leaves us with the question of bail."

The prosecuting attorney stood. "Having viewed literally hundreds of crime scenes over many years, I can say with great conviction that this one is by far the worst I have ever dealt with. And because of the heinous nature of this crime and the fact that Ms. Dawson has contacts outside the country, making her a flight risk, I request that bail be denied and that Ms. Dawson remain in custody until such time as a verdict is reached."

Garland Ramsey quickly came to his feet and turned toward the prosecuting attorney. "Exactly who are these contacts outside the country?"

The prosecutor ignored Garland, instead addressing his answer to the judge. "Your Honor, Ms. Dawson's parents are currently living in Thailand. If she would flee, which seems likely given the charges—"

Garland interrupted. "Your Honor, the relationship between Ms. Dawson and her mother and stepfather has been a very strained one. Ms. Dawson was adopted as an infant. Shortly after Ms. Dawson turned thirteen, her adoptive grandparents were awarded custody of her. I prefer not to discuss the grounds of that case. Suffice it to say that Ms. Dawson is unlikely to seek asylum with her mother and stepfather." He nodded toward the other attorney. "Furthermore, Ms. Dawson is currently employed and has many ties to this community. As such, I request that bail be waived."

Judge Meeks shook his head, and cracked a smile for the first time since entering the room. "I know you have to ask, Garland." He brought the gavel down. "Bail set at one million and the prisoner is remanded into custody of the state until such time as it is met, or a verdict is reached."

Garland cleared his throat. "Sir, my client doesn't have those kind of funds."

"The court is well aware that the amount is substantial, Counselor. But my duty is to the public." Judge Meeks rose and retreated through the door where only moments earlier he'd entered.

The level of conversation rose behind her, the words indistinct, but she could imagine them just the same. People began to shuffle out into the cool morning, into the fresh air.

What she wouldn't give to be able to somehow meld into that flow of humanity, once more become part of them. But she couldn't, could she? And even if acquitted, she would never be one of them ever again. She'd never be able to look at life as they naively did.

Never believe that being innocent was enough.

Lexie sagged in her seat. Again, Garland reached over, this time giving her forearm a comforting squeeze. "I'll make some calls."

She nodded, but held little hope. Most of her friends were working people. They weren't the type with money wallowing in bank accounts. Waiting for a lost cause.

At the same moment the guard arrived to take her back to jail, she heard footsteps just behind the bar, but didn't look up immediately, not until she heard Jack address Garland. "Is there some problem with raising bail money?"

The guard reached for her, but Garland motioned the woman back. Lexie was surprised when she complied.

Garland glanced at Lexie briefly, as if weighing how comfortable she would be with his being truthful about the need for cash. "Unfortunately, there is a problem."

Lexie scraped the chair back and hurriedly stood, fully intending to cut off Garland's plea for financial help. She held out the hand without the cast to Jack, forcing him to take it. "Thanks for coming." She needed his help, but she didn't want to take his money, too.

But as his fingers closed over hers, all she could think was that he looked good. Smelled that way, too, which reminded her of her own wrinkled orange jumpsuit, the lack of even lip gloss, and the knowledge that she hadn't showered since the day before.

"Sorry I ran late," he said. "How are you holding up?"

"Fine," she lied.

There was a small commotion near the courtroom door that jerked Lexie's attention away briefly, but she couldn't tell exactly what was going on or who was involved.

When she turned back, she realized that she'd missed what was being said between Jack and Garland.

"Then it's settled," Jack said. "I'll make the arrangements and contact you."

Arrangements? At first she was certain that she had misunderstood. That Jack couldn't be offering to put up the full amount of her bail. But when her gaze connected with his, she realized that she'd heard correctly. "I couldn't…I can't—" He was already doing enough for her.

Garland interrupted. "Lexie is very grateful for your assistance."

With no other choice, Lexie again reached for Jack's hand. "Thank you."

He offered a small smile, his hand still holding hers. "You

have to understand that it could take me some time to come up with that type of cash."

Her throat suddenly tight with relief, she nodded.

As she watched Jack walk toward the courtroom exit, Lexie felt Garland's gaze resting on her. She had allowed Garland to believe that the reason Jack had agreed to help her was because he believed a miscarriage of justice was about to take place. She suspected Garland now knew it wasn't quite as simple as that. But even if he asked her, she didn't think she could explain Jack's actions.

Because even she didn't understand them.

"YOU ARE GETTING YOURSELF in way too deep here, Jack. It's one thing to want to see justice done, another to put up that kind of money."

Jack had known his brother would disapprove. And in some ways, Jack had even surprised himself. It wasn't as if that kind of money was going to be easy for him to come by.

Though they were basically alone in the hallway just outside the courtroom, Jack kept his voice low. "It's just a loan."

"You may want to get that it writing."

Jack faced his brother. "What would you have me do? Leave her sitting in jail for the next few months?"

"What about family?" Alec asked as both men resumed walking toward the exit. "Surely she has someone who—"

"Only living relative is the mother. She couldn't be much of one if the grandparents were awarded custody of Lexie." He looked over at his brother. "As for friends, I'm sure they would have come through in time."

"You're assuming she has any," Alec said, as he reached for the front door. There had been a slow drizzle falling when they'd gone in, but now the sun had made an appearance.

Jack recognized that he was the one who had asked Alec along, but his attitude was beginning to get under Jack's skin a bit. "And you're making assumptions about a woman you don't know based on a twenty minute court appearance where you had no actual contact with her. I know you're good at profiling people, Alec, but don't you think that's a little fast for even you?"

His face revealing frustration, Alec suddenly halted just outside the courthouse doors. "Okay. Let's say you're right to risk that kind of money on a woman you barely know. Where in the hell are you going to come up with that kind of cash?"

"I'll close out my retirement account." It wouldn't be enough. He'd need to bleed his savings down to the last few thousand, too. And considering he was jobless and was likely to remain that way for some time to come, the move was probably financial suicide, but he didn't see where he had much choice.

"Don't do that." Alec settled the navy-blue jacket he'd taken off in the courtroom over his shoulder. "Some of the money from Jill's life insurance policy is still sitting in the account. I was making arrangements to donate it to a woman's shelter, but the paperwork hasn't come though yet."

Alec had received a large settlement from his first wife's murder, money he had used solely to bring her killer to justice.

"Those funds should go to the shelter," Jack said.

"Jill would want it to be used to help another woman. And as you said, it's just a loan."

Suspecting he was feeling what Lexie had when he'd made the offer of financial assistance—not wanting that type of help from him, but also recognizing that not taking it would be foolish—Jack held a hand out to Alec. "Thanks."

After the briefest of hesitation, his brother shook it. "Just be careful, Jack. And I'm not talking loans or jobs now."

"I plan to."

Though they'd arrived in separate vehicles because Alec was meeting his wife, they walked toward the parking lot across the street together. When they reached Jack's SUV, Frank Shepherd was leaning against the vehicle's front grille, his arms crossed and sunglasses firmly in place. He'd been in the courtroom, near the back, when Jack and Alec had arrived, and had obviously slipped out before them, so Jack was surprised to see him now.

"Morning, Shepherd," Jack called as he headed for the driver's door. He fully expected the detective to follow him, and he did.

"You plan to put up the bond money?"

"I can't see that it's any of your business." Jack opened the door, but didn't get in.

"Well, that's where you're wrong."

Jack turned to the officer, suddenly aware that the fastest way to end the conversation was to take control of it. "What is it that you want?"

"Where were you Friday night?"

"You know damn well where I was. I flew in from Philadelphia."

"What time?"

Jack refused to glance over at his brother. "The plane was scheduled to land at 10:08."

"Maybe the one you were initially booked on came in at that time, but you caught an earlier connecting flight out of Atlanta, didn't you? Got in before seven?"

Jack couldn't see anything to be gained by responding to the detective's question.

"So where were you between seven and, say, ten-thirty that night?"

After reading body language for so many years, Jack knew how to appear unfazed by the questions. And they wouldn't have bothered him quite so much if Alec hadn't been watching. "I went for a drive."

Out of the corner of his eye, Jack saw Fitz cutting toward them, his path taking him in front of the SUV.

Shepherd lowered his shoe from where it had been propped on the bumper. "After a four-hour flight, the first thing you did when you landed was get in your car and go for a long drive? Must have had some things on your mind, huh?"

Fitz, whose shirt sported large teardrop-shaped patches of perspiration beneath his armpits, arrived at that moment. Jack nodded at him, but immediately shifted his attention back to Shepherd. "That's right. I had some things on my mind."

"Any chance your drive took you through Thornton Park between eight-thirty and ten that night?"

When Shepherd smiled, Jack suddenly found himself wanting to wipe the smirk off the detective's face. Why stop there, though, he decided, when what he really wanted to do was wipe the pavement with the man?

As Jack shoved the car door closed behind him, Shepherd came toward him. If Fitz hadn't come between them, the detective would have thrown a punch. Jack wished Shepherd had gotten the opportunity. If only because it would have allowed him to throw a few of his own.

"Take it easy, Frank." Fitz kept his body positioned between Shepherd and Jack.

Shepherd stabbed a finger at Jack. "Your car was seen in the area that night."

Jack reached behind him for the door handle. "Like hell it was. If you're accusing me of having something to do with Dan Dawson's murder, Shepherd, at least have the damn guts to come out and say it."

The detective glanced over at Alec for the first time. "Maybe you know where your brother was that night?"

"I'm not my brother's keeper. You have questions for him, you ask him." Alec glanced at Jack. "You okay here?"

"Sure. Buzz me later and we'll firm things up for tonight."

Jack climbed in the SUV, but left the door open as he started the vehicle. "You used to be a good detective, Frank. I considered you the best on my force."

"It's no longer your force. It's mine."

"For how long? Keep making the mistakes you're currently making and they'll come back to bite you in the ass."

"I'm going to prove that Lexie Dawson wasn't working alone that night. That you were helping her."

"You can try." Jack slammed the car door and dropped the truck into reverse.

NINE HOURS LATER, Lexie paced her small cell. Her adrenaline continued to flow, making it impossible for her to stop the constant movement. She'd managed to eat a few bites from her lunch and dinner trays, but knew it wasn't enough to sustain her or to protect the health of the baby.

The guard who had escorted her to court earlier in the day had left several hours ago at the end of her shift, but not before telling Lexie that she was scheduled to get a cellmate.

She didn't want to share the small space with a petty thief, or a drunk, or a druggie or prostitute. Which was pretty damn funny when as far as the world was concerned, she was a murderer.

Most of her thoughts over the past nine hours had been centered on Jack. He'd quit his job and now he was putting up a lot of money. Why? What did he expect in return? There was no such thing as true generosity. Not when it came to a hundred thousand dollars, there wasn't.

Lexie sank onto the bench. She was just wasting energy here. It was a loan. As soon as she was free of the charges, she'd repay him.

Lexie's nerves tightened at the sound of approaching footsteps. She eased toward the back wall, expecting the worst. But the female guard was alone.

"Guess you won't be staying with us tonight, after all, Dawson."

The guard handed her the clothes she'd arrived in. After exchanging the jumpsuit for sweater and jeans, she was escorted to a room where she had to sign for the rest of her possessions. The shaky signature didn't even look like hers. She slid the form back to the man behind the counter. "Is that it?"

He nodded. Lexie grabbed her things, suddenly very anxious to escape, but uncertain what she was going to do once she did. She'd expected Jack or Garland to be waiting for her, but realized that she had no idea how any of this worked, and didn't particularly want to ask. She just wanted out of here. She checked her cell phone, but found the battery dead. If no one was outside waiting for her, she'd find a pay phone.

The clock on the wall indicated that it was just after 6:00 p.m., but because of the time of year, it was already dark.

Lexie was slipping on her sterling silver charm bracelet when Jack came in the door. He wore faded jeans, a black T-shirt and a black leather jacket—not a bomber, but one cut like a sport coat. He wasn't smiling. In fact, she couldn't recall ever seeing him look any more serious than he did at that moment, his blue eyes moving swiftly over her and then the rest of the room, stopping only when they reached the man behind the counter. "How's it going tonight, Art?"

"Chief," the officer replied in a tight voice. He immediately turned away.

Possibly realizing that Lexie watched to see his reaction to the snub, Jack grabbed the manila envelope containing the rest of her belongings off the counter and took her by the elbow. "Come on."

He released her just outside the door. "Sorry it took so long."

"Don't be. I can't begin to thank you. And not just for the bail money."

Having spent twenty-eight out of the past twenty-nine hours in a windowless cell, she dragged in fresh, crisp air. The night was still too young for a moon.

"Are you doing okay?" he asked.

"Better." She glanced back at the building behind her, once more thinking just how glad she was to be free, even if it was only temporary. "I'll pay you back."

"I know you will," he said simply, and motioned toward the sport utility waiting at the curb. "How about we get you something to eat? And maybe a double vodka to relax you. Then we'll start making plans."

She nodded. There was no question of who was in charge. And for the moment, she was more than willing to give up control. She wanted a long, hot shower, clean clothes, her own soft bed and about a dozen hours of sleep.

Jack got the car door for her, waited while she climbed in. As soon as he was settled behind the wheel, he opened the sunroof, almost as if he understood just how much she wanted to be free of any type of enclosure.

Since he had mentioned food, she'd expected them to stop

at a restaurant, but didn't say anything even when it became obvious that they were headed out to her place. When they reached the outskirts of Deep Water, the scenery made a sudden dramatic change from homes and businesses to undeveloped land that was either thickly treed or densely covered in palmettos. The striping on the road pretty much disappeared, as well. Night air poured in, and the long wails of Kenny G's sax filled the cab.

Lexie glanced over at Jack, her gaze skimming his handsome profile, the elegant nose, the well-shaped mouth that usually appeared to be one second from forming a smile, but which was now held in a stiff line. Even in the dimness, the shadow of his beard added a disreputable edge to his stern appearance. She realized in that moment just how little she knew about the man. And maybe that wasn't such a good thing, considering that she'd placed her life in his hands.

Not wanting to get caught staring, she turned and looked out the side window. The moon now hung low, just behind the distant oaks. The sky was intensely clear. Though it was already cool out, without the insulation of cloud cover the temperatures would continue to drop rapidly.

She looked back at Jack. "Mind if I turn on some heat?"

He reached to close the sunroof, but she stopped him. "Could we leave it open? I like the fresh air," she said.

He lowered his hand. "Make yourself comfortable, then."

She kicked the heat on, felt the dry, warm air pour from the vents. She hadn't given much thought to what she was going to do once she was released, but now she did. The idea of staying out at her place alone, something she had been doing for months and months now, suddenly left her feeling vulnerable.

Maybe because, if she hadn't killed Dan, which she hadn't, then whoever had murdered him was still out there.

Chapter Seven

By the time they reached Riverhouse, the moon had crawled higher, leaching away the velvety blackness and creating shade beneath trees.

"A hunter's moon," she said as they arrived. "That's what my grandfather used to call a night like this."

Was there someone out there even now, watching her arrival, hoping that, before too long, she'd be alone?

After turning off the engine, but still seated behind the wheel, Jack looked over at her. Their gazes connected and for a few moments they just watched each other. Her pulse hammered and she could feel a slight tingling along her nerves. When he'd brought her home before, they'd sat as they were now, the air between them charged not with uncertainty and fear, but with sexual hunger. Within moments, they'd been kissing. They'd stumbled out of the car. Remembering, she felt the unexpected thrum of awareness.

In the near silence of the interior of the car, the engine made subtle sounds of cooling. She looked through the windshield, toward the house, but it wasn't the structure she was seeing. It was the hood of the car, now bathed in moonlight. It hadn't been their intended destination two months ago.

Certainly not the most comfortable spot for sex. Things had just gotten away from them.

She recalled the sensation of the warm polished metal sliding beneath her like satin sheets as the cooler night air had briefly chilled exposed skin.

Lexie looked out the side window. That night had been a mistake, and yet she couldn't think of the results of it in those terms. But she wondered how Jack was going to react when she finally told him about the baby.

"You should be prepared," he said. "Cops aren't particularly neat when they do a search."

"Do you know if they found anything?"

"They didn't come up with a twenty-five-caliber handgun, which I'm sure they considered very disappointing." Jack reached for the door handle. "There will be a list inside of what was taken."

She hadn't realized just how worried she'd been, until she felt relief flooding through her. "I was afraid they might find it."

Sensing Jack's sudden stillness next to her, she looked over at him. "It's not what you think." But when their gazes met, she realized that even at this late date, he wondered if he had misjudged her.

"Then what is it?" he asked quietly.

If she hadn't been so tired and scared, she might have been able to work up some anger. But she was tired. And she was scared. And Jack was one of the few people she had to count on. So if there were moments when he questioned his decision, she was just going to have to cut him a lot of slack.

"It's just that planting a gun here at the cabin wouldn't have been all that difficult." Lexie rubbed her head. "So why wasn't it found? Why not hide the twenty-five for the police to stumble across?"

Instead of looking at her, Jack stared out the windshield. "Because the weapon is registered to the killer. Letting the actual gun be found was out of the question, but leaving anything else—knowing that a ballistic test would be run, and that when it was, the test would reveal that it was the wrong weapon..."

"But if no weapon turned up, the police would just assume I dumped it," she added, looking over at him once more.

Jack reached for the door handle again. "We'll talk about what the cops do and don't have after you've had something to eat and a shower."

She followed him up the walk and into the house, but halted just inside the door. Even after Jack's warning, she was shocked by the mess, which started at the front door and continued through the living room and into the dining room. The drawer contents of the entry cabinet had been dumped out on the cabinet top. The furniture in the living room showed signs that it had been shifted, and one chair was still turned over as if its underside had been searched. None of that mattered, though. Lexie plopped her purse on top of the mess on the foyer table. Furniture could be righted, the previous contents of drawers returned. The only thing that was important was that she was home. That she'd sleep in her own bed tonight.

Lexie walked into the room, pretending to scan it, but what she wanted to check was the fireplace. She'd thrown the directions to the pregnancy test into the grate. Turning toward it, she saw that it had been swept clean. Had the directions and packaging been fully burned? Or had their not-quite-decipherable remains intrigued the police?

Being concerned at this point was ridiculous. Eventually, she would have to tell Jack. Maybe she had wanted to pick the moment, but even if he learned it from the cops, did it really matter? It wasn't as if she expected a marriage proposal.

What did worry her was that his finding out from another source would damage the trust that was building between them. And the possibility that Jack might believe the baby wasn't his.

Lexie suddenly spun toward the front door as a solid rap landed on it, her heart slamming hard against her ribs, the hand with the cast resting at the base of her throat.

She nearly came out of her skin when Jack touched her shoulder.

"Take it easy. That's probably just the pizza."

Home delivery pizza? He may have made it sound as if there was nothing to worry about, but he still reached inside his jacket for his weapon. "You aren't actually going to open the door to some kid with a gun in your hand? You'll scare him half to death."

Jack motioned her to move to a position that would place her out of the direct line of sight when the door was opened.

"I'll just give him a good tip to make up for it." Standing to one side of the door, he opened it.

She was so unsettled that she didn't question Alec Blade's appearance in her home until he was already inside. He held a couple of plastic grocery sacks in one hand, a large bottle of wine in the other.

He was taller than Jack by several inches, and where Jack's hair was dark blond, this man's was nearly black. They didn't look like brothers, she thought. Not until you reached the eyes. Not the color, but the shape and intensity.

Lexie didn't miss the speculation in the brother's gaze when he looked at her. She was becoming accustomed to seeing it in the faces of people she passed. Did she do it? Did she kill her husband? Was she that kind of monster?

But with Alec Blade's background as an FBI profiler, there would be additional questions, too, wouldn't there? Was that why he'd accompanied his brother this morning and why he was here now? In hopes of dissuading him from helping her?

She lifted her chin slightly. "I don't suppose any introductions are needed."

"No," he said succinctly, and didn't offer anything additional, making it fairly obvious that he didn't approve of her.

"We just got here ourselves." Jack locked the door. "So I haven't had a chance to check everything," he said, as he tucked his weapon away. "Alec, why don't you inspect the windows and doors in here while I examine the other rooms?"

"Sure." Alec walked on through to the kitchen first.

Lexie followed Jack toward the short hallway that led to the two bedrooms and the cabin's one bathroom. Jack flicked on the hall's ceiling light. The door to the nursery was closed, as was the bathroom door. The door to her room, however, was standing open. Walking past the closed doors, he turned on the overhead light in her bedroom before entering.

Lexie remained in the doorway. Not because she wanted to, but because she couldn't seem to make herself move forward. The mess in the living room had been bad enough, but it was nothing compared to the way this looked.

Most of the dresser drawers stood open, and those few that were shut had been closed on bras, panties and T-shirts. The top surface was littered with more of the same. The lamp from the bedside table sat on the floor next to the pine piece, the contents of the single drawer dumped on top. She thought about what had been in that one drawer, the bits and pieces of her recent life that she had kept close at hand in case she woke at night and needed them. The self-help book written by a woman who had lost her child to SIDS. The book of her grandmother's poems that her grandfather had had bound for her on their fiftieth wedding anniversary. The bottle of Valium that her psychologist had prescribed and she had never taken. And then there was her journal, which she suspected the police had confiscated. She thought of everything she'd written in there and knew it wouldn't help her cause.

She'd made her bed the morning she was arrested, but someone had ripped back the spread, the sheets and even the mattress pad, exposing the bare mattress beneath. And amazingly, perhaps because it seemed so unnecessary, the action seemed to be the biggest assault of her privacy.

Jack crossed to the closet and looked inside briefly before moving on to the windows, making sure they were locked and that the drapes were drawn completely. When he motioned her into the room, she managed to enter.

"Stay here while I clear the other rooms."

As soon as the door closed behind him, she ripped open drawers, crammed whatever her hand touched into them. When one was full, she went on to the next, repeating the process, not even caring if she put things away where they didn't belong. As long as they were out of sight, as long as when she looked at the room, she didn't have to feel the violation.

She didn't hear Jack open the door. It wasn't until she had jerked the sheets from the bed that she saw him standing there watching her.

Lexie kicked the pile of linens out of her way. "What about the nursery?"

"The same," Jack said.

She turned away. They'd touched her baby's things. They had ripped open and riffled drawers where she had painstakingly arranged disposable diapers, pajamas and footies for a baby whose ashes she had already spread in the Atlantic.

"Damn bastards!"

Jack crossed to where she stood in the center of the room. He squeezed her shoulder briefly. "Why don't you gather up some clothes and go take a shower?"

Lexie offered only a nod. Her emotions were so close to the surface now that saying even one word might lead to a complete breakdown. She deserved to have one, a really noisy one with lots of hysterical crying, but the truth was that it wouldn't change anything, wouldn't help her situation. And getting overly distraught just might endanger the baby.

WHEN JACK ENTERED the kitchen, Alec was on his cell phone. "I shouldn't be here long." Alec glanced up and, seeing Jack, motioned toward the three wine-filled glasses on the counter. Grabbing one, Jack leaned against the counter a short distance away. The police had posted a list of what they'd taken on the refrigerator door, and he took it down and glanced at it. A personal journal—the kind that could be really damaging if Lexie had written how much she hated her ex-husband or wanted him dead—and given what Jack already knew, it seemed very likely that she had.

He glanced down at the list again. The other items were mostly records. Phone bills, charge card statements and the like. Jack was uncertain what his colleagues were really looking for. Maybe a receipt for a twenty-five automatic. Or maybe Shepherd was hoping to link Jack to Lexie, and in the process, to Dan Dawson's murder.

Jack slid the list into his jacket pocket and waited for Alec to finish his conversation with his wife. When would Alec get around to asking him where he'd been Friday night? When he did, Jack would have no other choice than to lie. He hadn't minded lying to Shepherd, figured if the detective wanted to know where Jack was that night, he could work a little harder for the answer. But with Alec, it was different.

"I love you, too," his brother said, and then flipped the phone closed.

"How's Katie doing?"

"Fine," Alec stated simply as he grabbed one of the wineglasses.

For several seconds Jack just watched his brother shape the pizza dough. He'd expected Alec to pick up something from Mama's Pizza, but realized he should have known his brother wouldn't settle for take-out anything.

Thinking just how good a cold beer would taste, Jack took a sip of the barely chilled red wine. "You really are a culinary snob."

"For wanting my pizza to be fresh and hot, instead of soggy?"

"Like I said." Jack plucked one of the slices of pepperoni from the cutting board and popped it into his mouth as he paced by. He'd been so busy making arrangements to get Lexie out of jail that he hadn't eaten any lunch. "Pizza is pizza to most people. Edible at all temperatures and even if it's been sitting uncovered in the refrigerator for a week."

"Why stop at a week?" Alec had anchored a tea towel around his waist as a makeshift apron, and had tossed a smaller one over his shoulder, which he now removed to wipe his hands. "Why don't you see if you can locate some Italian herbs?" He pointed to the cabinets next to the stove.

"Did you look over the packet I gave you?" Jack asked

as he nudged the small bottles aside. He'd put together everything he had—copies of Andy's notes, the 35 mm photos taken at the scene, the autopsy report, including the M.E.'s photos—and given everything to Alec to examine, hoping his brother might see something that he'd overlooked. Unfortunately, he didn't have a copy of Shepherd's notes, which at this juncture would probably have been more helpful. Especially in trying to determine where they needed to go first with their investigation.

Chopping onions, Alec nodded. "The evidence is as compelling as any that I've seen. With the medical examiner's window for time of death between eight-thirty and eleven-thirty, that leaves Lexie without an alibi and with multiple motives. Garland's a damn good attorney, but with that much circumstantial evidence, it's going to be tough to keep the jury open to the possibility that she didn't do it. Most juries love the kind of evidence the prosecution is going to present to them."

Alec sprinkled the onions over the top of the pizza. "The fact that she's beautiful and comes from a good background won't help either, because, if the prosecution gets its way, there won't be many of Lexie's peers sitting on that jury. There won't be a lot of college graduates." Alec opened a can of anchovies, but left them sitting on the table. "What there will be is a bunch of armchair criminalists. Folks who watch *CSI* seven nights a week and who believe that blood evidence, photos of crime scenes, ballistic experts all add up to guilt."

Alec added black olives. "By the way I didn't spot anyone in the courtroom today who looked particularly suspicious." They had been working on the theory that the killer might be compelled to see Lexie arraigned.

Jack handed him the basil, oregano and red pepper. His

brother looked at the containers and then at Jack, one brow climbing. "Watching the food channel lately?"

"Yeah. When I can't sleep." Jack flipped a chair around and straddled it.

They talked about the evidence in general terms for several minutes before focusing in on any one aspect as Alec slid the pizza into the oven. "It appears as if the killer either knew the door would be unlocked or that they would be let in."

Jack nodded. "I keep coming back to the fact that the bullet entered behind the condyle and that there were no signs of a struggle, suggesting he knew his killer."

"Tox report complete?" Alec asked.

"Not yet."

"Until it is, I'd have to go along with your position that it was a female offender, then. An organized one. From what I've seen so far the only loose end is the missing twenty-five automatic." Alec flicked the towel back onto his shoulder. "Was he seeing anyone?"

"One of his employees, but she works part-time over at the hospital and was on the critical care unit until midnight. A patient went code blue that night—one of hers—so there's no possibility that she managed to slip away."

"Okay. Then is there any possibility that she wasn't the only one he was seeing?"

"I suppose the fact that Shepherd didn't turn up a second girl-friend may have been because he didn't dig quite deep enough."

"Then that's where I'll get started tomorrow," Alec said.

Jack took a sip of his wine. He'd asked for his brother's opinion, but he hadn't asked for any help beyond that, so was surprised by Alec's announcement.

"Are you sure you can spare the time?"

"I was planning to stick closer to home for the next few

weeks, so yeah, I have plenty of time." Alec tossed down the towel and reached for his wineglass. "Where were you that night, Jack?"

Jack knew why Alec had waited until that moment to ask. Because he had hoped to catch Jack off guard. He hadn't.

"The surf was up. I decided to drive over to the beach." Frowning, Jack downed the last of the wine in his glass. He needed to change the subject, not let his brother dwell on his answer too long. "I think we can safely agree that the only way Lexie's going to avoid prison is if the real killer is found."

LEXIE STOOD IN THE hallway, her back pressed to the wall as Alec's and Jack's words rolled through her head. *Prison.* She was heading for prison unless they managed to find Dan's killer. It wouldn't be a matter of proving herself innocent. There was no way she was going to be able to refute the evidence…

Hearing a noise, she looked up and saw Jack standing five feet from her. He'd stepped into the hallway and out of the light coming from the kitchen, so she couldn't see his face.

She straightened immediately.

"I'm sorry you overheard that."

"Don't be," she said as she closed the distance between them. "I can manage the truth easier than I can deal with wondering what you're hiding from me because you don't think I can handle it."

His mouth tightened. "I'll remember that in the future."

Lexie stepped into her kitchen, already nervous about spending time in the same room with Jack's brother. She wasn't surprised by his offer to help. His reasons for doing so, though, didn't have anything to do with her, she knew.

"Whatever you're making smells delicious."

"Pizza," Jack said as he tried to hand a glass of wine to her.

She wanted it. There was no denying that. But she shook her head. "I can't. I took a pain pill a few minutes ago." She hadn't, but it was the only reason she could think of for turning down the wine.

As she was getting a bottle of water out of the refrigerator, the phone rang and Lexie automatically picked it up.

"You murdering bitch!" an unfamiliar female voice said.

Jack tugged the handset out of Lexie's hand, listened briefly before saying, "You have a good evening, too, ma'am."

Lexie tried to open the bottled water, but her hands were shaking too badly. She knew both men were watching her, waiting to see if she would fall apart.

She would have given anything just to be alone for a few minutes.

At her continued struggles, Alec held out a hand for the water. Passing it to him, she turned to Jack. He obviously knew what was going through her head.

"Your ex-husband's patient, most likely," Jack said. "It will probably continue for a few days. People typically give up after that."

While Alec and Jack ate pizza chased with a good Chianti, Lexie accompanied hers with the water. The conversation was anything but what was normally carried on during a meal. Both men asked her endless questions about her marriage, about Dan's habits, and hers, too.

It was nearly an hour later when, taking his plate with him, Alec got up from the table. "It's getting late and Lexie especially needs a good night's sleep."

She was surprised by those words, as she was when he held out his hand to her. Given the way he'd questioned her, it seemed an odd parting gesture.

As the men moved toward the front door, Alec having said goodbye, Lexie cleared the remaining plates. There was no automatic dishwasher, so she filled one side of the double sink with water and added soap and the dishes, stacking them neatly using her one good hand. What was being said at that moment in the foyer?

And then she realized that she really didn't care.

"You okay?" Jack asked, coming up behind her.

Was it her imagination that she could feel him reaching out to touch her? She waited heavy seconds for the contact, uncertain what she would do if it ever came. Welcome it? Retreat from it?

A slight trembling started low inside her and spread upward until it controlled even her lungs. Her breath became shallow and slightly labored. She needed to tell him about the baby, but didn't know how.

"Lexie?" His fingers fiddled with the ends of her hair. He probably didn't even realize that she could feel the contact, but it served to lessen her apprehension.

Turning, she lifted her eyes to his face. *Handsome* was too tame a word to describe this man. Jack's brother was handsome. Polished. Jack wasn't. But it was rough edges that set him apart, the slightly longer hair that, when he lifted his chin, slipped beneath his collar, and the hard, broad shoulders. The blue eyes that could go nearly black when he was inside a woman.

Courage suddenly abandoned her. "What if I asked you to stay tonight?"

He remained silent, his eyes not giving away anything of what he was thinking.

She lowered her gaze. "I don't want to end up like Dan. I don't want to be the next victim."

Jack reached out and rested his hand alongside her neck. He lifted her chin with his thumb. "I wasn't planning to leave you tonight, Lexie."

IT WAS PAST 3:00 a.m. when Jack awoke suddenly. He'd heard something outside, but sat there unmoving, waiting for the sound to repeat.

After his brother had left, Jack and Lexie had spent some time cleaning things up a bit. When Lexie turned in, Jack had settled on the couch, his weapon, a 9 mm, within easy reach. He hadn't been able to sleep, though, his thoughts so anchored on the woman in the next room.

He needed to watch himself around her. If he didn't, he'd touch her as he had in the kitchen earlier. Her hair first, and when that wasn't enough, a single hand stroking the side of her neck. And when that wasn't enough… His imagination took him places he couldn't allow his hands to go.

If he'd had to name what it was about her that got under his skin, it wouldn't have been her looks, which were sexy as hell. It would have been her strength. And her vulnerability.

He'd nearly decided that he'd imagined the sound when he heard careful footsteps out on the decking. Definitely not an animal.

Jack slipped off the couch and, keeping to the shadows as much as possible, moved to a position next to the closest French door.

Flipping off the automatic's safety, he waited. More sounds of movement. Because of Jack's location and the way the house was laid out, he couldn't get a good visual, but with the next sound it became apparent that, whoever it was, they used the deck to circle to the back of the house.

He moved quickly to Lexie's bedroom door. After knocking softly, he opened it. She was already sitting up.

"We have a visitor. Might just be someone out to harass you." She climbed off the bed. She wore what looked to be white boxer shorts and the same color T-shirt.

He waited for her to reach him. "I'm going out the front way. I need you to lock it behind me. Bring your cell phone and keep it handy."

She followed him, her expression worried. "Maybe you should stay inside."

He understood her fear. She didn't like the idea of being left alone. Dropping down, he retrieved the thirty-two from his ankle holster. He passed it to her there in the dark silence of the entryway, his fingers slipping off cold metal to reach the warmth of her skin. "You won't be able to operate the safety with your left hand, so take it off as soon as you hear anything."

They both knew that he didn't need to give her instructions, that she was well versed in the handling of a weapon.

She looked up at him just before he slipped out. "Be careful."

"If I'm not back in five minutes, call 9-1-1 and then Alec. The number is on the refrigerator."

Once outside, he waited until he heard the lock click into place behind him, then followed the same track their visitor had.

The night had cooled into the low forties. As he slipped past the first French door, he glanced inside. Where was Lexie? Still by the front door, or concealed in one of the living room's shadows?

He didn't really believe it was someone out to hassle Lexie. If that had been their goal, there would have been no reason to risk getting this close. A rock lobbed through a window or graffiti sprayed on her car would have been just as effective and far safer for the perp.

Reaching the corner of the house, he waited again for the subtle sounds of movement.

But what would Dan's killer gain by showing up? If the goal had been to kill Lexie's ex and frame her, why not just sit back and watch the show? At least until there were signs that the court wasn't going to handle things to your satisfaction?

The breeze that had been blocked by the house reached him, the scent of the nearby woods forced to mingle with that of the river. He leaned out just far enough to look down the length of the home, but immediately flattened himself again.

A bend in Deep Water Run meant the river pretty much wrapped two sides of the house. What wasn't enclosed by water was bordered by trees. Perhaps not closely, but the forest still presented cover for anyone's arrival or departure.

Jack scanned the area between the house and the woods. Instead of aiding him, the moonlight created shadows in the tall grasses that could easily hide a man. Was someone out there staring back? Perhaps using night-vision equipment? Something made Jack glance down at the deck he stood on. Or had they ducked underneath?

He crossed to the railing and dropped over the side. As soon as his shoes connected with the soft, slick ground, he crouched. He'd had to put his hand out to maintain his balance, and it was now coated with mud.

Jack trained the 9 mm on the darkened area beneath the boards. The moonlight, penetrating the spaces between, striped the ground and the water, but didn't reach the foundation.

The headroom was about four feet, tall enough for a man to move around. Which meant that Jack was going to have to get even dirtier than he already was. But five feet in, he came face-to-face with an opossum and realized there was no need to go any farther. The animal would have been long gone if anyone had crawled beneath the deck ahead of him.

He circled the house a second time, his gaze trained on the woods now. Maybe he was overreacting. Perhaps their visitor had nothing to do with Dan Dawson's murder. Most of the residences in the area were weekend retreats and would normally be unoccupied on a Tuesday night. Maybe it had just been someone looking for an easy house to break into.

But Jack didn't think so.

Chapter Eight

"Did you see anything?"

Lexie jerked open the door before Jack even had a chance to knock. She'd been tracking his movements the whole time, and she had watched him turn away from the door suddenly several minutes earlier, as if he had seen or heard something.

Jack closed the door behind him and locked it.

"Jack?"

He looked unsettled. "Maybe it was just a reporter. I don't really know." The hand he ran through his hair hesitated at the back of his neck, and then dropped away. "We'll stay here tonight, but we'll move to my place tomorrow."

THE FOLLOWING DAY Lexie and Jack arrived at Fleming Whittemore's office just after eight o'clock. The sun was barely peeking above the trees and the morning chill still lingered.

The brick-and-stucco building, built only three years earlier by Dan Dawson and Fleming Whittemore, was located on a quiet street adjacent to one of the older residential areas in Deep Water. The homes may have been smaller than those in Thornton Park, but the lots were just as large, as were the oaks draped in Spanish moss and the Formosa azaleas.

"You okay with this?" Jack asked as they headed up the wide sidewalk.

"I'll be fine." She wouldn't be, of course. She would have preferred to be just about anywhere else this morning. Besides jail. Even if the reason for the visit hadn't been to confront Fleming, just entering her dead ex-husband's office and facing members of his staff would have been difficult enough. How many of them actually thought she'd killed Dan?

Innocent until proven guilty sounded good in theory, but from Lexie's recent experience, that's not how it really worked. People loved to believe the worst about other people. Because it made them feel better about their own lives.

Jack held the door, and Lexie stepped into the overly cool reception area, where the aromas of antiseptic and fresh-brewed coffee seemed to coexist comfortably.

Because of the early hour, there wasn't a receptionist at the desk, but a nurse stood just outside the file room, her arms full of charts. She looked up as they entered, and her expression became troubled.

"I'm not sure you should be here," the woman said.

"We need to speak with Dr. Whittemore," Jack stated.

The nurse looked uncertain. "Please have a seat. I'll see if Dr. Whittemore can take the time away from his patients."

Instead of sitting in the reception area as she had suggested, Jack chose to wait next to the desk. Lexie felt too conspicuous just standing there, though, so she paced nervously. The room was mostly glass, the view outside one of expansive lawn and century oaks. Slickly framed photographs of babies filled the limited wall space. Advertisements. She'd always thought it was a bit cheesy, like an automotive repair shop hanging photos of race cars.

One of the photos had recently been removed. In its place, someone was creating a collage from snapshots of babies. Glass protected the work-in-progress. As she scanned the faces, Lexie thought of all the happy mothers who had donated them. And couldn't help but think about the baby she'd lost, and the one she carried.

Jack touched her on the arm. She flinched at the unexpected contact.

"Come on." He nodded to the nurse, who now waited for them.

The nurse who showed them into Fleming's office didn't close the door when she left, so Lexie did. For no other reason than she didn't want to feel as if she was on display to patients and staff when they walked past.

"Nice building," Jack commented as he checked out the framed medical diploma and board certification. "Did you have a hand in it?"

"Only financially."

He glanced in her direction. "Pharmaceutical reps make that kind of money?"

"No. My grandparents left me that kind of money."

"What about Dan? Did he have money?"

"Recently licensed doctors don't have money. They have sleep deprivation and debt."

She saw the speculation in Jack's eyes. Had Dan married her for the money? To be honest, there were times when she wasn't so certain that he hadn't.

"Dan received the office in the property settlement and I was to have retained the Thornton Park house and River-house."

"Alimony?"

"No. My attorney wanted to push for it, but I wouldn't let

him. It would have only served to exasperate the animosity, and I just wanted to put the marriage behind me."

She rubbed her arms. She didn't know if it was the room temperature or the conversation that had left her feeling chilled.

As if he sensed that she didn't want to continue the discussion, Jack checked out the alcove with the large window. They'd stopped by his place so that he could shower and change. And to leave the suitcase she'd packed in the center of his bed. She'd felt awkward sitting in his living room, listening to the shower run, and when it stopped, seeing him casually walk across the hall to his bedroom with a towel draped around his waist.

Jack was obviously very comfortable in his skin. Competent. Confident. She was none of those things anymore. Perhaps that was why she had been so drawn to him that night, and remained drawn to him even now.

They were both working hard at pretending that the intimacy of two months ago hadn't taken place. Or maybe Jack didn't need to try all that hard. Maybe she was the only one who couldn't quite seem to put it out of her memory.

And she could no longer put a name to the relationship. He'd been a lover briefly, in the most nonchalant sense of the word. They didn't even know each other well enough for the label of close friend to apply, and yet he'd pretty much flushed his career in order to help her. What kind of man forked over a hundred grand for a woman he barely knew? The crazy kind? The right kind?

Her conscience ratcheting the knot inside even tighter, Lexie glanced away. What was she going to do? Maybe she should just come out and tell him that she was pregnant. Get it out in the open. Deal with it.

As Fleming pushed open the door, she looked up.

"You've picked a really bad time to show up here, Lexie."

"Not nearly as bad as my timing Friday night," she said.

Fleming let out a harsh breath as he stepped the rest of the way into his private office. He almost looked embarrassed, as if he realized just how self-centered his statement had sounded.

"Sorry. It's been a bad week already. There were two detectives in here yesterday questioning the staff for hours. On top of that, there was no way to cancel Dan's patients, so I didn't get out of here until nearly nine last night, and I have half a dozen patients waiting in treatment rooms now." A patient and a dark-haired nurse walked by the still-open door.

Fleming pushed the door closed. "And to be honest, in the future I'd prefer you didn't come here. It just upsets the staff and the patients."

Fleming hadn't yet given any indication that he saw Jack.

"And you?" She took a deep breath, tried to corral her agitation. "Does my presence here make you uncomfortable?"

He frowned. "If you're here to ask why I refused to help with bail, you should have realized I couldn't."

"Couldn't, or wouldn't?"

"Dan was my partner. You're charged with his murder. How would that look?"

"As if you believed I was innocent?" She didn't quite manage to keep the sarcasm in check.

"Listen, Lexie, I am sorry about your current problems, but the last thing I need is to get dragged into a murder investigation on top of everything else."

"I think it's too late," Lexie said.

"What do you mean?" He was starting to move away from the door when he finally saw Jack. He pulled up short, and

Lexie could see the outward signs of irritation being suppressed.

"Good morning. I didn't realize Lexie wasn't alone." He rounded the desk and sat. As the office call system chirped, he glanced down at the box. After punching in a response, he met Jack's gaze again. "So what brings you here? Since you're no longer with the police department."

"The defense has hired me to investigate, and I wanted some clarification of your movements on Friday."

"I'd love to help you, but I've given answers to these questions already. To the police. And as I said a few moments ago, I have patients to see." He stood.

Jack also got to his feet. "I can get a subpoena."

Fleming rounded his desk on the way to the door. "Then I think you better get one. This is nothing more than harassment."

"You have any idea what the penalty is for perjury? That's what it's going to be when Lexie's attorney puts you on the stand and asks you where you were Friday night. Because I know for a fact that you didn't stop at Clive's." Jack stepped in front of Fleming. "You answer a few questions, and assuming I like those answers, you don't get subpoenaed. At least not by the defense."

Still seated, Lexie looked up at Fleming. She didn't recognize him. He had always been someone she felt she could turn to. She'd considered him a friend. But the look in his eyes assured her that he wasn't. "Wouldn't it be easier, Fleming, to just answer the questions?" She got to her feet. "Unless you have something to hide. Unless you were somehow involved in Dan's murder."

Fleming reached down for the phone. "If you don't leave now, I'll have you arrested for trespassing."

Jack did something Lexie didn't expect. She suspected Fleming hadn't, either. Jack smiled. "You're hiding something, Whittemore. And I'm going to find out what it is."

Stepping aside, he escorted Lexie out the door. They were nearly to the reception area when Lexie nodded toward the restroom. "I need to make a quick stop." She was still shaking inside.

After washing the hand without a cast, she reapplied lip gloss somewhat awkwardly. She was getting better at doing things with her left hand. Buttons and bras were still on the tricky side, though. She was sliding away the tube of gloss when Marian Glefke, the officer manager, stepped in.

Marian was one of those women who was rarely noticed until your eyes connected with hers. Then there was no looking away. She'd been one of Dan's favorites. Lexie's, too, actually.

But today, Lexie steeled herself for the coming confrontation.

Marian's hand remained on the door. "I wanted to tell you how sorry I was about Dr. D. And about what is happening to you now."

Surprised and relieved, Lexie tossed into the trash the paper towel she held. "Thanks, Marian." She managed to halt the emotion that welled up inside her. "You can't imagine how much that means to me. Dan always thought so much of you."

The office manager hadn't moved away from the entrance. Was she standing in front of it to keep anyone from walking in on them? Did she worry that being kind to Lexie was going to put her at odds with the rest of the staff? With Fleming?

"The respect was mutual," Marian said. "He was a good doctor." She paused. "The police were in yesterday, talking to all of us about last Friday. I didn't mention it to them."

"Didn't mention what?"

"Actually, with everything else, it slipped my mind until my husband brought it up last night. He wondered if there had been any fallout."

What was Marian talking about? "What kind of fallout?"

"Dr. D got a call just after lunch on Wednesday. Maybe three or four o'clock. I think something about the call upset him because a few minutes later, he requested his patients for Thursday afternoon be moved to another day."

"Do you know who it was that called?"

"Nidia Rivera."

"From the Pierson Clinic?"

"Yes."

Dan and Fleming had taken over the Pierson Clinic two years ago. The clinic had been struggling financially, largely due to poor collection. Had the call Wednesday just been about another unprofitable month?

"Dr. D. phoned me from out there the next afternoon. He wanted to know where Dr. Whittemore was."

"And where was he?"

"Seeing patients here in this office. He wasn't scheduled to be out in Pierson until Friday morning."

"But you don't know why he wanted to know where Fleming was, or why Nidia had called on Wednesday?"

"No. But in four years, the only other time Dr. D had me change his appointments was for the baby's memorial. He always put his patients first. Didn't want to inconvenience them."

Dan hadn't attended Lindy's memorial, though. And Marian would know that. As she would know the lies that Dan had spread about the reason he hadn't attended.

Someone pushed at the door. Marian immediately moved

away from it to the sink, where she washed her hands. Both Lexie and Marian smiled at the newcomer, a patient, and then exited, but almost if by unspoken agreement, not together. Fortunately, when Lexie stepped out into the hall, Fleming was nowhere in view.

She caught sight of Jack waiting next to the front door and hurried toward him. Her footsteps echoed on the limestone floor. Out of the corner of her eye, she saw a woman rise and follow a nurse toward the exam rooms. Something about her profile seemed familiar.

Turning, Lexie watched the woman. All she could see now, though, was the trim back, the very straight posture. The long dark hair. Instead of an exam room, she was ushered into Fleming's office. Who was she?

The private office was used to discuss either the good news of pregnancy or the bad news of a medical complication. Or to interview job applicants. Did Lexie know her from one of the medical offices she called on in the area?

Fleming came out of an exam room across the hall and headed for his office. As he reached for the knob, he glanced toward the reception area, his gaze connecting with Lexie's. She expected trouble, but instead he walked into his office and closed the door.

It was only then that the answer came to her. The woman in the office was Amanda, the young woman from her support group.

Was it possible that she was pregnant again?

Marian walked up. "I'm sorry, Lexie. You need to leave. Otherwise, I'm to call the police."

Lexie nodded in understanding and started to turn away, then faced Marian. "The patient in Fleming's office. Her name's Amanda. Has she been Fleming's patient for long?"

"No. She was one of Dan's. From the Pierson Clinic."

"Is she pregnant?"

"You know I can't discuss a patient's medical history or current condition."

"Yes. I know."

Jack held the outside door open for Lexie as she approached. "What's going on?"

"Marian said that Dan got a call from the Pierson Clinic last Wednesday. She seemed to think it upset him. Enough that he cancelled an afternoon's worth of appointments with patients. And Dan wasn't the type of doctor who did that kind of thing."

"I guess that means we should take a ride out there."

Pierson, a small community sitting on the edge of the Ocala National Forest, held the distinction of being the Fern Capital of the World. In spite of that, with the high unemployment rate and an average annual income of less than thirty thousand, it was one of those rural areas that seemed to survive, but never to prosper.

The Pierson Clinic of Drs. Whittemore and Dawson was nothing like the Deep Water office. The strip mall where it was located was on Highway 17, the roadway itself poorly maintained, the median filled with dry weeds and trash. The actual medical facility was sandwiched between an auto parts store and a bakery.

Where professional photographs of babies hung in the reception area of the other office, the only thing on the wall here was a framed poster titled: From Conception to Birth.

The furniture was basic doctor's office, and the flooring was a gray, multitoned commercial carpet that showed wear. But there were flowers at the front desk, and a small carafe of water and disposable cups sat at one end of the counter.

A young girl dressed in jeans, a hoodie and flip-flops was talking to the woman behind the reception desk.

Jack and Lexie took seats against the back wall to wait.

"A little different than the Deep Water office," he commented.

"These people aren't looking to be impressed. They just want good care at a fee they can afford. There was another obstetric office in Pierson, but high malpractice premiums forced it to close its doors."

"So how often are patients seen out here?"

"Two days a week."

As the girl turned to leave, Jack and Lexie approached the counter. "Hello, Mrs. Dawson." The woman, a Hispanic lady somewhere in her forties, with long dark hair and flawless skin, looked uncertain.

Lexie introduced Jack to Nidia Rivera.

Nidia seemed nervous. "Dr. Whittemore called a little bit ago," Nidia said. "I've been instructed not to talk to you."

Jack ignored the statement. "You made a phone call last Wednesday to Dr. Dawson. What about?"

"I make lots of phone calls to Dr. Dawson. For the past month, I've had to report to him almost daily."

"What about?" he repeated.

"People around here depend on the fern industry. When the hurricanes destroyed the shade structures, they lost their jobs. Without work, they can't pay their bills." She slipped the two dollars the girl had given her into the top drawer of the desk. "Dr. Dawson said I wasn't working the account receivables hard enough. I told him to come try and collect money from people who don't have it. See how he did."

"What about Wednesday? Anything different about that call?"

"Sure. About two weeks ago, Dr. Dawson asked me to pull the charts of any patients he or Dr. Whittemore had seen in this office once or twice who had failed to return for further appointments. The computer system at the Deep Water office evidently tracks that kind of thing, but the crap system here doesn't. I had to go through each chart." She motioned toward a file room wall-to-wall with records. "On Wednesday I called to tell him I had them ready for him, and to ask if he wanted me to have them couriered to him or wanted to look at them the next time he was out here at this location."

"Why would that interest him?"

"Lose a patient, lose their money. That's all these people were to him." She looked at Lexie. "It got worse when you left him."

"So when he came in on Thursday, what happened?"

"He called me into his office and accused me of doing a bad job. It was my fault that the clinic wasn't doing well. That so many patients had left after their first or second visit. He actually chewed me out. Like I was a nobody. I don't take that from no man. I gave him my two-week notice that afternoon."

Jack nodded, as if agreeing that the woman was right to be upset. Nidia seemed to relax some.

"Do you still have those charts?" he asked.

"He took them with him."

"How many?"

"Twenty-three."

"Did you keep a list of the patients?"

"No reason to," she said.

"Perhaps you recall some of the women?"

"No. Because they were only in once or twice, they were

just names to me, and I have a hard time remembering names. I'm much better with faces."

"Okay. What about Friday? Dr. Whittemore was here seeing patients until what time?"

"We were scheduled to five, but he had me reschedule his last few patients. Said he was meeting someone."

"Could he have been meeting Dr. Dawson?"

"I don't think so. Dr. Dawson called just before three and Dr. Whittemore had me tell him that he was with a patient. That they'd talk on Monday."

"So Dr. Whittemore didn't want to talk to Dr. Dawson?"

"No." Nidia glanced down as the phone rang, but didn't answer it. "If you ask me, he was meeting a woman. Before he left here, he brushed his teeth, trimmed his mustache. I went in to empty the trash in his bathroom, and there was toothpaste and hair in his sink. And he nearly knocked me over with the smell of his cologne as he walked past me on his way out of the office."

"Did he often have dates that required him to take off early?" Jack asked. "Or did you ever see him leave with anyone?"

She glanced toward the front window. "I once saw him give a ride to one of Dr. Dawson's patients." Lexie followed Nidia's lead and looked out the window, toward the overgrown field across the highway.

"What exactly did you see?" Jack asked.

"This patient, a young girl, was standing outside as if waiting for someone to pick her up. He was on his way to his car. He stopped and talked to her for several minutes. She followed him to his car and got in."

"And they drove away?"

She nodded. "Yes."

"Do you recall who the patient was?"

"No. Just some young girl with long brown hair."

The outside door opened and a young man walked in, dressed in work boots, jeans and a dirt-streaked T-shirt.

"It's my lunch hour," she told them. "My husband is here to pick me up."

Jack and Lexie walked outside, but didn't get into the SUV. "A wasted trip," she said.

"Maybe not. There was a pile of charts sitting on the corner of the desk Friday night. Maybe we can spot something in them that points to another suspect."

Of course she'd seen them. They'd been splattered with blood. As had everything else.

Lexie took a deep breath and looked away. She'd tried desperately to forget everything about that night, and had pretty much managed not to think about what she'd been confronted with in that room. Except at night. When the nightmares found her.

Jack's strong fingers closed over her shoulder, their warm pressure bolstering her, but not quite chasing away the fear that curled tightly inside her. Nothing could, she suspected. After a brief squeeze, he let go, and by the time she looked up, he was opening her car door.

They passed a barbecue place on the way back and decided to stop. She wasn't particularly hungry, but realized Jack must be. One look inside at the nearly packed interior told them that, despite the rough appearance of the building and the gravel parking lot, the food was probably good. But it was unlikely they'd get a table in the dining room anytime soon.

Lexie figured they'd just move on up the road until they reached the next restaurant, but Jack pointed to a window marked Take-out Orders.

"I'll order us a couple of sandwiches. On the way in, I saw two outside picnic tables. Why don't you go grab one?"

Because the day was cool, both tables were available. She chose the one in the sunshine. As she sat, she noticed the plank top had been heated by the sun.

Closing her eyes, she enjoyed the moment of solitude. It was the first time in days that she had been truly alone.

Lexie inhaled slowly, deliberately, trying not to think about anything.

Opening her eyes and discovering Jack watching her from five feet away, she offered a weak smile. She found being around him easy. There was a calmness in him that she hadn't noticed in many men. A certain confidence that was appealing and gave her some measure of hope. And hope was something she was having a real hard time holding on to.

"Too late." Jack placed the take-out containers on the table and pulled a couple of soft drinks from the pockets of his jacket.

"What is?"

"That smile. As I was walking up, you were frowning."

She reached for one of the napkins trapped under a soda can. "I was thinking about my night in jail."

His expression turned serious. He sat, the wood beneath her buttocks and elbows rocking as his weight settled on the opposite side of the table. "You're not going back to jail, Lexie. We'll figure this out."

With the hand in the cast, she swiped at the loose hairs that floated forward onto her cheek. "As much as I want to believe that, it doesn't feel as if we have all that much to go on."

"We're just getting started." Escaping carbonation hissed as he opened the drink. "Our investigation is still in its infancy."

She'd been attempting to open the food containers with her good hand, but suddenly looked away, the word *infancy* seeming to hang in the air between them. At least in her mind it did.

Reaching across, Jack undid the lid on the box in front of her, obviously assuming she'd become frustrated at her inability to do something so simple.

Lexie picked up one of the French fries. "Thanks."

"Sure. We need to eat and get back on the road. I want to get to our next stop before midafternoon."

She lifted the top half of the bun. "We're not heading back to Deep Water to check out the charts?"

"It'll take Garland some time to get them. Day or two, or maybe even longer."

"Then where are we headed?"

"Whittemore has patients until four today, so I thought it might be a good time to check out his cabin." Jack took a bite of his sandwich. "Ever been there?"

"No."

"What about Dan? Did he ever go there?"

"Not to my knowledge. Having been raised in Boston, he wasn't exactly the outdoor type. In the three years we were married, he only came out to Riverhouse a few dozen times."

Jack was about to take another bite of his sandwich, and then didn't. "I got the impression that the place was a regular weekend retreat. Because of the way the second bedroom is set up as a nursery."

"I was hoping that we would spend more time there. As a family."

As she smoothed her napkin in her lap, her fingers brushing her abdomen, she didn't think of the baby she lost. She thought of the one she carried. The tightness in her chest eased. Her emotions confused her. It was as if she was on some crazy theme park ride. One moment she was shooting downward through a dark twisting tunnel, certain she wouldn't survive, and then the next she was sailing out into liquid sunshine, everything inside her filled with joy.

Jack laid the sandwich down. "To the outside world Dan appeared to have it all. The successful practice, the nice home, the beautiful wife."

Even though his tone had dropped with the last of his observations, Lexie didn't read anything into the compliment. "Dan came from a poor background. He worked his way through college and med school. He was a very good doctor. But for all his success, he always saw himself as that kid struggling to get out. In his mind he never arrived."

"What about the pregnancy? Was he happy about it?"

Realizing she'd already said more than she was comfortable with, she reached for a rhetorical question instead of the truth. "Isn't every father-to-be?"

But Lexie knew that not every man was excited by the prospect of children. Especially if the pregnancy wasn't planned. Or made the man feel trapped. She took a bite of sandwich, but no longer tasted the pork and barbecue sauce and bread. "What about you? Any children?"

"None that I'm aware of."

It took a cola chaser to push the food past the knot in her throat. "Ever married?" She realized she probably should have asked sooner.

"No. And no close calls." He shut the empty foam box. "When you work undercover, you don't meet many women who are looking to settle down in suburbia to raise children. Even if you are lucky enough to meet one between assignments, the divorce rate for cops is one of the highest for any profession. I had a gal pal who claimed the only way to be certain you didn't end up in divorce court was never to get married in the first place."

"And you believe that?"

"It's been working so far," he said as he climbed to his feet. He was grinning, which made it difficult to tell if he was serious and used the smile to take some of the edge off his words.

Locking the cover closed on the food container, she couldn't help but wonder where he would go after the trial. He'd moved to town to take the job and now there was no more job…and no reason for him to stay.

Chapter Nine

Even with the address and a map, finding Fleming's cabin took longer than Jack would have anticipated. Several street signs were missing and some of the roads were pretty much dirt tracks.

The driveway to Whittemore's place wasn't any different. Long and narrow, a dark tunnel of foliage. There was no light at the end, just more shadows.

The cabin was large and modern, with wide decks circling the upper levels. Instead of wood railings, thick, tubular metal coated in red paint had been used.

Huge chunks of window glass interrupted the cypress siding, but appeared to be almost random.

Leaning forward, Lexie peered through the windshield. "From the way he always talked about it, I was picturing something small and rustic."

"What do you think it's worth? Three or four hundred thousand? A lot of money to have tied up in a weekend getaway for a man with money problems."

There were no cars in sight and no lights on inside the house. As he stepped out of the SUV, Jack looked around the clearing. He glanced to where Lexie stood next to the vehicle.

"Well, if he was here Friday night," Jack said, "it wouldn't be surprising that no one saw him."

He closed the door, unconcerned that the sound would alert someone to their arrival.

"What do you know about Whittemore's love life?" Jack asked.

"Nothing really. The times that he came over to the house for dinner, he always had a date, but it never seemed to be all that serious. I've heard him say that he had no intention of getting married."

Lexie followed Jack as he walked around the lower level. "What are we doing here?"

Because of the deep shade beneath the tree canopy, there was no grass, no lawn. Just sandy soil covered in a loose loam that left perfect indentations of their footsteps. Jack wasn't particularly concerned that Whittemore would notice their tracks.

There were no windows on the lowest level, only a single steel door around back fastened with dead bolts. Two of them. Which seemed a bit extreme, but perhaps because of the remote location, there had been problems with break-ins.

Only after making a complete circle of the structure did he climb the front stairs.

"You're not thinking about going in there, are you?" Lexie asked, trailing behind, obviously nervous.

"No." As appealing as the idea was, Jack wasn't ready to break any laws quite yet.

He looked in the windows one by one. The first revealed a large two-story space with wood floors and dark leather sofas, the next was the dining room. Nothing looked particularly out of place. Had Fleming been here Friday night as he insisted? With a date of one gender or the other?

Jack turned and stared back down the driveway. Maybe he was wrong about Fleming Whittemore. Perhaps he was protecting the identity of a male lover.

Lexie wandered to the metal rail. "Can we go? This place is really beginning to give me the creeps. I guess it's all the shadows and the silence. Or the sense that just about anything could happen out here and no one would ever know it."

Facing him, she rubbed her arms slowly. She was wearing black slacks and a black turtleneck sweater. Both seemed to hug her curves—the fullness of her breasts, the soft flare of her hips, the nicely rounded, firm derriere. Jack's fingers curled.

Last night, lying there on her couch, knowing she was just in the other room, sprawled in the very bed where he had made love to her that night…

And tonight it would be his bed in which she slept. Alone.

Jack withdrew his phone from his pocket. "I just need to make a quick call." He dialed the Deep Water PD number and asked for Frank Shepherd.

When the other man picked up, he said, "Hey, Frank. Just thought you might want to know that the cellular reception out at Fleming Whittemore's cabin is better than good. I'm standing on the front porch right now."

There was a slight pause. "Maybe he just didn't want to talk to her, Jack. Or was too busy in the sack."

So Frank had known about the supposed date. "Maybe. Or maybe he was showering off the blood from murdering his partner. Whittemore had dried mud on his clothes, but his hands had been scrubbed until they were pink. Don't you even wonder about that, Frank?"

Before the other man could say anything, Jack hung up. His intent with the call was to give Frank something to stew about. Jack figured that, unless the charts turned up something useful, he'd already spent as much time as he dared chasing after Whittemore. He'd leave him to Frank. No matter what else Shepherd was, he was the kind of detective who would go to great lengths to prove he was right.

Jack was nearly to the car when the cell phone rang. He expected it to be Frank, so he was surprised to hear Garland Ramsey's voice.

"Those charts should be here by five-thirty."

"How'd you get them so quickly?"

"The prosecutors are playing it safe. And, at this point, they don't see the evidentiary value of these records to their case."

THE LAST TIME Lexie had been in Garland Ramsey's office, she hadn't yet been charged with Dan's murder. But she had still been nervous, having just come from the confrontation with the woman at the end of the support meeting.

Lexie thought about Amanda. Why had the young woman been in Whittemore's office this morning? Was there some way she could get the girl's last name?

As she approached the building's front door, Lexie sidestepped a well-dressed man and a toddler. The office was located on the second floor of what had been the county's government building in the early 1900s. The structure had been completely restored to its former glory, a hundred years' worth of bird droppings, grime and mildew sandblasted away to reveal the aged patina of the limestone and the craftsmanship of European workers.

Jack pulled open the front door. Their footsteps echoed on the marble floors and resonated in the cavernous space as they crossed to the wide, central staircase that led to a broad landing where politicians had once pontificated. From there, two narrower sets of stairs continued upward. The law firm of Ramsey, Peterson and McGuire took up the whole floor.

There was a sense of hushed silence as the receptionist showed them into a conference room. "Mr. Ramsey will be with you in a few moments. He suggested that you might want to go ahead and look through the documents that were sent over."

The space was done in what Lexie called lawyer decor. Muted moss-green paint, lots of dark trim, mahogany table, plush carpet.

The artwork depicted natural Florida: the beaches, the Everglades, the deeply shaded oak hammocks and piney plains dotted with longhorn cows. All of the canvases looked expensive. The signature on the cow painting caught Lexie's attention. "K. L. Blade?" She glanced toward Jack. "That would be your sister-in-law?"

"It would."

"She's talented."

Jack unsealed the box in the center of the conference table. "Yes."

When he didn't elaborate, Lexie wondered if he was too preoccupied with what he was doing, or if he wasn't all that crazy about his sister-in-law. Lexie didn't know Katie Blade, but she'd seen her around.

She moved toward the narrow table at the opposite end of the room. A carafe of coffee and pitchers of water had been set up.

She glanced back at Jack. "Would you like something?"

Looking up, he shook his head. "No thanks."

Lexie helped herself to water, then returned to where he had unloaded the patient files. She pulled out a chair, intending to sit, but was brought up short by the sight of them.

After only seventy-two hours, the blood splatters had faded to a point it would have been hard to say what had made them. The rusty-brown shade could have just as easily been paint or some type of food. But the sight of them drove Lexie to the large window overlooking Laishley Park.

If Jack noticed, he didn't say anything. Sipping water, she stared out at the descending dusk. For obvious reasons, she hadn't thought about the coming holidays. Sometime in the past few days, though, wreaths had been added to the lamp-posts surrounding the city park. On several of the large catalpa trees, clear lights had been haphazardly strung in patterns that somehow managed to resemble constellations. On the smaller trees and the two gazebos, the twinkling lights were placed closer together and more evenly, so that from where she stood looking the overall illusion was that of a fairy tale village sprawled beneath the Big Dipper.

A couple ambled along the brick walkway, pushing a stroller. Kids ran about in one of the open areas, playing a game of tag, the coming holiday adding another level to their limitless energy.

As Lexie's eyes returned to the couple pushing the stroller, she reached out, pressing her fingers to the window. Longing expanded inside her. That's what she'd wanted when she married Dan. That sense of completeness. Like the fairy tale village beneath the Big Dipper, she now realized that happily-ever-after was an illusion, born of naiveté.

Or maybe some people actually did find it. Her grandparents certainly had. But she wouldn't. She was no longer naive about anything. And most especially about the likelihood of future relationships. Even if she was acquitted, how was she going to put this behind her? When people looked at her, they would always wonder if justice had truly been served.

And if she was convicted…

Topping up her glass of water, she returned to the table. This was her life they were talking about. No matter how uncomfortable the blood made her, she needed to be involved in what Jack was doing.

"Have you found anything yet?"

He looked up as she sat. "There are some similarities between the patients. They all appear to be between the ages of eighteen and twenty-one, and unmarried." He slid a chart across so Lexie could read it. "Do you recognize the handwriting?"

"The first two entries belong to Dan. The last one, I don't recognize. Possibly a nurse." Disappointed, she leaned back. "So there's really nothing here?"

"And it's what's not here that may be the most telling. There are only twenty-two charts instead of twenty-three."

"Maybe Nidia miscounted."

"Given the importance of these charts to her job, I doubt she would make that kind of mistake."

Lexie inhaled sharply and then let her breath out slowly. "You're right. So where's the missing one?"

With a heavy sigh, Jack looked up. "It could be just about anywhere. And the fact that it's missing may mean absolutely nothing. Welcome to police work. Lots of leads, lots of dead ends."

As he flicked the cover on the chart closed, the photo in front caught Lexie's attention. On a patient's first visit, a photo was snapped and placed in the front of their file. It served two purposes—to help alleviate the possibility of any type of record mix-up, and to help foster the illusion that a patient wasn't just a number and a medical condition.

Pulling the file toward her, she flipped the cover open and

stared at the young woman with the long dark hair and wide-set brown eyes. Not a stranger, as she had expected.

Jack, who already had gone on to the next chart in the pile, stopped what he was doing. "Do you know her?"

"Yes. She was at the Sisters-in-Loss meeting on Saturday, and she was going into Fleming's office this morning. She was one of Dan's patients. At least that's what Marian said."

"Wouldn't they need the chart if they were seeing her today?"

"Sure. Ideally. But charts do go missing sometimes." Lexie ran a finger along the series of numbers on the end tab. "Out at the Pierson Clinic, every patient is assigned a number that matches her file. The color coding helps when it comes to a misplaced file, but if one goes AWOL, it can still take some time to locate it."

Returning to the treatment notes, Lexie's eyes narrowed. "This can't be right. The last entry says that she miscarried at eleven weeks." She glanced back at the photo a second time to be sure she wasn't mistaken. "But Amanda said that she gave her baby up for adoption."

"Are you sure?"

"Yes." Lexie looked up. "Do you think it means anything?"

"I think it means we're not done for the night."

MORE THAN FOUR HOURS later, Lexie looked around the small bedroom, at the mission style furniture that was obviously new, at the neatly made bed where she would sleep tonight. Jack's bed. The only one in the house.

Even after nearly two years, a dozen unpacked boxes still filled the second bedroom. Almost as if Jack hadn't wanted to get too comfortable. As if the years of working undercover had made it impossible for him to relax into a place, to accumulate the "stuff" that most people had by the time they reached thirty.

Lexie ran the brush through her wet hair a final time and then tossed it into her open suitcase. Disappointment and frustration battled inside her. And right below both of those there was the ever-present fear about her future.

After leaving her attorney's office, they'd driven to Pierson, hoping to talk to Amanda. Finding the house dark and a For Sale sign in the front yard, Jack had knocked on the door of two neighboring homes. He'd been told that after her mother passed, Amanda had moved away. They didn't know where, though. And no one seemed to recall a pregnancy. What they did remember quite clearly was that Amanda had gone off the deep end after her mother's funeral, had even been admitted briefly to a mental health facility.

So which was it? Had the grieving young woman lost touch with reality, created a story where she hadn't miscarried? Instead, had given her baby up for adoption? Lexie scrubbed her face with her hands. Or had the neighbors failed to notice the pregnancy?

And was there any reason to believe that there was a connection between Amanda Wilkes and Dan's murder? Wasn't it just as likely that the reason Dan was dead had nothing to do with anything in those charts? That Lexie and Jack were going miles and miles down a dark road that led nowhere but to prison?

Despite the heat duct spewing warm air, she shivered.

She'd left the bedroom door open, and the subtle creak of a floorboard made her glance toward the opening. Jack stood there, his chest bare, a towel wrapped around his middle, his hair a darker shade of blond because it was still wet. The scent of clean male skin and shampoo filled the room.

"Finding everything?" he asked.

"Yes. Thank you."

"I just want to grab a few things. Then I'll clear out of your way. Let you get some sleep."

He crossed to the dresser and opened a top drawer. She couldn't quite stop herself from watching the play of muscles across his shoulders. The way the damp towel clung to his firm buttocks. She remembered her fingers curling into their hardness two months ago, urging his thrusts deeper, faster.

Some hint of motion in the mirror jolted her, and when she lifted her gaze, she met Jack's. She felt as if she'd been caught with her hand in the cookie jar.

Sparks of awareness danced along her skin and heat pooled low and heavy in her body. It had never been like that with anyone else. The sharp spike of physical need brought on by close proximity, by a simple look. By a not-so-simple memory.

Jack closed the drawer, the sudden movement and sound causing Lexie to jump slightly.

"I think I have everything I need. I'll just go—"

She should have offered to get out of his way sooner, she realized. "No, I can—"

Both made a move for the door at the same moment. They collided. When she tried to retreat too quickly, she backed into the bed. Jack caught her by the shoulders to steady her. Even when the support was no longer needed, he continued to hold her.

Lexie looked down at her hands. Trapped between their bodies, they curled from the need to touch him. His chest was well-muscled, covered in honey-toned hair that reached from tight male nipple to tight male nipple, before trailing down his hard abdomen and disappearing into the thin towel. There was no disguising that he was aroused.

Jack inhaled sharply. His fingers shifted. He probably hadn't intended it as a caress, but it had that effect. Her already shallow breathing halted. And when she lifted her gaze again, she realized just where she and Jack were headed.

As she stared into his eyes, his fingers flexed on her shoulder as they had earlier. The last time, their pressure had conveyed understanding. This time they communicated something far different.

There didn't seem to be any reason to stop. She didn't know what the future would bring. But she did know what she would find in this man's arms. The ability to forget for a few hours the nightmare that had become her life. To be held. To be warmed by another. To fill the emptiness. And most importantly, not to feel quite so alone.

Jack's mouth descended to within a whisper of hers, the craving inside her expanding so that she could barely breathe now. Closing her eyes, she ran her hands down toward where the towel wrapped his waist. His harsh intake of breath as she reached terry cloth tightened the sexual hunger inside her.

She swayed into him, her breasts brushing against his chest, her fingers loosening the towel. Abdominal muscles bunched—not just Jack's, but hers, too.

And then suddenly, his hands wrapped around her wrists, halting their action.

Startled, Lexie opened her eyes. No matter what his hands said, his gaze said he wanted her. But that he wasn't going to act on that want.

"Jack?"

Releasing her, he backed away. "I think it would be best if we didn't do what we were just about to do. It will only complicate matters."

With that, he turned and walked away.

Chapter Ten

It was still dark out when she was awakened by Jack digging through dresser drawers again. She rolled up onto one elbow. "What's going on?"

The bedroom door was half-open, the light from the hallway reaching across the room, but falling well short of both the bed and the dresser.

"We're meeting Alec," Jack said without turning to look in her direction.

"In the middle of the night? Did something happen?"

"Happen? No. Alec and I run most mornings."

"Could you define 'morning' in this case?"

"It's nearly six."

She groaned. "That late?"

Reaching up, she turned on the lamp beside the bed. When Jack didn't go running from the room after one glance at her, she figured she must look better than she felt. Bolstered a bit, she eased up into a sitting position. For the past two mornings, her stomach had behaved, but there was never any guarantee with morning sickness.

As she had last night, she watched Jack rummage in

drawers. At least he was dressed this time, in a navy blue or black T-shirt and boxers of a similar color.

She hadn't slept well. Mostly because she couldn't seem to let go of her embarrassment over the way she'd acted last night. Two months ago, he'd briefly pursued her, and she'd said she wasn't interested. That was before the murder charge, though. It shouldn't surprise her that, though he intended to help her, he didn't want to get mixed up with a woman whose next address might be the state penitentiary.

Lexie bowed her head and scrubbed her face again. What would her life be like now if she hadn't turned Jack down when he'd called the morning after? The same? Different? What if she'd stopped by Jack's that night instead of going to Dan's?

She'd have the best alibi a girl could—the chief of police— that's what. She'd still have a job. Enough money in her account to meet financial obligations. Credit cards that weren't nearly maxed out. Friends who called with happy news instead of asking about her problems. Not that she'd talked with many of her friends over the past few days. The fact that she hadn't was her fault. They'd left messages. She just didn't have it in her to pretend that everything was going to be okay when she was becoming more and more certain that it wouldn't.

Jack tossed her running shorts and a blue sweatshirt with National Academy done in yellow lettering. "You better get into those. Alec is on his way over."

Arching her back, she yawned. "Sounds like a boys outing to me."

"Maybe. But I need the exercise and I have no intention of leaving you here alone."

"If you're worried about the killer stopping by, I don't think that's likely to happen. I can't imagine he or she is in any hurry to get rid of me. Not as long as I'm scheduled to take the fall. Kill me and she or he has to worry about the police getting it right the next time around."

"An 'I told you so' doesn't make the grave any more comfortable." Jack turned and headed for the door a second time. "Besides, a few endorphins kicking around your system are bound to help." As he left the room, he pulled the door shut behind him.

Still bleary, she sat on the edge of bed and tried to get her bearings. She'd always been one of those people who rolled out of bed with energy to burn, but six nights of either too little sleep or no sleep had finally taken a toll on her reserves. Her body wasn't just coping with the sleep deprivation. High stress and the pregnancy had also exacted their pounds of flesh—from the way her clothes were fitting, she would guess at least five or six.

As for the stress, she needed to get a handle on it somehow, and exercise was a good place to start. Maybe she should have asked how many miles they typically ran. When she'd been carrying Lindy, she had jogged well into her seventh month, so it wasn't the exercise that worried her, but her ability to keep up.

After stumbling into the running shorts and fighting her way into the sweatshirt, she crossed the hall to the bathroom. Maybe cold water would replace what she really needed, a bottle of vitamins and ninety-nine hours of sleep.

She took one look in the mirror, leaned in closer when she didn't recognize the face. Sunken eyes. Skin that was dry and lifeless. Freckles that didn't seem so much sprinkled as troweled across her nose and along her cheekbones.

Jack rapped once on the door. "We'll meet you outside."

"Okay." As he walked away, she glanced at the makeup kit balanced on the edge of the pedestal sink. Why bother?

Anything she put on now would be sweated off in the first half mile.

Lexie used an elasticized band to pull her hair back into a thick ponytail. It wasn't a good look for her. With the loss of weight, it made her cheekbones appear too prominent and emphasized the squareness of her jawline.

She grimaced at the face in the mirror. So she wasn't a beauty queen. Whoopdeedoo. She'd grown up a tomboy, and even as an adult hadn't quite outgrown the tendency.

Jack and his brother looked up as she closed the front door behind her and stepped out onto the front porch. It was still mostly dark out, but wouldn't be for much longer. She was thankful for the sweatshirt. The temperature couldn't have been much above fifty, the chill attacking her bare legs.

She jogged stiffly down the steps. "Morning."

Both men nodded but remained mute. Must be a family thing, she decided. Even if they didn't exactly look like brothers, there was no disguising that they were. They used the same mute nod as a greeting. During most conversations, they would leave silence hanging as if it were an interrogation they were conducting. And she suspected neither one of them missed much when it came to their surroundings. Or to people.

Both men were already going through their warm-up with the rhythm of those who did it often and knew which muscle group came next. Lexie chose a position off to the side and followed suit.

After stretching each calf muscle, she moved on to the quadriceps. As she was working her hamstrings, she became uncomfortably aware that both men had stopped to watch. Lexie released her foot. "What's the distance this morning, boys?"

The men exchanged amused smiles. They didn't think

she'd be able to keep up. Maybe she wouldn't be able to, but it wouldn't be from lack of trying.

Jack stretched an arm above his head and bent to the side. "Alec and I usually do six."

"Then six it is." Lexie took off at an easy pace.

She'd managed to catch Jack and his brother off guard, but they caught up quickly and pushed ahead. Jack grinned as he passed. "If you need to stop, just yell. If we're still close enough to hear you."

"I'll be sure to do that."

They both knew it was an empty threat, that no matter how poorly she performed, Jack would be only steps ahead.

She quickly realized that she didn't like being the one to bring up the rear, but experience said that if she pushed now, the guys would probably just speed up. By mile five, she'd most likely be struggling to maintain the pace they'd set.

When it came to competing with males, it wasn't just about physical prowess; it was also about mental prowess. The guy was always going to get you with the first, but the second, if used properly, could easily level the field. Jack and Alec expected her to be the weaker gender, so she would sandbag for a while, set them off their usual pace.

Besides, bringing up the rear wasn't so bad when you had two fine male specimens ahead of you. Great butts. Nicely muscled legs and broad shoulders. Yeah. A girl could do a whole lot worse than chasing after the Blade brothers.

As dawn stole onto the streets, the colors around them seemed briefly washed in gray, but sharpened quickly. They kept to quiet neighborhoods, dodging puddles left by overnight rain. The sharp bark of a dog and the sound of a car being gunned to life overtook the morning stillness. But it was her breathing and that of the two men that seemed the loudest now. And the rhythmic slap of rubber soles on blacktop.

Because of what she considered her innate laziness, the first mile was always the toughest for her.

In recent months, having taken to running the old turpentine trails out near Riverhouse, Lexie had grown accustomed to rural scenery. The tawny hip-high grasses that waved gracefully in a breeze, or less often stirred noisily as her approach startled an armadillo or opossum. Trees that from a distance seemed to be covered in gigantic white flowers, but as dawn brightened, the "blooms"—the egrets—would fly away, sailing out into the new sky like hope.

And then there was the absence of manmade sounds that could clutter the mind at times. More than anything else, it had probably been her early morning runs that had helped her hang on during those dark days after losing Lindy.

As they made a wide synchronized swing out into the roadway to avoid a man getting into his car, almost like schooling fish evading a predator, Jack glanced back. Lexie closed her mouth, pretended that her breathing was a little easier and smoother than it really was.

Sweat coated her rib cage, and her hair band loosened. Normally she would have stopped to deal with it, but was afraid if she lost any ground, she would never be able to regain it.

By mile three, the endorphins made their appearance. She had never been so glad to feel them.

Jack dropped back around mile four. "Doing okay?" His face carried the sheen of his exertions and his hair was damp around the edges, but she found both oddly sexy. As she did his grin.

"Doing fine." In need of more oxygen, Lexie had resorted

to breathing through her mouth, so it took great effort to make her words come out smoothly. "How about you?" She managed a smile. "If you two need to stop or anything, let me know."

His grin spreading a bit, he shook his head. Instead of rejoining his brother, he stayed with her. She liked running beside Jack. But then she was beginning to believe that doing any physical activity with him would be enjoyable. Dan had never been particularly active, certainly never into any kind of physical challenge.

But a man like Jack Blade would challenge a woman on many different levels.

They were now into the downtown area, running along the wide, deserted sidewalk in front of Jan's Antiques and Seminole Stationary and Gifts. Past a women's clothing shop and a toy store. Lexie's breathing was coming hard now, and she could feel the burn, not just in her muscles but in her chest, as well.

She would have liked to ask how much farther, but was afraid that Jack would think she was looking to stop. And for some reason she wanted to be seen as tough. Maybe because she sensed that it was the one attribute that both men admired.

And one of the most indelible characteristics that linked these two men. Not just physical stamina, but intellectual and moral strength. She saw Jack's willingness to help her as an indication of just how tough he was morally.

It wasn't until Alec broke down to a walk, and she saw the only business with lights on just ahead, that she realized their destination. Being the coward that she was these days when it came to public appearances, she would have preferred to keep running.

Jack and Lexie halted beside Alec just outside Alligator

Café. As much as she probably needed to eat, the thought of food wasn't appealing. And she was also worried that some of the cooking smells might set off her stomach.

Lexie glanced inside at the few people sitting at tables. At least two of them were doctors that she called on. Colleagues of Dan's. What kind of reception could she expect? Still fighting to even her breathing, she loosened her hair, smoothing it as best she could, before pulling it back into a ponytail again. Her legs were slick, her sweatshirt damp with perspiration. The running had left her dehydrated, and she suspected her eyes probably appeared even more sunken.

Alec held the door for her. For the first time since they met, his eyes didn't seem quite so remote. "You did well this morning."

"You mean for a girl, don't you?"

She saw amusement in his face. "For a man or a woman. How far do you normally run?"

"Three or four miles, three times a week."

Grinning, Jack stepped past his brother, who still held the door open. "I told you that she'd keep up."

The fluorescent lights offered a benign hum. As soon as the three of them entered, the only waitress who seemed to be working hooked an index finger through the handles of a trio of mugs at the same time that she grabbed a coffee carafe. On the way past the cash register, she snagged a menu.

Lexie glanced over her shoulder. "Eat here much?"

"Seven mornings a week."

As she passed the two doctors, she offered a smile.

Neither one of them returned it. Before she could even really feel the snub, though, Jack touched her briefly and lightly in the middle of her back. "Come on. I could use a cup of coffee."

Lexie had thought she was going to be okay. That she

could deal with the aromas of grease and raw egg. But as she was about to slide into the booth, sudden nausea sent her running for the ladies' room.

The scent of disinfectant got her even worse as she dived into the first stall. By the time she straightened, her abdominal muscles felt as if they'd worked as hard as those in her legs had.

Lexie stood at the sink, staring at the woman in the mirror again, wondering how long she could continue to keep silent. She'd thought waiting was the answer, but realized now that the longer she did so, the more difficult it was going to be to come clean.

"So you think you're tough?"

Another diner pushed open the bathroom door and walked in—a thin, lively looking woman with curly gray hair, dressed in jeans and a heavy sweater. Lexie offered a smile and immediately received one in return. Which pretty much guaranteed that the stranger was a tourist. Locals either looked right past Lexie, as if afraid to meet her eyes because of what might happen to them, or they stared.

"I sometimes give myself pep talks, too," the woman said. Then she noticed the cast on Lexie's right hand, and her smile faded.

Lexie held it up. "In-line skating."

The woman actually looked relieved. Lexie wasn't certain if she'd lied for the woman or for herself. But either way, she didn't like it. She wanted her life back.

When she returned to the table, Jack stood so that she could slide in. "You okay?"

She managed a tight smile. "Yeah. I just pushed myself a little too hard, that's all."

There was a small pot of tea already waiting for her, and she assumed Jack must have ordered it for her. The other morning she'd been drinking the beverage, so he probably assumed that was what she preferred.

As the bacon, eggs and grits were delivered to the brothers, Lexie reached for the tea, first with her injured right hand and then with her left. Jack took the pot from her and filled her cup. She smiled in thanks.

The waitress pulled out her pad. "I don't have to ask anymore what these two want, but what can I get you?"

Having never opened it, Lexie handed the waitress the menu. "Rye toast, please. And can you make it dry, but with a little butter on the side?"

"Sure, honey."

Lexie stirred three teaspoons of sugar into the tea. She wasn't so worried about Jack guessing the reason behind her sudden inability to handle food as the brother with the pregnant wife.

She spent some time blowing on the tea before taking that first sip. Only then, believing she was prepared, did she allow her gaze to connect with Alec's. And didn't like the speculation she saw in his eyes.

Jack leaned back, rested an arm along the seat back behind her in an almost protective gesture. As he did so, Alec's mouth tightened. If she hadn't been watching closely, she wouldn't have seen it. Alec's opinion of her obviously hadn't changed completely. He still saw her as a problem for his brother. A complication.

Using his knife and fork, Alec sliced up the over-easy eggs, the yolks leaking out over the plate.

Feeling a resurgence of the nausea, Lexie took another sip of tea. *If you make a dive for the restroom again, he's going to guess.* He was a keen observer, just as his brother was. The difference was that Alec wasn't quite so close to the situation. And because he wasn't, he might recognize her condition more easily.

All Lexie wanted to do was survive breakfast.

"So who makes the hit list today?" Alec asked, shifting his attention to his brother. "I've dug pretty deep into the victim's life. I have a few more details to run down, though. I plan to fly down to Miami tomorrow to talk to some of the people he worked with during his residency. Probably won't get anything useful, but it's about the only aspect of his background I haven't covered."

"Talked to his parents again?"

Alec nodded. "Yeah. Nothing new there."

Jack finished off his orange juice. "I'll try to chase down Amanda today and question her. Do the same with the other women whose charts were on the desk that night."

Lexie picked up her spoon and dipped it in her already-stirred tea. The shoptalk made her uncomfortable. Everything about this morning made her uncomfortable, especially Alec.

"Maybe we should start interviewing friends, mutual acquaintances of Dan's and Lexie's," Jack suggested.

"Sure," Alec said, "but it might be best if I handle those interviews. Even if someone knows something, they're not going to talk in front of her."

Jack nodded. "You're right. She can work up a list for you to work from. And I think with this much ground to cover, it might be a good idea to hire some help."

"I have a private investigator I sometimes use."

"Sounds good." Jack grabbed a paper placemat from the next table, flipped it over and handed Lexie a pen. "Put down names, and perhaps type of contact. Keep it simple."

Writing with her left hand was difficult, but she'd already listed quite a few when Alec added, "And any male who asked you out recently and that you turned down. Even if it was just for an ice-cream cone."

Without looking up, Lexie nodded. She jiggled the tea bag in the small pot as she ran back through her mind one more time.

Catching Alec watching her, she passed him the list. He briefly scanned it, then folded it and slipped it into the pocket of his sweatpants. "I talked to the woman Dawson was seeing. They were supposed to meet Wednesday night, but he cancelled. She said that he seemed upset. She assumed it was the situation with Lexie, but he didn't give her any real details."

Alec was looking at her again. "She did tell me something that I found interesting."

Having finished his breakfast, Jack shifted his plate to the side and reached for the coffee. "What's that?"

"Dan Dawson believed the baby Lexie lost wasn't his."

Stunned, Lexie's chin popped up. "That's absolutely ridiculous!"

Alec's eyes narrowed. "Is it?"

The gazes of both men were on her now, the silence at the table heavy, like a wet mattress flung down on top of her. She felt her facial muscles stiffen. What must Jack be thinking now? That she was easy? That she lacked morals? That she had been cheating on Dan all along? Lexie forced her spine straighter.

Jack removed his arm from the seat back—a withdrawal of support.

"Is it, Lexie?" Alec repeated. "Or was the father of the last child the same as the one you're carrying now?"

Lexie felt Jack stiffen beside her, but she didn't glance in his direction. She didn't want to see his face just then. Didn't want him to see hers.

"No. I was never unfaithful. No matter what Dan thought,

Lindy was his daughter." She took a deep breath. "Dan made the accusation only once. He'd gotten Lindy's autopsy report that day and I assumed he was just looking to strike out."

"Did he say anything else?" Alec asked.

"If he did, I was too angry to listen." She looked down at her hands.

Alec didn't say anything. It was obvious that he was waiting for her to go on. As the man sitting beside her was.

Lexie forced her gaze to meet Alec's. "As for the father of the baby I'm carrying now, it's none of your damn business."

"But it is my brother's business." Alec's tone was harsh, filled with disdain. "He's put his career on the line and you haven't even been honest with him. Isn't it possible that your lover might have killed Dan?"

"No!" Realizing just how loudly she'd said it, Lexie lowered her voice. "No. I'll say it again, Alec—the baby I'm carrying has nothing to do with my ex-husband's death."

Jack turned toward her. "How far along are you, Lexie?"

She realized that his voice didn't sound any different from his brother's—cool, with an edge of contempt.

She lifted her gaze to his. No reason to continue hiding it. He'd already guessed. And from the hard look in his eyes, it wasn't good news.

It didn't matter. At least that's what she'd been telling herself. But like so much recently, she was wrong about that, too. She wanted Jack's understanding, but she suspected she wasn't going to get it.

"Eight weeks and six days."

Chapter Eleven

Jack ran a hand over his face, trying to figure out how he was supposed to feel about the two-ton bombshell that had been dropped on him. God. What was he going to do? All these years. Never a slip. Never once had a woman shown up on the doorstep with this kind of news.

Needing privacy, he and Lexie had walked across the street to the park and now made use of the gazebo. The early hour and the fact that rain came down in hard, gray sheets meant that they weren't likely to be interrupted.

Lexie stood on the opposite side of the structure, her back to him, staring out at the rain.

How was he supposed to act toward her? About the situation?

"I would have been less shocked if you had admitted to murder."

"It was a shock to me, also." Facing him, she folded her arms in front of her. "I planned to tell you."

"When?"

Her eyes were bright. Not with tears, though. With anger. "I don't know! When I was ready. When I knew what I wanted!"

A knot formed in his gut.

"What in the hell is that supposed to mean? That you considered terminating the pregnancy?"

"You say it as if that's no longer an option. As if now that you're involved, decisions will be made for me." She turned and paced to the steps, almost as if she contemplated making a run for it. "Well, I've got news for you, Jack Blade. Most of the decisions about my life have been ripped away. They're beyond my control. But not this. I will not relinquish this. This is my decision."

He grabbed her by the upper arm. "Like hell it is! What becomes of that baby is as much my concern as yours."

She removed his hand from her arm. "One night, Jack. That's all you really have invested in this child right now." She took a deep breath and let it out slowly. "You don't know me. If you did, you would know that I wouldn't harm this child or any child."

"Were you thinking about raising the baby alone, then? Never telling me?"

"Yes. As a matter of fact, I was."

Life had been so easy before he'd met this woman. He'd had a good job. A future in law enforcement. No real personal problems other than the sometimes-strained relationship between him and his brother. Yeah. Perhaps life had seemed a little too tame at times, but it had also been uncomplicated. Which was what he'd been looking for when he left the Atlanta PD. A chance at a regular life.

"And you thought that was okay? Not to mention to a man that he was about to be a father?"

"To be honest, right now, I don't know what I think about a lot of things. I just found out on Monday. With a trial date set for two months from now, I figured the murder charge was more urgent."

"Three days? You've known for three days? Two words. That's all it would have taken." He raised two fingers. "I'm," he said, and lowered the first. "Pregnant." He dropped his hand. "If you'd managed one word a day for just two of those days, I wouldn't have had to sit across from my brother and have this kind of revelation dropped into my lap."

He paced away. Hell. He'd nearly made love to her last night. Had nearly taken advantage of her vulnerability. Just as he had the first time. She'd been needy and he'd been a convenient shoulder. He had fully intended to keep his distance. At least until she was cleared of the charges. But last night, if there'd been a condom in the house…

"How in the hell is this even possible? I protected you each time." Jack glanced away, embarrassed by his words. "Okay. I know it's possible."

What he didn't know was what he was going to do now. What a man was supposed to say when a woman he'd slept with only one night turned up pregnant, demanding…

That was the problem, wasn't it? Lexie wasn't demanding anything of him. Didn't seem to expect anything of him.

He was the one doing the demanding here.

Lexie stopped in front of him. Her hair had come loose again, her face was void of any makeup, but he still found her the sexiest woman he'd ever met.

"Look, Jack. I'm not asking you to decide right now if you want a relationship with this baby. Or, if you do, what kind of relationship." She rubbed her arms. "And I'm sorry you found out the way you did. That was never my intention."

She caught her lower lip between her teeth briefly, and he realized it was the first time he'd ever seen her do it. "I would have expected you to ask for a paternity test."

He shook his head. "It never even crossed my mind."

"Why?"

"I'm not sure." But he was. He'd never doubted the baby's paternity because he trusted Lexie.

There were a few people, perhaps even his brother, who would question his judgment. But Jack realized that he no longer did where Lexie was concerned.

THE CALL CAME IN JUST after nine o'clock that night. Jack was helping himself to a beer, but recognizing crime scene tech Andy Martinez's cell number, he left the beer unopened on the counter and picked up the phone. Though he and Andy were friends, Jack didn't figure it would be a social call.

"You didn't hear it from me, Jack."

"Didn't hear what?"

"The tox screens came back earlier today."

"And?"

"It showed Talzepam. A presurgical dose. Dan Dawson probably didn't even know what was happening to him."

"How'd it get in his system?"

"Shepherd went back over this afternoon and found a sample packet, one that's distributed to doctors. There was a pristine thumbprint dead in the center of the packet."

"Lexie's, I assume?"

"You got it." Andy sighed.

"That still doesn't explain how it got into his system. And if it was a sample, it's not surprising that the thumbprint of the rep would be on it. Since it wasn't collected during the initial investigation of the scene, there's no way to be certain that it was even there that night or that it's the actual package. Arguably, it could have been placed there at a later date."

"That's not keeping the state attorney from taking the tox

report to the judge. I hear that he's going to ask for the charges to be upped to murder one and that bail be revoked."

And when she went to trial, she'd be facing the death penalty. In the state of Florida, that meant lethal injection.

Jack's gut sickened as he thought about giving this news to Lexie. Maybe he wouldn't. Maybe the judge wouldn't go along with the state attorney.

"But you didn't hear it from me," Andy repeated.

"Thanks, Andy. I owe you one."

"You don't owe me nothing. Just watch your back. There's been a rumor circulating that maybe Lexie didn't act alone. That she had help."

"Help? As in me?" To be honest, he wasn't even surprised. Once it was established that Lexie and he had been seen leaving a bar late at night together and that he was now helping her, it wasn't all that far a leap to believing that he might somehow be involved in the murder of her ex-husband.

"Shepherd hasn't turned up anything yet, but he's working the angle really hard."

"He's not going to find anything." Even as Jack said it, he knew it wasn't completely true. If Shepherd dug deep enough, he'd find out that the reason it had taken Jack so long to get to the crime scene that night wasn't because he'd been out driving. That Jack didn't have an alibi for the time of the murder. At least not one he was willing to reveal.

"I know that, Jack. Do you need anything? I have some extra time on my hands."

"I appreciate that, Andy. And I appreciate the heads-up. But if anyone finds out that you're helping me, your ass will be out on the street."

"If you change your mind…"

"I won't."

Jack hung up the phone. Now what? How was he going to tell Lexie? Turning, he saw her standing in the doorway and realized that she'd overheard the conversation. At least his side of it. Enough to know that things had gone from bad to much worse.

They'd spent most of the day trying to get a lead on Amanda Wilkes. The address on her Florida driver's license and the one the social security office had on file was her mother's home in Pierson. There hadn't been any withholding taxes reported in the past year and a half, leaving him to wonder how Amanda was supporting herself. And there were no records of utilities under her name. Which meant she might have a sugar daddy who paid all the bills, or she was working in some profession that the IRS wasn't able to regulate—cleaning houses, maybe—and had a place where the utilities were part of the rent.

Lexie had seen the inability to track the girl as a real setback; Jack still wasn't certain if she was even one of the pieces they needed.

Their attempts to talk to some of the women represented by the charts hadn't been any more successful. Of the three they'd managed to find either at home or at work, two had said they'd miscarried, and the third had refused to talk to them.

Lexie closed the distance between them. "What happened?"

Again, he briefly considered not telling her all of it, then realized withholding information was what he'd accused her of that morning.

"The tox screen showed Talzepam."

To her credit, she filled in all the blanks. That it was just another piece of circumstantial evidence that would be piled with the rest. Another link between her and the murder of her ex-husband.

Maybe Garland Ramsey would be able to convince the jury that it was rare in a murder for all the pieces to fit together quite so seamlessly. But Jack felt fairly certain that the lawyer would fail.

Moving past him, Lexie sat at the kitchen table. She'd showered and changed. He was beginning to find the shorts and T-shirt that she favored as sleeping attire to be sexier than silk lingerie. It was the juxtaposition between the male-like attire and the female body it covered. He realized her contradictions intrigued him. He liked her competitiveness. Possibly because it challenged him. There was nothing artificial about Lexie. She could be one of the boys, but she was totally feminine. In bed, most of all.

Her hair had been left down after she washed it, and was full, glistening beneath the lighting. It also lent a softness to her face that was absent otherwise. There was worry in her eyes, and shadows beneath them.

He poured her a glass of grape juice and grabbed the beer before joining her at the table. "Judge probably won't let the packet with your fingerprint be admitted in evidence," he said.

"But he'll allow the tox screen. It will prove that I have easy access to a drug that was in Dan's system," she said.

"He was a doctor. He would have easy access to Talzepam, too," Jack said as he sipped his beer. "You said Dan liked to take Valium occasionally?"

"Yeah. If he was really uptight about something at the office or if he was up all night with a delivery." Lexie pulled the glass of juice toward her. Without picking it up, she slowly rotated it. He wondered how she managed to keep herself together, was beginning to wonder if she might not be quite as strong as she wanted everyone to believe.

"Any possibility he got his hands on some of your samples and decided to give it a try? Maybe the bottle of Valium was empty? We know he was upset about something that night."

She didn't look up. "Maybe. But he'd know to cut the dosage in half."

"Did he ever have access to your samples?"

"No. I wasn't repping Talzepam when we were married. Maybe the hospital."

"Where the woman he's been dating works?"

WITH A HARSH GASP, Lexie shot to consciousness like a scuba diver with a near-empty tank seeking the surface.

Even as she struggled into a sitting position, the sound of a crying baby lingered in her subconscious. Lexie pulled her legs up and rested her forehead on her knees. She didn't even know which was worse anymore. The nightmares as she slept where Lindy was crying and Lexie couldn't get to her, couldn't save her daughter, or the nightmare she faced daily while awake.

Lexie climbed out of bed, taking the blanket with her. She needed fresh air. The room was dark and she wasn't completely familiar with it yet, so she moved forward cautiously. Reaching the door, she opened it as silently as possible.

The hall was marginally cooler. She snugged the blanket around her shoulders. The living room wasn't as dark, light from a streetlamp reaching inside the house, turning the chair near the front door into a black cube, the couch into a long, narrow silhouette. The back of the couch faced her, so she couldn't see Jack, but she heard his soft, even breathing.

She glanced at the front door. No good. Too much exposure. She'd have to walk past Jack. Risk waking him. No one could see her like this. Especially Jack.

She headed for the kitchen and the back door. There was a brick patio behind the house that would give her privacy. Her fingers became desperate as she worked the dead bolt. Releasing it, she jerked on the handle. The sound as the security chain caught and held was loud in the silence, but escape was all that mattered now. Banging the door shut, she released the chain, and in the next instant shot out into the cold air—she'd finally reached the surface. Now it was just a matter of breathing deeply, of mastering the panic.

The night was cold and carried the scent of fresh grass. She sank onto the steps, the bricks damp beneath the cotton boxers and her bare feet. She stared out into the small yard with the bed of overgrown roses and the untended birdbath. The moonlight leached the night sky of stars and created shade beneath the oaks. In the distance, a train let out a long, mournful wail.

What was she going to do? She'd failed Lindy.

She locked her eyes shut. And now she held another life in trust. A child's life. What if she went to prison? What if she was sentenced to death? What if… It seemed as if her whole life was up for grabs. That there was nothing she could hold on to these days. Perhaps the only constant, the only thing she was certain about, was this baby. That she wanted it.

But what became of babies born to women behind bars? Born to a woman on death row? Would Jack take the baby? Or would he want her to put it up for adoption?

"Lexie?"

She stiffened at Jack's voice, but didn't turn around. "I'm okay."

But as she said those words, the first harsh sob slammed against her chest wall. She swallowed it and, bending forward, tried to push it down inside her. The trembling in her shoulders became the hard racking of bone and flesh as a second sob struck higher this time, climbing to the back of her throat. It was the third one that made it past her lips.

Lexie wrapped the blanket tighter around her. To muffle the sounds that kept coming out of her, she forced the material against her mouth. It was as if now that even one of them had escaped, there was no stopping, no controlling the rest.

The ache behind her ribs expanded, the pain, the misery, the fear crowding her chest so completely that there was no room left for breathing.

And all the while, all she could think of was the man who'd followed her out here, who now stood watching as she splintered apart into a million fragments that she could never hope to reassemble. She thought of the nursery tale of Humpty Dumpty, and cried harder still. For herself, for the damn egg or whatever it was that Humpty was made of, and for the baby growing inside her.

It wasn't until Jack's arms wrapped around her and pulled her back against his chest that she realized he'd gotten on the ground behind her, that his legs were stretched on either side of her.

"I've got you." He rocked her slowly, his arms tight around her, the firm wall of his chest at her back, radiating the warmth and strength that she so desperately needed.

"Shush," he said, his voice pitched low and roughened. "I'm not going to let anything happen to either one of you." His arms tightened around her.

They stayed like that until her sobs faded. Until her

muscles loosened. Until she became aware that Jack's hands ran slowly up and down her arms beneath the blanket, their warmth gliding over her cool flesh, warming her. Though it was just over two months, it felt as if an eternity had passed since she'd been held.

She wiped her eyes. "I'm sorry."

His hands stilled. "There's no reason to be."

"I don't usually do this kind of thing."

"I know." His hands began to move again. She found herself relaxing into him. She should get up, go back inside, but somehow she didn't want to. She wasn't foolish enough to believe Jack's words. Not because he didn't mean them, but because he was only a man, and no matter how much he wanted to help her, he could do only so much.

She didn't know how long they sat there, long enough that everything went silent inside her. The nightmare faded. It never really went away, just became a pale shadow sifting somewhere between conscious and unconscious thought, almost like a ghost that was trapped between earth and heaven.

Jack began to move even before he spoke. "Come on."

He pulled her to her feet and led her back inside. He didn't reach for any light switches, and she suspected it was because he understood that in the dark she felt less exposed. Which was really crazy, since she couldn't be any more exposed than she had been out there on the patio. No one had ever seen her like that before. Not because she hadn't fallen apart, but since childhood, she'd been careful not to let anyone see it. Weakness equaled vulnerability, and vulnerability led to emotional pain.

But somehow, it hadn't seemed so bad this time. Not to be alone. As she followed behind, her fingers linked with his, Jack moved through the house without hesitation, as someone sure of his surroundings, of his direction. But it wasn't just his home that he seemed to move through with certainty. It was his life. She still found it difficult to understand him. His sense of justice. What he was willing to risk personally just helping her. How many men were there like Jack Blade? The answer was simple. Not enough.

He nudged the bedroom door wider. "I'll get you another blanket."

As soon as he left her there, she felt everything begin to close in on her again.

Jack returned. "Lie down. I'll cover you up."

Instead of following his orders, she looked up at him. "Stay with me tonight. I don't think I can handle being alone."

She sensed hesitation in his sudden stillness.

He passed her the cover. "Okay. Go ahead and get in, and I'll be back in a moment."

When he returned, he was carrying his Glock, and slid it into the drawer of the bedside table. He briefly sat on the edge of the bed, his knees splayed wide, his elbows resting on his thighs.

When she shifted, he looked over his shoulder at her but didn't say anything, just slid beneath the sheet and blanket.

Even as he settled on his back, she could feel the tension in him.

"Thanks, Jack." Because she thought it was what he wanted, she turned on her side away from him and managed to fall asleep.

When she woke, it was still dark, dawn hours away. And Jack held her, spoon-fashion, his hard body following the contours of hers. Or perhaps it was her body that unconsciously and willingly adapted, seeking the warmth and firmness of his.

It didn't take her long to realize what had awakened her. Jack's right arm was wrapped across her shoulder, his hand resting over her left breast. Every time she inhaled or exhaled, the tips of his fingers dragged across her nipple. With each brush, the unrelenting tension coiled a little tighter in her.

Her breathing came a little faster, a little more irregular. Almost as if she'd lost control over her own body, her backside settled against Jack's groin. He was already hard.

When Lexie tried to create more distance between their bodies, though, the required motion only forced her buttocks even more intimately against his erection.

She couldn't stop herself from imagining what it would feel like if there was no clothing between them. If she arched only slightly and he thrust, he could be inside her, taking her as he had that night. Driving her to the edge of reason and beyond.

As the images played in her mind, her hips unconsciously shifted, seeking the right position. She could feel her own wetness. Felt that slightly swollen sensation that only penetration could relieve. She was imagining the sweet glide of Jack's erection when his hand closed over her breast. Her breath caught, then escaped with a harsh sound as, gathering up her fullness, he kneaded her breasts through the T-shirt. Her abdominal muscles quivered and flexed as his hand moved downward across her rib cage.

She could think of a million reasons why what they were doing wasn't wise, but she wasn't willing to listen to any of them.

Reaching the hem of her T-shirt, his fingers stilled, and this time when they shifted upward there was only skin.

There was no more pretending either one of them was asleep, but Lexie chose to remain silent.

Jack's fingers caressed and teased as they went. She felt him shifting, so that his mouth could reach the side of her neck. His breath was warm, as ragged as hers now, but his lips as they found skin were firm and practiced. They gently assaulted her senses as his fingers continued to stroke. She breathed shallowly.

When she started to roll to face him, Jack's hand slipped lower, held her hip so that she couldn't. His breath fanned her ear, his voice as rough and ragged as his breathing. "Just relax."

Relax? She felt herself smile, but the chuckle that climbed her throat died as he pushed her boxers down.

His open palm skimmed upward. As his lips continued to work their magic, he slowly dragged the back of his fingers across her belly in slow circles that crept lower and lower. As his fingers reached pubic hair, her legs began to shake and ease apart, giving him what they both wanted. She moaned softly as he lightly rubbed the heel of his hand against her, but Jack caught the sound in his mouth.

He deepened the kiss, his tongue slipping past her lips at the same moment that his fingers slid into her wet heat. She opened her legs and her mouth fully, welcoming both assaults.

She immediately came hard and fast, her hips lifting and grinding against his hand. And as his teeth closed tenderly where her neck met her shoulder, the orgasm she thought nearly finished found new life. She panted in sharp bursts. Felt her heart hammering in her chest as it seemed to go on and on.

She barely caught her breath, was barely aware of Jack removing his shorts. His erection brushed her buttocks. He pulled her back against him, eased into her by slow degrees until he filled her completely. Rising on one elbow, he turned her face so that he could see her. He smoothed the sweat-dampened hair off her cheek, lowered his lips to hers and for the first time kissed her with a restraint that she hadn't expected, and was so different from previous kisses.

She came apart inside at the unexpected tenderness.

He raised his head, seemed to study her face in the soft light filtering in between the blinds. It wasn't enough illumination to read his expression, but it revealed his masculine features. The well-defined lips. The small cleft in his chin. The blond hair that was lighter on top and darker around the edges. Like the man himself. On the surface, he looked more like a beach boy than anything else. But when you reached the edges, to what was barely exposed, it became apparent he wasn't quite so uncomplicated. That there was a darker, not-so-sunny edge, just out of sight.

Still watching her, he started moving inside her, not driving, demanding thrusts, but slow and easy. Inviting.

She could feel her body climbing toward release. Her hips began to move, greedy now, focused on only one thing. Jack let her take control, let her set the pace.

She closed her eyes.

He immediately reached out and smoothed the hair away from her temple. "No, Lexie. I want to watch you come."

He followed the line of her jaw with his lips, ending at her mouth. His breath was unsteady, and she could feel the restrained tension in his body.

"I want to see you and feel you."

He pushed the T-shirt up and out of his way, the cool air as her breasts were exposed oddly erotic. As he had earlier, he cradled a breast in his palm. She watched his features sharpen, the sheen of moisture that collected across his brow as he tugged on her nipple. Sensation shot through her, carrying her closer to what her body craved.

"Come for me, Lexie. Come now."

With a small cry she did, her muscles closing around him. She was still coming when Jack drove into her hard, his hand dropping to her hip, holding her in place as he filled her, as he followed her.

Both of them rested back on the mattress, hearts hammering, skin slick with moisture, but neither one of them made a move to extricate themselves from the intimate connection.

And neither of them spoke of what had just happened.

Chapter Twelve

When she woke again, she was alone in the bed.

Pushing the covers off, she realized that while she wore a T-shirt, the lower half of her was naked.

She glanced toward the door. Where was Jack? He wouldn't have left her alone in the house.

Because she was listening for him, he startled her when he came walking in dressed in jeans and a sweater. Lexie tugged the sheet across her lap and waited for some clue on how she should act.

When he looked at her without hesitation, without any hint of embarrassment, she decided that he wanted to pretend it hadn't happened. It wouldn't be easy, but she'd manage.

"Morning." She scanned the floor for her shorts, found them draped over the footboard, but chose to leave them where they were for the moment.

"Why don't you catch a shower? We'll get some lunch. Garland Ramsey called and wants to see you at three."

"Did he say why?"

"The State Attorney is seeking to have your bail revoked." He stopped in the doorway on his way out. "Tell Garland you're pregnant. The prosecution won't want to believe it, but when the test comes back positive, they'll have to."

"What will that accomplish?"

"The judge will most likely allow the bail to stand. The state is required to pay for the medical expenses of inmates, and they'll do just about anything they can to avoid that expense."

Lexie lifted her chin. "And if they ask who the father is?"

"You tell them the truth."

She sat there on the edge of the bed for several minutes after he'd left the room. No matter how hard she tried, she just couldn't get a read on Jack. He still hadn't mentioned what his intentions were where the baby was concerned. And yet, there had been that moment last night, as he'd wrapped his arms around her....

AFTER GRABBING A DELI sandwich, they headed out to her place for additional clothes.

As she opened the front door, she realized it felt as if she'd been gone for weeks instead of only two nights. The heat had been left off, so the house was cold and damp.

Without waiting to see if Jack followed, she headed for the kitchen. On her way by, she hit the play button on the phone recorder, but kept moving until she reached the wall of windows. Unlike the past few days, it was sunny, but it was also chilly again. The sky was that sharp blue that seemed to accompany cold fronts, or perhaps it only seemed bluer because of the gray days that had preceded it.

Jack had followed her into the kitchen. She could feel him at her back. The news of the pregnancy had been the big white elephant sitting between them all day yesterday, but after what had happened last night, there were two elephants in the way. She snugged his arms around her. The coming meeting with Garland Ramsey also made her nervous. She wasn't really ready to announce the pregnancy. But if it would keep her out of jail, she really didn't have a choice—as much for the baby's health as her sanity. It felt as if she was being slowly and thoroughly backed into a corner.

"I'll be right back," Jack said. "I just want to take a quick look around outside." She glanced over her shoulder and watched him walk away. She wondered if sometime in the not too distant future she'd watch him do the same, only for good this time.

As the front door closed behind him, she turned her attention to the window again. Even though it was sunny, you could still tell the time of year by the color of the grass beneath the pines. Everywhere she looked these days, she saw things that she hadn't really seen in years. She recalled her grandfather telling her how, shortly after he'd learned that he had cancer, life had taken on a new glow. That some of the simplest things became the most meaningful when you faced death.

At the time, she'd thought that she'd understood what he was saying, but she realized that she hadn't. Not until now.

She barely paid attention to the first ten or so phone messages, which were mostly from the media. The next few were from friends. It was comforting to know that she still had some. That some people knew her well enough to know she hadn't killed Dan.

The eleventh call was from her employer. She'd been fired. Several days ago, losing her job would have devastated her. Now it seemed inconsequential.

There were several hang-ups in a row. Only half listening now, Lexie reached for a water glass.

"Mrs. Dawson, this is Amanda Wilkes. We met at the meeting last Saturday."

The glass Lexie held slipped from her fingers and, hitting the wood floor, exploded. Stepping over the mess, she crossed to the machine.

"I...I need to talk to you." There was a long pause where Lexie thought something might have happened to the rest of the message, and then, "It's about my baby. I...I...don't know how to say this, but I think it's possible your baby's not dead. That it was my baby..." Another long pause. Lexie stood over the machine, wanting to turn the volume up, but afraid if she did, if she hit the wrong button by mistake, she might erase it.

Not dead. The words echoed in her head. How was that possible?

"I live at 1316 Banyan Court, unit 5." There was a final long pause before Amanda hung up. As if she'd wanted to say even more.

Lexie stabbed the rewind button. She rewound too far, though, and as the other messages replayed, she tried to make sense of what the young girl had said. Lindy alive? Her baby? Lexie rubbed her forehead. What was she doing even letting herself believe that was possible? Obviously, the young woman was delusional.

"Mrs. Dawson, this is Amanda Wilkes. We met..."

Lexie looked up and saw Jack standing there. When the message finished, he reached past her to turn off the machine. "Is there any way that any of that is possible?"

Frowning, she rubbed her forehead. She needed to think clearly, logically, which was difficult because of the excitement welling up inside her. "I don't see how. I saw her body. There was an autopsy."

He remained unmoving, as if not wanting to distract her. "Tell me everything you can recall about that night."

Lexie forced herself to think back. Dan had been plopped

in front of the television, glued to one football game after another. She didn't know when he'd started drinking, because she'd recently noticed that he tried to hide it from her by opening a Coke, pouring half of it down the drain and then refilling the can with rum.

It had been one of those gray days, raining off and on, so she'd spent most of the afternoon working on the nursery, putting away some of the things from the baby shower her coworkers had given her the day before.

She'd been sitting on the room's window seat. One of the gifts had been a book where you wrote in all the important dates and included several pages for the mom-to-be to talk about her excitement over the coming birth and about being a mother. Looking up from what she'd been writing, she'd seen Dan wobbling in the doorway. She had frowned, and as soon as she had, he'd stormed off, accusing her of all sorts of crazy things. She'd caught up to him as he was unlocking the front door, the car keys in his hand.

She'd gotten in front of him, tried to stop him. He'd pushed her. She'd ended in a pile at the bottom of the steps. Dan hadn't even looked at her, had kept going. Had gotten in his car and left her there on the ground.

"Lexie?" Jack prompted.

She hugged herself. "I was in hard labor when I arrived. I banged on the front door instead of using my key." Only when the broken glass crunched under her foot did she remember it, but she still made no attempt to clean it up. "Fleming should have been waiting by the door when I arrived. I had called him." Her gaze connected with Jack's. "Why wasn't he?"

"Maybe because he was already busy. Maybe because you weren't the only woman in labor that night."

"But why wouldn't Amanda have gone to the hospital?

The office isn't really set up for deliveries, and she wasn't trying to hide anything."

"Maybe she was. You said she put her baby up for adoption. Did she say anything about how the adoption took place?"

"All I know is that she doesn't know who the family is."

"Did she say how the adoption was arranged?"

"From what I recall, the doctor who delivered her baby assured her that she was making the right decision by giving her up for adoption." Eyes narrowing, Lexie glanced back at him. "You think Fleming switched the babies?" It was just sinking in. She'd been so overwhelmed by the idea that Lindy might be alive that she had failed to focus in on how any of that might be possible. "And that it was intentional?"

"If it happened at all, it was intentional."

"But why? How could he do that? How could he steal my baby? Give my child to another woman? Let me believe Lindy was dead?"

Pacing now, she shook her head. "No. It doesn't make any sense." She stared out the window. As much as she wanted it to be true, it wasn't. Lindy was dead. She'd spread her ashes just over two months ago, believing that doing so would help her let go. And here someone, a young woman who had gone through a mental breakdown, and who had seemed to be having a hard time coping with guilt over giving her child up for adoption, was telling her that Lindy was alive. That it had been her baby who had been born dead. Was this Amanda's way of coping with her guilt?

"Why now?" Lexie asked. "What would make her suddenly think that the baby she'd put up for adoption wasn't hers? And how would she have known that I was in the office that night?"

"Because Fleming told her. He couldn't afford for you to

know what he was doing there that night. And don't forget, he wasn't the only one breaking the law with that adoption. Amanda was and is just as guilty."

Jack walked up behind Lexie and cupped her shoulders. "What do you remember about the actual birth?"

"I remember Fleming helping me to one of the exam rooms. He kept saying he was just going to stabilize me and then call an ambulance. But I was already in full labor and that he couldn't. I remember that as soon as Lindy was born, he cut the cord and took her away. I was scared, really frightened, when he didn't say anything."

"How long was he gone?"

"Five minutes?"

"What happened then?"

"He brought her back, cleaned up and wrapped in a scrub top. He told me that he'd tried to revive her, but that he hadn't been able to."

"Did he let you hold her?"

"Yes." She shivered. "I couldn't believe how cold she was."

"After just five minutes?" Jack asked quietly.

Lexie stepped out from beneath his touch. Was that why she hadn't been able to let go? Because subconsciously she had known the baby she held wasn't hers? Had Amanda experienced the same sensation? Had she known the baby she held wasn't hers? Had she known all along what Fleming had done? Was her appearance that morning at the support group a coincidence? Or had Amanda followed her there?

"So it was Amanda's baby that he brought me to hold? As I was crying uncontrollably, my heart feeling as if it had been ripped from my chest, he pretended to comfort me. How could he do that? What would make him do that?"

"Maybe because he had a buyer for Amanda's baby?

Selling babies isn't just illegal, it's also very profitable, especially if you know where to find the right buyers."

Lexie looked up at Jack. For the first time in days, she wasn't thinking about the murder charge.

"If Lindy's alive, I'm going to find her."

THE APARTMENT WAS ONE of those that rented by the week, a long block building that had probably been a mom-and-pop motel in the 1960s. If it had been maintained, it wouldn't have looked half-bad maybe, Jack decided, but the paint job was a dingy white and there were quite a few shingles missing from the roof. He guessed that most of the units probably coped with leaks every time it rained, and flourishing colonies of mold and mildew even when it didn't. It was the kind of property you expected to see in a third world county, but not in your backyard.

"I can't imagine living like this," Lexie said as they approached Amanda's apartment. Unit five was on the end, right next to a weed-filled lot and a retention pond of green scum water where trash floated. "This makes the house out in Pierson look palatial."

"Makes you wonder why she would move out and into this." Jack knocked on the gray door, and then stepped back several feet and waited.

When Amanda didn't answer after a reasonable period of time, he tried the door, but found it locked.

Lexie was already walking around the side when he caught up. "This isn't the kind of place you want to go wandering around back."

Lexie looked determined. "Because of snakes and rats?"

"No. Because of what you just might walk into."

"Like a drug deal going down? A meth lab?"

"Yeah."

"Look, there's no way I'm just knocking on the door and leaving when someone doesn't open it up. Not when there's the slimmest chance that my daughter's alive."

He'd known she wouldn't be willing to let it go. "Just stay behind me, then."

The back of the building actually looked better. The grass, or weeds, had recently been cut, and most of the units had tidy patios. Amanda's held a couple of plants in plastic pots, a cheap white-plastic chair and a plastic crate turned upside down being used as a table.

Jack knocked first. He didn't expect anyone to answer. As he had out front, he tried the door. When it, too, appeared to be locked, he lifted the one panel up off the track as far as it would go and shook it enough to release the catch on the door lock.

He slid the door open.

"Is this legal?"

"No. But I didn't get the impression that you were willing to hang out and hope Amanda comes back."

"You're right."

He wasn't doing it just because Lexie was anxious for answers. He was getting a really bad feeling about the girl. It was always possible that she had a job or was shopping, but it didn't seem likely that she would make that kind of call, then go off. At least not willingly.

Jack pulled out the 9 mm and flipped off the safety. "Stay here."

He pushed aside the drape, but didn't enter right away. Instead, he listened. Even with a weapon, walking into a dark building without soft body armor or backup was dicey.

He glanced at Lexie again, felt fairly certain that she was

going to listen to him and stay put. Of course, with Lexie, you never knew.

As soon as he crossed the threshold, he dropped into a crouched position next to a large chair just inside the unit. He waited again, listening, absorbing his surroundings. The drape hadn't fallen completely closed behind him, and allowed a small amount of light to filter in. Even in the dimness, he could make out a couch and another chair, a television set and a small coffee table. There were magazines on the floor, as if they had been thrown there after they'd been read. It wasn't the room of a tidy person.

Which worried him, because someone had recently used chlorine in the apartment. Bleach was one of those chemicals that criminals favored, mostly because they believed it would destroy blood evidence. It didn't, but he didn't like to think about what that might mean for Amanda.

Careful not to touch anything, he worked his way through the apartment, moving from the living area to the kitchen, where the scent of bleach seemed equal to what was present in the living room. The bedroom was next to the front door, and the chlorine smell seemed slightly less strong. Of course, after a matter of minutes the olfactory sense tended to adjust, no longer registering what had previously been a strong, offensive odor.

When he was convinced that the unit was unoccupied, he turned on the bedroom light. The room was tidy, the bed's swaybacked mattress covered in a pink spread. There had been other attempts to make the room comfortable. A poster with some roses hung over the bed, and a piece of cloth covered the top of the old dresser. He opened the closet door and looked inside. The clothes were arranged by type and by color. He glanced at the floor. Only four pairs of shoes, but they were lined up like piano keys. He checked the bathroom. Towel hung up. All the surfaces, if not shiny, certainly cleaned. And wherever the bleach had been used, it wasn't in this room.

Jack swore as he headed for the living room.

Lexie stood just inside the back door. "Is that bleach?"

"Yeah. But I don't know where it's coming from yet." When she started to step toward him, he held up a hand. "You better stay where you are, and whatever you do, don't touch anything."

The living room didn't look exactly as if it had been tossed, but it did appear as if someone had maybe been in a hurry looking for something, or as if someone had been taken by surprise and quickly subdued.

He checked the kitchen again. Counters cleared, no dishes in the sink.

"Do you think something has happened to Amanda?" Lexie had followed him into the room.

"I don't know." Jack glanced at her. "You don't follow instructions very well, do you?"

"I don't like to be left in the dark. Or behind."

He could understand that. For the past week he felt as if he'd been spending most of his time uncertain of what was going on around him, and he hadn't liked it much, either.

"Just don't come any farther." Jack squatted to study the front of the sink cabinet. The raised profile of the hinge was probably responsible for the small amount of blood next to it being missed during the cleanup. Jack bent down farther. There appeared to be more blood in the joint where floor met the kick plate. Still didn't mean it was the girl's. Maybe after cutting up a chicken for frying, she'd decided to eradicate the possibility of any lingering salmonella risk by using bleach.

He straightened.

"Stay here. I have some evidence swabs in the car."

When he returned, he collected the spot on the cabinet and ran a second swab in the corner where cabinet met floor. Maybe they'd get lucky. Maybe it wasn't human blood. He slid each swab into a separate container and marked them.

"Should we call the cops?"

"And say what? That we broke into the apartment, found some blood that we don't know is even human yet? I don't think that's such a good idea."

"But what if something has happened to her? Shouldn't we report her missing?"

"We don't know anything about Amanda. Her habits. If she's employed. Who her friends are. Even if we knew all those things, unless we also had evidence of foul play, the police wouldn't do any more than take a report."

"So what do we do?"

Jack straightened. "I get Andy to check this out. He'll be able to determine if it's human and not just from the last time she did some cooking. He can get us a blood type, too. We have Amanda's, so we'll be able to tell if it's the same as what we have here."

He sensed Lexie's frustration and fear, and felt powerless. Because he couldn't alter either emotion. And he wanted to, he realized. More than he'd wanted anything in a long time.

"What about Fleming?" she asked. "Maybe if I went to him and told him—"

"That Amanda phoned you? What if she's okay right now, but just off working or shopping? You could be putting her at greater risk."

Lexie's chin came up, and her eyes met his. "You think Fleming might harm her?"

"Yes. And I think there's a possibility that he murdered his partner because your ex-husband discovered something in those files."

"But we've been through them a dozen times," she said. "And Alec has talked to some of the women."

"But not all of them."

Lexie threw up the hand with the cast. "So what are we going to do? Wait to see if Amanda shows up?" She paced toward the back door. "I don't think I can do that. If Lindy's alive, I have to find her." Returning to where Jack stood, she stopped. "Don't you see? She's my daughter."

He pulled her into his arms. He understood what she felt, but he also understood what they were up against. They needed proof.

And then one of the pieces suddenly dropped into place for him.

"You said Dan accused you of being unfaithful?"

She lifted her chin. "Yes."

"I think maybe when Dan read the autopsy he realized that the baby's blood type was wrong. He assumed the discrepancy was because he wasn't the father, that you had slept with someone else. He certainly wouldn't have suspected that the baby wasn't yours. No one would."

"So all we need is the autopsy report?"

"To go after a respected doctor? It'll take more than that."

Chapter Thirteen

Shortly after they left Amanda's apartment, and just after Garland Ramsey postponed the appointment until Monday morning, Alec phoned Jack on his cell phone, suggesting they meet at a small restaurant a short distance away.

Instead of inside, they sat outdoors at the picnic tables, where they would have more privacy. Jack told his brother about Amanda's phone call and their visit to her apartment.

Jack took a bite out of his hamburger. "So what did you come up with on your end?"

"Something that's both interesting and disturbing." Alec wiped his mouth. The breeze had messed up his usually neat hair, and he was dressed in jeans and a blue oxford shirt. "One of the women on my list was reported missing nearly ten months ago by her family," Alec said. "Her body turned up three weeks ago in a shallow grave."

Jack lowered his sandwich. "Jesus."

Horrified, Lexie closed her eyes. When she thought it couldn't get any worse, it just had.

"And here is where it gets interesting," Alec continued. "The record shows that she miscarried, but the medical examiner's report indicates that there were signs that she gave birth just prior to her death. Which makes her the second woman whose chart showed a miscarriage, but who carried full-term."

"Cause of death?" Jack asked.

"After ten months, the heavy rains of last summer and the heat, there wasn't much for him to work with, but no obvious signs of trauma. The M.E. thinks it may possibly have been a medical complication from the delivery. The local authorities have been investigating, but it's a small department and they're poorly equipped."

"Had they talked to Whittemore or Dawson?"

"Whittemore only. And not because they considered him a suspect. They went to him early on, trying to determine if she had been a patient."

"And what did he tell them?"

"That she wasn't."

Jack rubbed his hand over his face as if that might clear his head. "So we have one dead and another possibly missing or possibly dead?"

"Did you report Amanda missing?" Alec asked.

"Report what? That she called and suggested we stop by to talk? And when we got there, she wasn't home?" Jack's frustration was obvious. "I reported it, but we both know that nothing will happen. Maybe after Andy runs the swabs. If they come back as human and the ABO typing matches Amanda's, maybe they'll take it seriously."

"But for now, as far as they're concerned, she's not even missing," Alec added.

Jack nodded. "You got it."

Alec seemed to mull over some aspect of what he'd just been told. "So you believe Amanda was in the office when Lexie arrived that night? And that when Amanda's baby was stillborn, he made the switch? Ostensibly, because he had a buyer lined up for Amanda's baby and didn't want to disappoint his client?"

"There's not much evidence yet to back up the theory." Jack glanced toward Lexie. "But it gives a possible motive for Dan Dawson's murder and suggests a reason why Fleming Whittemore declined to help Lexie. It also gives a possible explanation why the text messages Lexie received that night appeared to have come from her ex-husband. Whittemore would have known which buttons he needed to push to get Lexie over there."

Alec balled up the wrapper from his sandwich. "So where do you want to go from here?"

"While we wait for Andy to get back to us? We look for Amanda and go after Whittemore, preferably without letting him know what we're doing. The last thing we want is for Whittemore to disappear. If he does, we lose our best hope for finding not only Amanda, but Lexie's daughter, too."

"It might not be a bad idea to establish that the child Lexie believed to be hers was actually Amanda's."

"Unfortunately, we have no way of doing that," Jack said. "The body was cremated, and the ashes scattered."

Alec's mouth tightened. "Well, that's going to make it difficult to do anything until we've located the other baby. Which means we're going to need to be very careful. If Whittemore believes we're getting close, he'll destroy any records associated with the babies. He may already have done so." His expression turned even grimmer. "To be blunt, I think we have to consider the possibility that Whittemore may already have killed Amanda to keep her quiet. Just in case she's still alive, it wouldn't hurt to consider where he might take her."

"The place out in the Ocala National Forest," Jack suggested.

Lexie felt a slight chill climb through her. Once any man lured a woman out to someplace as remote as Whittemore's retreat, she would be at his mercy.

JACK AND ALEC MADE a quick stop at Alec's house, just long enough to drop Lexie off. She wasn't happy about being dumped, but there was no way Jack intended to take her with them out to Whittemore's place. Not when he didn't know what they'd find.

They'd already determined that Whittemore was staying at the house in town, and they'd left the private investigator watching to make sure the doctor didn't decide to go for a midnight drive.

Jack glanced over at his brother. "I want to thank you for all the help," he said.

Alec nodded but didn't show any other signs that he'd heard him. They were already on the gravel and dirt roads leading out to Whittemore's place, and it had been more than ten minutes since they'd passed a car.

After several more minutes of silence, Jack turned to his brother. "Talk."

"Katie told me about last Friday night."

Jack tensed at those few words. He'd known going by Alec's that night was a mistake. That if Alec found out about it, he'd think the worst. That Jack was making a play for his eight-months-pregnant wife.

But he wanted things out in the open for once between him and Alec. "Katie was upset. Lonely. She asked me to come have dinner with her." He looked over at his brother. "It wasn't the first time she's asked, and I was out of excuses. I suppose I could have told her the truth, that the reason I wasn't willing to come over was because if you showed up, you'd think the worst. Not just of me, but of her, too."

Alec's expression went from troubled to grim. "I know I deserve that. I want to apologize for my behavior the night I came home and saw you and Jill on that couch. It just hit me wrong. Not so much that you were sitting there with her, but that it had been months since Jill and I had sat together."

"She believed all you really needed was your work."

"She was wrong."

"You should be more truthful with yourself," Jack said quietly. "Back then, there was nothing but the job. You lived, breathed and ate it."

"And you didn't?"

Jack chose not to respond. It took two to get a really good pissing contest going, and he wasn't really in the mood for one, was thinking about what they would find when they reached their destination.

Alec reached for the radio, flicked it on, but immediately turned it back off. "You're right. I was a lousy husband. Jill deserved better. I don't plan to let that happen again." He looked at Jack. "About last Friday. I want to thank you for being there for Katie when I couldn't be. It meant a lot to her, and it means a lot to me, too. She means a lot to me."

His expression grim, Alec stared at the road. "All those times that I knocked on doors and gave the kind of news that no husband or father should ever have to receive, I told myself that I understood their pain. But when I look at Katie sometimes and think about what I would do if anything happened to her or to the baby, I realize what a condescending prick I was back then."

Jack was stunned by Alec's words and by the emotion he heard in his brother's voice. He had never expected him to be so candid about his feelings. Alec had always been so calm and analytical. Except with Katie, Jack admitted. There was no question in his mind that his sister-in-law loved his brother.

"You won't lose her," Jack said quietly. "Not because you won't screw up, but because she loves you every bit as much as you love her."

They were silent after that. Jack realized that he envied Alec his wife, his child, the life he'd created. He found himself thinking about Lexie and his baby.

Alec pulled into what appeared to be a small turnoff partway up the drive. "How do you want to do this?"

"If she's there at all, she'll be on the lower level."

Jack was the first to get out. As he moved forward, he checked his weapon, made sure the two additional magazines were within easy reach in case he needed them.

They followed the drive the rest of the way to the house. Once there, they walked around the house once, ending up in front of the entryway to the lower level.

Jack ran his flashlight over the door. "Looks as if someone tried to break in recently. It doesn't look as if they were successful, though."

"Let's hope we are," Alec said.

Jack passed Alec a pair of vinyl gloves and the flashlight, before pulling out his tools.

It took him nearly ten minutes, partly because the locks were some of the best on the market, and partly because he was out of practice.

When both dead bolts were opened, he put away his tools and pulled out his weapon again. Alec handed him one of the flashlights. When Alec started to go through the door first, Jack stopped him. "Why don't I go in first? You've got a baby on the way."

Alec moved forward. "So do you, brother."

They went in like two seasoned law enforcement officers entering a building where they were uncertain what they would be facing. Alec taking the lead, sweeping ahead, but Jack only a short distance behind, protecting his brother's back.

Once inside, both men scanned their flashlights over the furniture. The sofa and two chairs were arranged in front of a large cabinet that held a television and DVD player and stereo equipment. On either side of the entertainment center there were doors. Off to the right was a small kitchen with your basic Formica table.

"Looks like a small apartment," Jack said.

"Without windows?"

Jack moved past Alec and opened the first of the closed doors. "Bedroom." He stepped inside. "Doesn't appear to be in use. There's an attached bath."

By the time he emerged, Alec was already at the second door. "We've got another dead bolt." Alec allowed his flashlight to travel over the room again. "Why a dead bolt?"

"To keep nosy guests out?" Jack passed his flashlight to his brother. "We're going to feel damn stupid if it's a wine cellar or a woodworking shop."

"I'm not particularly feeling that way at the moment. How about you?"

"Unfortunately, no." At least this lock wasn't quite as burglarproof as the last two. As soon as it clicked open, Jack nodded for Alec to take cover against the wall on the other side of the entrance. His shoulders pressed to the wall, Jack pushed the door inward.

He looked over at his brother. "My turn to go first."

LEXIE PACED around Alec and Katie Blade's living room with its tall ceilings and deep moldings. The pine floor was polished to a satiny finish. Several thick, burgundy rugs, around which sofas, chairs and love seats had been arranged, anchored the space. In one corner a large Frasier fir was covered in small lights.

And in the fire grate, the last embers sizzled and hissed toward extinction.

Though large, the house felt cozy. It was the kind of home that welcomed. That said family. And having seen Alec and Katie together, Lexie knew why. She'd thought Alec to be rigid, intense, and perhaps he was with other people, but Katie only had to walk into the room for his whole face to change.

Lexie glanced at the painting over the fireplace. Two boys sitting on their surfboards, waiting for a wave. She leaned in to read the title: *A Long Boarder's Right of Passage.* Though she liked the painting, it didn't seem to match the room. The scale seemed off for the space above the mantel.

Katie, who had excused herself moments earlier, walked back in. "I gave that to Alec shortly after we met. He said it reminded him of the times he and Jack went surfing as boys." She sat on the sofa. "I had originally done it for my sister, so it has meaning for me, too."

Even at nearly nine months pregnant, Katie Blade was one of those women who radiated energy and kindness.

"I'm sure everything is fine," she said.

Lexie was growing more frustrated by the moment. More desperate. She shouldn't just be sitting here. Her daughter was out there somewhere. She should be doing something.

She walked to the French doors and looked out. "I think I've always known Lindy was alive." She turned and looked at Katie. "Do you think that's possible?"

"Yes."

She gazed outside again. "I've been having these nightmares for months where she's crying, but I can't reach her. It was never the same nightmare. There were always subtle differences. Sometimes she'd be crying hard. Other times she wouldn't be. And once, she was even cooing softly." Lexie smiled sadly. "I even went to a psychologist. He said I had them because I blamed myself for what had happened. I think I was having them because, deep down inside, I knew she was out there somewhere."

Katie approached her, stood beside her, both women now staring out into the night. "I lost my twin sister in a car accident when I was seventeen. Even now, I sometimes feel her with me." She looked at Lexie. "I believe that there is a strong connection between mother and child." She rested her hand on her rounded abdomen. "Everyone else meets the baby on the day its born, but the relationship between mom and baby begins long before that."

"I'm pregnant," Lexie said. She realized it was the first time she'd volunteered those words, and that, instead of the mixture of elation and panic she'd felt in the past, this time there was only joy.

"Jack's a good man," Katie said quietly, and then turned away.

Lexie nodded. He was a good man. And she was in love with him. But she knew it wasn't enough.

WITH HIS FIRST STEP into the room, Jack cursed.

When they'd made the trip out to Whittemore's place tonight, he'd hoped to find Amanda unharmed and maybe even to find some records of Whittemore's baby-selling. And if they were really lucky, something that would tie him to Dan Dawson's murder.

Jack certainly hadn't expected what he was now looking at.

Sitting in the center of the room was an exam table, the stainless steel stirrups extended. Just to the right of it was a rolling cart, the top of which held an array of instruments still sealed in their sterilization bags.

He heard Alec step into the room behind him, but didn't turn to look at his brother.

"He kept them here," Jack said. "In the apartment until it was time, and then brought them in here." He flicked the only light switch he saw, the one on the fixture over the exam table. A daylight glare beamed down onto the surface, almost as if it were stage lighting. "Can you imagine being a young woman, pregnant and unmarried, and uncertain what to do? And then this doctor approaches you. He tells you that he'll give you a place to stay, he'll take care of you, he'll deliver your baby. All you have to do is agree to give your baby up for adoption."

Jack slowly walked around the room. Greed. That's what this room was about. "Maybe he doesn't even tell you about the adoption at first. Maybe he tells you that, if you want to keep the baby, you can. Maybe the story is never the same. Maybe it's whatever he thinks you need to hear. Whatever it takes to get you to say yes. And once he has you…"

Jack ran his gloved hand over the edge of a stirrup. There was a length of nylon strapping attached. As if occasionally he resorted to restraining them. "Can you imagine the first time the girl sees this room? She's alone. Maybe she's beginning to worry that after he gets the baby, he plans to kill her. Her terror is complete then. She's not sure if she's facing the delivery of her child or death.

"And afterward, to keep her from talking, he tells her that she could go to jail if anyone finds out."

"Or that her baby was stillborn," Alec added, an edge of anger in his quiet tone.

Jack opened a cabinet against one wall. It contained paper products and other medical supplies: disposable gowns, paper booties, sutures and a box of drug samples. He picked one up. "He's got Talzepam samples," Jack said.

Alec, who had been investigating the other side of the room, swung to face his brother. "And I bet we'll find Lexie's prints on some of them. But he wouldn't have given that prior to a delivery."

"What about after? To knock her out? He'd have to transport the baby, collect his money. Or perhaps he even uses it to kill some of them."

Alec motioned toward the ceiling.

Jack wasn't prepared for the blood splatter. Someone had done a mediocre job of scrubbing it off, but to a poor young girl who climbed up on the table and spread her legs, it must have looked like a chamber of horrors.

But if Amanda's baby was born out here, there was no way Whittemore could have made the switch. Either Amanda delivered at the office in town, or she was mistaken about the babies having been swapped. If that turned out to be the case, Jack knew it would destroy Lexie.

"We need to do a quick check of this room. If there are any records on this level, they'll be here."

While he went through the remaining cabinets, Alec searched the rest of the lower level.

"Anything?" Jack asked.

"No. You?"

"No records," Jack said, pulling his cell phone from his pocket. Opening it up, he took half a dozen shots of the room, including the Talzepam samples.

They left everything as they found it, but if Whittemore was observant, he would recognize the tool marks left behind on the locks. There was no telling what his response might be if he realized someone had gained access.

Jack and Alec were nearly back to Deep Water when Jack received the call from the private investigator. "Whittemore just left his house."

"Where's he going?"

"He stopped at the service station and filled two five-gallon cans, and now it looks as if he's heading out toward the forest."

"Stay with him, but whatever you do, don't let him see you."

Disconnecting from the P.I., Jack looked at his brother. "He just purchased two cans of gas."

"There was a generator in a room off the kitchen," Alec said. "Fuel might be for that."

"Or getting rid of the evidence," Jack said as he punched in a new phone number.

Frank Shepherd answered on the fifth ring. It sounded as if he'd been asleep. "You're damn lucky I picked up. Do you have any idea what time it is?"

"Yeah. Time to possibly save a life," Jack said.

"What are you talking about?"

"Earlier today, I stopped by and filed a missing person report on an Amanda Wilkes. I'm sure nothing has been done."

"I don't know anything about it."

"Amanda Wilkes left a message on Lexie's voice mail suggesting that Lexie's baby may not be dead. That Whittemore made a switch that night."

"What in the hell are you saying?"

"That Fleming Whittemore appears to be into black-market adoptions. And may be responsible for the death of the young woman whose body those hikers found six weeks ago."

"You have any proof?"

"There's plenty of it out at his place in the Ocala National Forest. He's got an apartment where he keeps them locked up and a fully equipped delivery room. Trick is coming up with probable cause for a search warrant. Find the girl alive, and you'll have it. But you better hurry because he's on his way out there with a couple of full gas cans."

"How the hell do you know any of this?"

"Let's worry about that later. After we make sure another young woman doesn't end up in a shallow grave."

Jack glanced at Alec. "With Whittemore out of the way, that leaves both the office and his condo unprotected. If we assume he did switch the babies that night, he would have had his hands full. Chances are he probably has some place that he takes the baby shortly after birth. He may also have a woman who provides care until the adoptive parents show up. Or perhaps he contacts the adoptive parents when the woman goes into labor, and they take custody directly."

"You're thinking he'd have to make at least one phone call?"

"And most likely it would be a cell phone that he uses."

Jack made another call, this one to Andy. "Any luck with the swabs?"

"It's definitely human, Type B."

"The same as Amanda's," Jack said. "We may already be too late."

Chapter Fourteen

It was nearly 3:00 a.m. when Lexie, Jack and Alec parked a block and a half from Fleming's office. The cleaning crew was still inside.

A nearby streetlamp filled the interior of the SUV with enough light so that Lexie could see Jack's expression as he cast a glance at her over the seat back. "Any idea what time they usually finish up?"

"No. But I think on weeknights they only spend about an hour. Just getting the trash and cleaning the bathrooms."

"We can't stay here," Alec said. "It looks as if we're casing the area."

Lexie's fingers found the door handle. This was crazy. If there was even a remote possibility that there was something inside that office that would tell her where her daughter was, or help find Amanda, they shouldn't be sitting out here. They should be in there. Getting answers.

"I'm not waiting any longer," she said as she hopped out.

During the short time they'd been in the car, the night had turned colder and the moon had climbed higher. The surrounding homes had been silent only seconds earlier, but she now heard a dog barking, the muffled sound coming from inside one of the nearby houses. Lexie turned and started walking in the direction of the office.

She'd taken the Blade brothers by surprise, so it took a half second for Jack to climb out, the closing of his car door fueling more barking.

Even when his footstep came close, she didn't look back, just kept walking. "You might as well save whatever it is you're planning to say. I can't just stay put and do nothing."

He drew even with her on the sidewalk. "It would be safer."

She looked at him now. "Maybe. But she's my daughter."

He wrapped his fingers loosely around her forearm, forcing her to stop momentarily. "And what about the child you're carrying?" He let go of her arm. "Is that child any less important?"

Lexie tried to shove her hands into her pockets, but the one with the cast was too bulky, so she left them both at her sides. She knew what he was trying to do, and she wasn't going to allow it. "You know damn well how I feel about this child."

Lexie turned and continued walking toward the office. "What neither of us knows is how you feel!"

If she hadn't been so angry, she would have found the idea of Alec witnessing another informative blowup between her and his brother embarrassing.

Jack caught up with her again. This time he took her hand. She tried to pull away, but he managed to keep his fingers firmly knitted with hers. "It gives the illusion that we're just a couple out for a late night walk."

She jerked free. "And now we're a couple who just had a fight while on a late night stroll." Lexie lengthened her stride, forcing him to do the same. Jack slid his hands easily into his pockets but didn't say anything.

When they reached the office, the cleaning crew was still inside, so they kept walking. Lexie didn't even glance toward the SUV as it slipped slowly past them, but watching the taillights disappear around the next corner made her feel nervous.

If something went wrong, there would be no speedy getaway. She and Jack would be on foot, and while she was in good physical shape, if escaping meant scaling any type of structure, a fence or a wall, with the cast on her dominant hand, she was going to be in real trouble. And since Jack wasn't the type of man just to leave her behind if she couldn't keep up, she was putting him at risk, too.

Suddenly stopping, she faced him. "Don't use this baby. In an attempt to control me, or to beat yourself up. What happened, happened."

When she would have walked on, Jack stopped her. "You're wrong, Lexie. I do know how I feel about the baby."

She waited, no longer noticing the cold, uncertain of what he would say, or what she wanted him to say. No. That wasn't true. She knew what she wanted to hear. That he loved her. That he wanted her. That he wanted their child.

"I want this baby, Lexie. Just as much as you do. I want to be there to watch my son or daughter grow up."

Well, he'd gotten one out of three right. "Okay. We'll draw up paperwork." She started to walk away for a third time. Until his next words drew her to a halt.

"I don't want visitation rights, Lexie. I think we should get married."

She turned to face him. He stood there, five feet from her, his expression hidden in the shadows. She loved him. To the point that her heart would ache for a long time to come if she walked away.

But he hadn't said he wanted her. He hadn't claimed to love her.

She took a deep breath, let it out slowly. One out of three just wasn't good enough. For her. Or for Jack. Or the child she carried.

As she stood there thinking about what she was about to do, the pain inside her expanded. Was she making a mistake? One that she would regret? The sound of a car engine forced Lexie to glance at the office. The cleaning crew was pulling out of the parking lot.

She immediately started walking back the way they'd come.

"Lexie?"

"I don't think marriage is the answer," she called over her shoulder. When Jack caught up, he remained mute. She didn't look at him, afraid that if she did, she'd change her mind.

The breeze sent the small leaves off the surrounding water oaks rattling across the sidewalk. Lexie pulled her jacket closer around her and forced herself to move a bit faster, but was uncertain if it was because she was eager to get inside or because even now she desperately needed to escape the decision she'd just made.

She kept to pavement as she circled the building. She knew Jack was a half step behind, but didn't glance around even once. She needed to get her mind back on the reason they were here tonight. When she reached the double plate-glass doors, she looked inside to where security lights lent a hushed glow to the reception area.

Jack handed her vinyl gloves. After pulling one on, she slid the key in the lock. It turned easily, but as soon as she opened the door, the security system's soft warning beep sounded. She crossed to the keypad and stood briefly looking at it, praying that the code hadn't been changed. She pressed in 1-7-9-9. Her finger hesitated over the 7 key. What if it had been changed? How long would it take the cops to get there?

"Lexie?" Jack said nervously.

She pushed down on the final key. The beeping stopped. As soon as it did, Jack locked the door behind them.

"Where to?" he asked. His voice had an edge to it. There was no way to tell if it was the situation that was making him uptight or if he was upset over her refusal to marry him.

"Marian takes care of the bill paying in the practice, but Dan and Fleming keep personal records in their offices."

She led the way back to Fleming's office. As soon as she turned on the light, the picture window behind the desk became a large black square. Because there were no blinds or curtains, they were going to be pretty much on display for as long as they were in the building. Lexie turned her back to the glass.

Jack stepped past her and, sitting in the desk chair, tugged on the top left file drawer. "I don't suppose you know where he keeps the keys?"

Lexie was looking for something sharp to jimmy the lock when she realized Jack had placed a small leather case on the desk and was in the process of unzipping it. He pulled out what she supposed was a lock pick.

It took him a matter of seconds to open the drawer. "Why don't you start there, while I do the one on the other side?"

She scanned the tabs. Most of the files appeared to be standard reports. Which might assist the police with nailing Whittemore but wasn't going to help them find Lindy or Amanda.

Jack had already opened the opposite drawer and now worked on the one below it.

"Did they teach that at the police academy?"

"No. I learned it from a drug dealer." He opened the last file drawer.

At the tone in his voice, she looked up. Their gazes connected only briefly before he turned away. "You better keep looking. We have thirteen minutes."

"What do you mean?"

"If anyone saw us, it'll take them a few minutes to decide that we don't belong here. Once they make that decision, assuming they're not carrying a cell phone, we have the time it takes them to walk home and make the call to the police. Stay too long, we'll both be spending the night in jail."

Lexie started digging faster. She slammed the second drawer closed. "Nothing here." Straightening, she checked out the room. "I'll go try Marian's office."

Lexie moved quickly, across the reception space and into the administrative area. The file cabinets in Marian's office were unlocked, perhaps because they weren't of a sensitive nature, but there was a whole wall of them. And none of the drawers were marked.

Uncertain where to start, Lexie ripped open one at random. She ran a finger down the line of tabs. The company the office contracted with for medical waste removal. Several suppliers of disposable products. A company that repaired equipment. She slammed the drawer shut. The next one contained files on the different insurance plans the practice participated in. She closed it immediately, assumed it would just be more of the same.

She grabbed the next drawer.

"Come on. Damn it, come on," Lexie said softly to herself. She could feel the tightness inside her escalating. How much time was left? What would they do if they didn't locate what they needed?

She opened three more before she discovered what they were after—the statements for Fleming's cell phone and those for the office. She grabbed the contents of the hanging files. There was a pile of incoming mail on one corner of the desk. She opened and emptied out a large manila envelope. There was a law against reading other people's mail, but at this point, she'd lost track of exactly how many they'd broken in the past twenty-four hours.

After shoving the statements into the envelope, she returned to the open file drawer. She transferred a handful of statements for Dan's cell phone into Fleming's file and the one for the office. Eventually the records would be missed. She just wanted to buy some time before Fleming became aware of what they were doing.

She was closing the drawer when she noticed Jack in the doorway.

"Time's up."

She grabbed the manila envelope from where she'd left it on Marian's desk. "I've got what we need!"

They were four blocks away when they saw the blue strobe of rack lights on the first cruiser. A second one flew past a few seconds later.

When she turned to watch them disappear in the direction of the office, Jack grabbed her arm. "Just keep walking. We're going to take a right at the next corner. And then I think it's time for some late-night jogging."

AN HOUR AND A HALF LATER, Jack sat at his kitchen table, studying the phone records. It had taken repeated attempts to convince Lexie that for the moment there was nothing she could do. She was now stretched out on the couch, not yet asleep, but resting.

He didn't know which of them had been more surprised by his suggestion that they get married—him or Lexie. He realized now that the proposal had been a mistake. He cared about her, more than he had ever cared for any woman, but what about Lexie? How could he expect her to know how she felt? Given everything she was going through, he didn't doubt that she had feelings for him. Gratitude most of all. But he would be foolish to think what had happened last night had necessarily been based more on love than on physical attraction and emotional neediness.

He briefly closed his eyes to clear their grittiness. He was accustomed to working long hours when needed, but he was also human, and his mental faculties dimmed with fatigue.

Opening his eyes again, he stared down at the numbers. Lexie had gone into labor just after ten-thirty on December 9. If they went with the theory that Amanda delivered at the office and not out at the cabin, the birth would have needed to take place prior to Lexie's arrival. But how much before?

Did Whittemore enlist some type of nanny to take care of the baby, perhaps even for several days afterward, or did he expect his clients to take possession within minutes of delivery?

If they weren't local, though, the adoptive parents would need reasonable travel time. How much would depend on whether they were coming from somewhere in Florida or out of state, maybe even as far as the West Coast.

Jack settled on a window of time from forty-eight hours prior to the birth until midnight the night of the delivery. Unfortunately, Whittemore must have been a real talker because he managed to log seventy-eight calls during that period.

Tracking down that many addresses would take too long, so Jack hunted for a pattern that had initiated shortly after June 2 when Amanda was seen at the Pierson Clinic for the first time by Dan Dawson. It was fairly easy to guess how Whittemore chose his targets. That some of them were Dan's patients wouldn't have greatly concerned him. Perhaps the lack of a documented doctor-patient relationship even played to his advantage.

When Jack narrowed the list to five possibilities, he flicked on his laptop computer, accessed an online reverse directory that also had a background search option. When he was done running all five, he was still left with two possibilities. He didn't have a printer attached to the computer, so jotted down addresses and some additional info on the households. Both belonged to people with the financial wherewithal to afford a black market adoption. The usual going price for a healthy baby of good background could reach up into the six figures.

He glanced at the stove clock. Nearly 6:00 a.m. He hadn't realized that he had been at it that long. Leaving everything spread out on the table, he wandered into the living room, intending to let Lexie know that he was stepping outside for a few minutes to clear his head. Finding her still asleep, he left her like that.

He was checking the wall-mounted mailbox next to his door when the patrol car pulled up at the curb.

The first officer out of the car was Faith Bair, a seasoned officer. She was attractive and had a good sense of humor, but more importantly, she knew how to handle herself and could take a grown man down to the ground.

Unfortunately, Shepherd was the second man out of the car. Seeing no other choice, Jack walked out to meet them.

He nodded at Faith, then turned his attention to Shepherd. "Did you find Amanda Wilkes?"

"No. Not yet. But I'm sure we will. I did check into her background, though. Seems she has a habit of making up stories to get attention."

"Talk to Whittemore?"

"As a matter of fact, I did. And that's the reason I'm here." Shepherd nodded at the front door. "Is she in there?"

Instead of replying, Jack stepped in front of him, blocking his way.

Shepherd smiled. "You know how this works, Jack. Bail had been rescinded. I'm here to take Lexie Dawson into custody."

"Have a warrant?"

"Sure do." He pulled it out and passed it to Jack. "Look. Right now I'm willing to overlook the fact that she wasn't acting alone last night when she broke into her ex-husband's office—I figure I owe you that much. But if you don't get out of my way, she won't be the only one in the back of the cruiser."

If Jack had thought there was some way he could legally keep Shepherd out, he would have. It wouldn't help anyone for him to get detained, too. And maybe it wouldn't be all that bad if Lexie was put on ice for a few hours. He was becoming increasingly concerned that she might do something to put herself and the baby in danger.

He handed the document back to Shepherd.

When Jack pushed open the door, the scent of fresh brewed coffee filled the living room. But it was the empty couch that he noticed first and the sound of the running shower.

Motioning for Faith to check out the bathroom, Shepherd turned to survey the room. The blanket that had been covering Lexie was now wadded up at the end of the sofa.

"I was up late watching a movie," Jack offered as an explanation.

"What movie would that be?"

"Jaws," he answered. Lexie had flipped on the television briefly when they'd returned last night. "Coffee?" Jack asked as he headed toward the kitchen. He didn't really need the caffeine now, his adrenaline having kicked in again, but figured it would be better if he could at least hide the stolen phone statements.

When he reached the kitchen, though, Shepherd was right on his heels once more. Instead of the fully loaded table Jack expected to find, the surface was clear. Even his laptop was missing. As were his cell phone and all his notes. Lexie's shoes were still where she'd kicked them off beneath one of the chairs.

Hoping that Shepherd hadn't already noticed the two mugs on the counter, Jack added a third. She'd obviously gone out the back way, taking time to gather up everything they'd been working on, but without her shoes.

She wouldn't get very far. He tried to imagine where she might head at this time of morning with bare feet. Would she use his cell phone to call a friend to pick her up? Assuming the battery wasn't dead. Or had she grabbed it knowing that he'd contact her when it was safe?

He'd taken the first sip of coffee when he heard the SUV's engine turn over out on the street. Shepherd gave no indication that he even heard it.

Faith Bair walked in at that moment. "I've searched both bedrooms and the bathroom. There's no sign of the suspect."

Shepherd rounded on Jack. "What are you trying to pull here, Blade?"

"Absolutely nothing. I never said she was here."

"You never said she wasn't, either."

"And if I had, you wouldn't have believed me. I just figured it would be easier to let you look around."

"And now that I've had a look, I'm ready for a nice long talk. Down at the station."

"Are you arresting me?"

"We can do it that way if you prefer."

Chapter Fifteen

"Have a seat, Jack. I'll be right with you."

As Shepherd left, pulling the door closed behind him, Jack grabbed a chair.

It had been a while since he'd sat on the wrong side of an interrogation table. There had been times when he'd been working undercover that vice would haul him in and screw with him to keep his cover intact.

Jack glanced at his watch in frustration. What he had failed to recognize immediately was that the phone bills, the computer and his cell phone weren't the only things on his kitchen table this morning. The final two names from the original seventy-eight had also been there, along with their phone numbers and addresses.

One may have been a Fontana, California, address, but the other had been an Orlando address belonging to Reid Nicholson, a criminal attorney who, up until two years ago, Benito Binelli had kept on retainer. Now serving two life sentences in a federal prison for money laundering and the murder of a federal agent, Benito no longer had need of Nicholson's services. Undoubtedly, the attorney had found some other lowlife to support him.

Given Lexie's desperate determination to find her daughter, it only made sense that once she had a name, she wouldn't hesitate to make use of it. But just how foolish was she? Would she do something as stupid as approach the Nicholsons?

Jack stood and paced. He needed to get to a phone and warn Lexie, but he needed privacy to accomplish it. As he walked by the door, he tried it but found it locked from the outside. Shepherd was screwing with him. Because he could.

The cop stepped back into the room.

"Would you mind if I made a quick phone call?" Jack asked, and tried to appear more calm than he was feeling. "I was supposed to meet my brother for breakfast this morning."

Shepherd passed Jack his cell phone. Jack flipped it open and dialed Alec's number. Alec answered almost immediately. "Morning. Did you get anywhere last night?"

"Yeah. I did." Now came the tricky part. "I won't be able to make it to the café this morning. Frank Shepherd asked me to stop by the station. It looks as if I might be here for a little while."

"Tell Frank it's not polite to eavesdrop."

"Maybe another time."

"Since we weren't planning to have breakfast, I assume this call has a purpose. Did you need me to do something?"

"Maybe you could give Reid Nickel's son a quick call and let him know that I won't be able to make it into Orlando this morning."

There was a slight pause, as if Alec was trying to place the name. "Are we talking about Reid Nicholson, Benito's man?"

"Yeah."

"Am I to assume that the reason you're using Frank's cell is because Lexie has yours?"

"Thanks, Alec." Ending the call, Jack handed the phone

back to Shepherd. "Now what is it you want to know?" he asked as they both took seats at the table.

Shepherd folded his hands in his lap and cocked his head to one side. "I want to know where she is."

"And what makes you think I know?"

"The women's shoes are under your kitchen table."

"Okay. She was staying with me, but she left."

"And you have no idea where she went?"

Jack nodded. "That's right."

"You don't look too worried about the bail money you put up."

"Just because she's no longer sleeping under my roof doesn't mean she intends to run. Things just got a little uncomfortable."

"Because of the baby?"

"Now you really have lost me."

Shepherd leaned forward, resting his hands on the table between them. "We found partially burned packaging from one of those over-the-counter pregnancy tests. I thought perhaps the reason you were helping her was because she was pregnant with your kid."

Jack settled back as if he wasn't in a hurry, propping an ankle atop the opposite knee. "Any good detective," he said, the inference being that Shepherd wasn't, "knows that taking a test is indicative of absolutely nothing unless you have a result. Maybe she was cleaning out her medicine cabinet."

"And decided to build a fire with it?"

If Jack hadn't been worried about Lexie, he might have been able to enjoy playing with Shepherd. "Maybe she was out of kindling."

"You have an answer for everything, don't you?"

At that moment, Fitz pulled open the door. "Amanda Wilkes just walked in."

THE SUV'S HEATER BLASTED onto Lexie's bare feet. Shoe stores didn't open at six-thirty in the morning. She could either go barefoot or drop by her place, but she figured Riverhouse would be the next location Shepherd showed up. He might even have someone watching the house already.

She used a fast-food drive-through to grab some orange juice and a pastry, enough to hold her until later. Instead of getting back onto the interstate, she pulled into one of the parking spots. Leaving Jack's computer on the passenger seat, she turned it on. She had no idea how his wireless connection worked, but was hoping that there might be some type of Internet access. After several minutes, she realized there wasn't, and turned it off.

She'd have to stop at a service station when she got closer to Orlando. Shoes might be optional, but a map of Orlando wasn't. She picked up Jack's cell phone. She knew he'd call her as soon as he broke free.

What if he hadn't by the time she reached the Nicholson residence? Should she just cruise by, see what she could learn without actually knocking on the front door?

She pulled back onto the highway. While she admitted to a strong urge to confront the Nicholsons, she realized doing so would be very risky, and would probably result in the cops being called. Something Lexie couldn't afford.

She eased her foot off the accelerator. She wasn't the only one who wouldn't want the cops called. Was there some way she could use that to her advantage?

Though she tried to keep it in check, excitement built inside her. In a few hours, she could be holding her baby in her arms for the first time.

"This is departmental business," Shepherd said as Fitz motioned for Jack to join them in the interview room where Amanda waited.

"She wants him there."

"I don't care what she wants—"

Fitz got in Shepherd's face. "The kid is scared witless. If she wants Jack in there, I can't think of a good reason why he shouldn't be."

Fitz motioned Jack out the door ahead of him. Shepherd looked as if he considered pulling rank, but then nodded with a grimace.

When all three men stepped into the interview room, the young girl already seated at the long table looked up. Fitz had characterized her as scared, but Jack's first impression was that she looked as if she'd reached the end of her rope and was just about to let go.

Her hair was uncombed, her jeans and jacket wrinkled as if she'd been sleeping in them. Her hands were folded on the table in front of her, but even as she met their gazes, she was peeling back the dried cuticle on her left thumb.

"You're the one who's been helping her, aren't you?"

He nodded as he took the only remaining seat.

Shepherd placed a tape recorder on the Formica surface in front of her. As Fitz went through the usual rundown for the taped interview, detailing the time and those present in the room, Amanda continued to fiddle with the injured cuticle.

"Okay, Amanda," Fitz said. "What can you tell me about Dan Dawson's murder?"

It wasn't the line of questioning that Jack had been expecting to be pursued.

"I was following Dr. Whittemore because I had gone to see him earlier that day about my baby."

"What about the baby?"

"I was having these really bad nightmares." She stared down at her hands again. "I kept dreaming that my baby was dead, the dream always the same. I was strapped to this table in a room full of medical machines. My baby was only a few feet away on this rolling cart. When she wouldn't move at all, I'd reach out and touch her. It was then that I'd know she was dead."

"Do you remember anything about the birth?" Fitz asked in a kind tone.

"Not really. Dr. Whittemore had given me something." She shifted in her chair, attempting to sit straighter. "When I went to see him, I thought if I could see my baby, the nightmares would stop."

"And what did he say?"

"That he would talk to the people who had her." She looked over at Jack. "I figured they'd say no. Just made sense that they wouldn't care about what I was going through. They had what they wanted." She caught her chapped lower lip between her teeth.

"Go on," Fitz said.

Her eyes remained on Jack. "I figured if I followed him, he might lead me to my baby."

"And did you follow him?" Shepherd asked quietly. "Did he lead you to the baby?"

"No. He went to Dr. Dawson's house that night. I figured that maybe Dr. Dawson was also involved with selling babies. They sat there and talked for a while. Dr. Whittemore had a bottle of wine with him." She glanced away. "There must have been something in the wine because Dr. Dawson suddenly seemed to pass out at his desk."

"Where were you when this was happening?"

"Outside. In the bushes."

"But you could witness what was going on in the room."

"Not really. I could only see if I got real close to the window, so I mostly listened."

"Was the window open?"

"Yes."

"What did the men talk about?" Shepherd asked, the look on his face suggesting that he was no longer skeptical of her story.

"About illegal abortions. Dr. Dawson thought someone must be doing them out in Pierson."

"Did he say why he thought that?"

"Because of the number of women who came in, but didn't return after one or two visits. He thought their receptionist might be somehow involved." Pausing, she looked away as if what she planned to say next might be difficult for her. "Dr. Dawson said the girl they found buried out in the woods a month or two ago had been in the office. Had seen Dr. Whittemore."

"What did Whittemore say?"

"That he obviously had no idea that she'd been his patient." Amanda pulled closed the front of her jacket, sort of hunching into it. "I knew he was lying. That she was probably just like me. When he approached her about giving up the baby, she saw it as a way out. And when he offered the apartment out there for her to stay in…"

"Did you live out there?" Jack asked.

"I did for the last five weeks. My mom had died. I didn't want to stay at her house anymore."

"Where did you give birth?" Jack asked.

"There's this room attached to the apartment that's set up like a hospital. I was supposed to deliver there, but the power was still off from when the hurricane came through a couple of days earlier. He brought me into town. To the office."

"The room off the kitchen, Amanda. Was there a generator there when you were using the apartment?"

"No."

So the generator had been added, possibly after Amanda

gave birth. Perhaps because Whittemore realized that without it he might have to transport another girl into town. He'd been lucky the first time. He might not be the next.

"Let's get back to the night of the murder," Shepherd said. "Did you see Whittemore shoot his partner?"

"No. It was the woman who did it."

All three men sat forward, but it was Jack who asked, "Lexie Dawson?"

"No. Not her."

"Then who?" Jack asked.

"I didn't see the woman. At least not that night."

"What do you mean?"

"By the time she showed up I was afraid to even look inside the room."

"How did she arrive?"

"She must have come in through the back door like Dr. Whittemore."

"So you didn't see a car?"

She shook her head.

"The statement you made earlier. Does it mean that you saw this woman at a later date?"

She nodded. "I'm really good with voices. The morning after the…after Dr. Dawson died, I went to a support group that meets over at the hospital. I needed to talk to someone. I thought maybe they'd be willing to listen."

From her facial expression, Jack assumed they hadn't.

"That was the first time I saw Mrs. Dawson. She was the only one who was nice to me." She rubbed her cuticle. "After the meeting was over Mrs. Dawson tried to talk to me, but I just wanted to leave. And then this woman grabbed Mrs. Dawson. She'd been the mannequin sitting across from me. I thought the reason she kept looking at me was because, like the rest of the women, she didn't think I belonged there." She pressed her lips together briefly. "When I realized who she was, I realized she must be following me. I got out of there really quick after that."

"I don't suppose you have a name?"

"No. You only introduce yourself if you get up and speak."

"Why did you call her a mannequin?" Fitz asked.

"Because she was dressed like some big-city model."

"So you can describe her?" Jack asked.

"Yeah."

Fitz stood. "I'll call over to the hospital and see if they keep a list of who attends those meetings."

"Let's get back to the night of the murder," Shepherd said again. "You're sure the woman was the one who pulled the trigger?"

She nodded. "As soon as the gun went off, Dr. Whittemore started freaking out and yelling at her about how Dr. Dawson didn't know anything about the switch, that she'd had nothing to worry about. They were still screaming when the other man came in."

Jack and Shepherd looked at each other.

"What man?" Shepherd asked.

"The woman's husband. He ordered Dr. Whittemore to get the woman out of there. That he'd take care of everything."

"And did he?" Jack asked.

"There was a second gunshot five or ten minutes after the woman and Dr. Whittemore left."

Jack sat back in his chair. Dawson had probably been still alive when his partner had left him there. The second round would have been meant to kill him and at the same time possibly destroy any sign of the previous one. It wasn't just any man who could walk in on that type of situation and know what to do in order to create the illusion of a suicide.

Shepherd leaned back in his chair. "Why didn't you come to us sooner?"

Amanda looked as if she would like to cry, but she didn't. "I was afraid to. Dr. Whittemore must have told her who I was. I thought maybe if I just pretended that I had changed my mind about seeing the baby, everything would be okay. I even went to see Dr. Whittemore at the office. Not after hours as I had before, but when there would be other people around." She tightened her arms across her chest.

She looked up at Jack. "I wouldn't have let Mrs. Dawson go to prison. I want you to know that."

"I believe you," he said, simply, and then leaned forward. "Think back to the night of the murder. To when the second man arrived. Did you ever hear a name after that?"

"I think I may have heard the name Reid."

Swearing, Jack nearly knocked Fitz over as he tried to get out the door. "Reid Nicholson," he yelled back as he raced down the hall.

"Lexie may already be there."

BY THE TIME LEXIE PARKED several doors down from 1393 Mandalay Way, she was wearing flip-flops, the only thing the convenience store carried.

The neighborhood was one of those with elephant-size houses, packed tightly on lots that left only enough room for a driveway on one side and a ten-foot-wide swath of grass on the other. The only trees were queen palms and a few over-trimmed ligustrums.

It was the kind of neighborhood where the only people out

walking at this time of morning were the domestic help who didn't live in.'

She glanced down at the dead cell phone. She'd stopped at a pay phone three or four miles back to try Jack's home number. She hadn't left a message, afraid the police might get it. She had next attempted to call Alec Blade, but his number was unlisted.

Which meant, if Lexie wanted answers, it was up to her to get them.

At 7:55 a.m., a woman collected a newspaper off the front walk. Another fifteen minutes went by, and then the garage door went up. The same woman backed a silver SUV halfway down the driveway, so that it was even with the front door. She popped the back open, left it that way while she went back inside the house.

Seconds later she reappeared, so quickly that it suggested the two large suitcases she dragged outside and slung into the back of the vehicle had been waiting just inside the door. She was moving faster now. The next thing that came out was a portable crib. She stowed that with the suitcases.

Lexie was getting a very uneasy feeling. The woman was about to run. Lexie glanced down at the damn phone. What should she do? Should she try to stop her? Should she follow her? But what if she lost her? Lexie wasn't an expert at tailing people. And if the woman managed to give her the slip, what then? What if she was never able to find her again?

As the woman pushed a stroller in front of her as if she were in some kind of relay race, Lexie made her decision. She was already at the end of the drive the next time the woman emerged. Seeing her, the woman backed toward the house.

Lexie was close enough to see her features, and the realization that she wasn't a stranger startled her. Reid Nicholson's wife was the impeccably turned-out Eurasian woman from the support group last Saturday. Not that she appeared all that impeccable this morning. If anything, she looked downright panicked.

Lexie followed her up the walk, and when Mrs. Nicholson tried to shut her out, she managed to get a foot in the opening. Lexie realized too late that flip-flops weren't much protection against a solid wood door.

They were pretty much nose to nose now, and she recognized desperation in the other woman's eyes.

"I just need to talk to you," Lexie pleaded. "About the baby you adopted."

The shoving match with the front door continued for several seconds more before Lexie managed to force her way inside.

The woman backed away, silent tears streaming down her face, taking with it the carefully applied makeup.

Lexie stayed where she was just inside the door. Maybe, if she didn't make a move toward her, the woman would calm down some. "I just need to ask you some questions about the adoption. And then I'll leave."

The woman glanced over her shoulder as if she had heard something. Suddenly, she just turned and walked away, as if Lexie wasn't even there. Or as if she were headed to a phone to call the cops. If they came, they'd arrest Lexie. And when they did, the woman would disappear, taking the baby with her.

In her mind, Lexie had already decided the baby was Lindy, but she knew it might not be so. That what she was doing here in this house was wrong. But she couldn't stop herself. Her daughter had been crying out for her for eleven months. Nothing was going to hold Lexie back.

Or so she thought until the small twenty-five automatic suddenly appeared in the woman's hand.

Lexie lifted her arms out to her sides. Dan had been shot

with a twenty-five. Was this the weapon that had been used? Had this woman killed Dan? Was it possible Dan had known about Lindy?

None of that mattered right now. What did was survival. Hers. The baby's.

More than five yards separated them. At this range, a well-placed bullet could be deadly, but the way the woman's hands were shaking and the way she could no longer meet Lexie's eyes suggested she was likely to miss altogether, or that Lexie would end up with only a flesh wound.

"I'm sorry. I'm really sorry." She was crying again. "I didn't mean for any of this to happen."

Lexie was uncertain what it was Mrs. Nicholson was sorry about. Her part in stealing another woman's baby? Dan's murder? The fact that she intended to harm Lexie?

At the sudden loud sound of two men's voices, the gun clattered to the floor. Both women dived for it at the same time. Lexie wasn't the first to reach it, but she wrestled it from the other woman's fingers. Still seated on the floor, the woman moved backward, sliding along the floor on her butt as she tried to escape.

"Get up," Lexie said.

The argument in the other room briefly grew louder, then tapered down to a more normal level of conversation, but not before Lexie realized that one of the voices belonged to Fleming. Lexie motioned the woman toward the voices, stopping her just short of the opening into the kitchen, where the two men were talking. She assumed the second man in the room, the one sitting at the granite bar eating his breakfast, was Reid Nicholson. He was a large man—six-three or six-four—but with his heavy features and craggy skin, he wasn't an attractive one.

Fleming paced. "I helped those girls. I gave them options when they didn't have any. Why can't anyone see that?"

"Are you worried they'll tie you to the girl they dug up a few weeks ago? She was in the ground too long, Doc, for there to be much left for them to work with."

"She was my patient. If they search the cabin, they'll find something of hers. A hair. Some DNA." Fleming stopped in his tracks. "I tried to save her. There was nothing I could do! Even if she'd been in the hospital, chances are she wouldn't have made it."

"I'm sure you're right. If you're worried about evidence, burn the place. Take a couple of those five gallon containers of kerosene out in my garage and burn it to the ground. They'll know it's arson, but they won't be able to tie you to the accelerant." He shoved a triangle of toast into his mouth and talked around it. "Collect from the insurance and build you a new place."

"But the medical equipment. They'll see it."

"You were storing it."

Fleming crossed to the sink suddenly and doused his face with water, used only his hands to wipe the excess away. Fingers splayed wide, he shoved them through his hair, curling them into his scalp at the back of his head. "I took an oath. To heal. I won't take the fall for what you two did to Dan."

Nicholson pushed the plate away. "I told you I would handle it, and I will."

Fleming slid back onto the stool. "I know you did." Closing his eyes, he lowered his head. "I'll be okay. I just never expected things to end up like this."

He never even knew the gun was pointed at his skull. As the sound of a single gunshot faded in the room, Nicholson laid the twenty-two next to his plate, and using the last triangle of toast, sopped up egg yolk.

"No one ever does."

LEXIE OR NICHOLSON'S WIFE must have made some sound because in the next instant the gun was pointed at them. Somewhere in the house, a baby wailed, but Lexie could barely hear it because of the roar of blood in her ears.

The woman beside her sank to the ground in a sobbing mess.

It took Lexie several seconds to realize that she still held the twenty-five in her left hand. And that the man holding the gun on her couldn't see it. But the safety, which was now on, was a right-hander, made to be easily taken off with a slight downward motion of the thumb. It wasn't so easy left-handed. But even if she could get it off, she didn't think she could use a gun on another human being.

In her peripheral vision, she could see Fleming slumped at the bar, his head resting on the granite surface. As if he was tired. There wasn't much blood. There probably wasn't even an exit wound, the round having ricocheted around inside the skull, destroying brain tissue as it went. Bringing death.

As she was watching, Fleming slid onto the floor, taking the stool down with him. The sudden movement freaked Lexie and her body jerked.

Nicholson chuckled slightly and winked. "Fast and clean. It's not a bad way to go."

He glanced down at his wife. He was smiling when his gaze connected with Lexie's. "Can you believe anyone would think she could kill a man? Look at her. The sweetest lady on this earth." He motioned with the gun. "Help her up."

Lexie pulled the woman to her feet using only her right hand, but Nicholson didn't seem to notice. "Pauli, listen to me," he said. "You go on and get the baby and take it on out to the car."

After she left the room, he came toward Lexie. "I wish I could make this so you wouldn't see it coming, but we both know that's not possible."

Lexie wobbled slightly on her feet, almost as if she was somewhat drunk. There was nothing for her to reach for, no one there to steady her. Nicholson's words echoed in her head. *No one ever sees it coming.*

But it wasn't until now, when she knew her fate would be the same as Dan's and as Fleming's, that she realized how many things she hadn't done in her life. Like really lived.

She hadn't even seen her daughter. She'd come so far, paid a really big price, but she would have to wait to see Lindy in heaven, hopefully many years in the future.

As the nausea brought on by her fear crawled through her, she doubled forward, her right hand coming up to cover her abdomen. As it did, she thought not of her life, not of Lindy, but of the life she carried. The life that grew inside her.

Lexie worked the small automatic's safety off. She had no idea what type of round was in the gun, but even if it was hollow points, chances were it wouldn't be enough to take down a man the size of Reid Nicholson.

But she was going to damn sure try.

As she brought the muzzle of the gun up, she saw Jack standing next to refrigerator, the 9 mm pointed at Nicholson's head.

She'd been wrong. There was something…someone to reach out to. Someone there to steady her.

Her last thought as she pulled the trigger was not of hate, but of love.

Chapter Sixteen

The house was silent and dark. Peaceful.

Leaning over the crib, Lexie watched her daughter sleep. DNA testing would be done to verify to the world what Lexie already knew—that this child, this beautiful little girl with the smooth, plump cheeks and the soft, curly blond hair, was hers.

Sensing Jack in the doorway, she looked up and offered a smile that she knew he wouldn't be able to see. He was back in uniform. She realized just how much she liked seeing him in it. Not because it made him look handsome, but because it made him happy to be doing what he did best.

Glancing down again, she smoothed a hand over the back of Lindy's head. "So many times before tonight I found myself standing where I am now, feeling such sadness. Such anger. My chest still aches. But it's with joy."

Jack moved away from the door, stopping only when he stood opposite her, the crib with the sleeping baby between them. But it wasn't the only baby between them.

The moonlight slipping in through the large window behind her highlighted the strong, graceful lines of Jack's face. "It wouldn't have happened without you. This crib would still be empty. I would still be empty, Jack."

Lexie reached down and touched her daughter again. "You know what I think?"

Even when he didn't say anything, she went on. "I think Amanda's baby was a little angel. I think our paths crossed because she knew that without you I would never find Lindy."

Reaching out, Jack captured her chin and lifted it. "As much as I want the child you're carrying, I want you more, Lexie. Marry me."

She had intended to answer him as she had the other night, but as their gazes met, she heard herself telling him not what was in her head, but what was in her heart.

"I love you, Jack Blade. So very, very much."

Leaning across the crib between them, he took her mouth in a kiss that seemed to empty the air from her lungs and to fill her heart to brimming. And perhaps even made her a bit dizzy, too. But as her fingers closed around his forearm, seeking the support of his strong body, she thought of this morning. About how, when she'd been certain that she wouldn't survive, it had been Jack she thought of. And he had seemed to appear almost magically.

Entwining his fingers with hers, he walked around the crib until he reached her. His other hand slid beneath her hair to the back of her head. Pulling her to him, he kissed her again.

"I'll take that to be a yes."